ANNA'S CROSSING

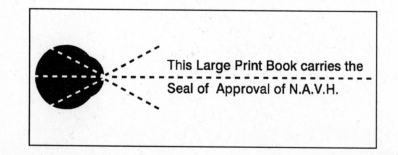

This Large Print Book carries the
Seal of Approval of N.A.V.H.

AN AMISH BEGINNINGS NOVEL

ANNA'S CROSSING

SUZANNE WOODS FISHER

THORNDIKE PRESS
A part of Gale, Cengage Learning

GALE
CENGAGE Learning·

Farmington Hills, Mich • San Francisco • New York • Waterville, Maine
Meriden, Conn • Mason, Ohio • Chicago

GALE
CENGAGE Learning®

LIBRARY OF CONGRESS CATALOGING-IN-PUBLICATION DATA

Fisher, Suzanne Woods.
  Anna's crossing : an Amish beginnings novel / by Suzanne Woods Fisher.
— Large print edition.
    pages cm. — (Thorndike Press large print Christian fiction)
  ISBN 978-1-4104-7630-2 (hardcover) — ISBN 1-4104-7630-8 (hardcover)
  1. Amish—Fiction. 2. United States—History—18th century—Fiction.
3. Large type books. I. Title.
PS3606.I78A83 2015b
813'.6—dc23   2014048881

Published in 2015 by arrangement with Revell Books, a division of Baker Publishing Group

To those "keepers of the faith" who have gone before us, risking their lives, seeking to worship God in peace. We don't appreciate enough what you have done to preserve and protect religious freedom. May we all use our freedom for the Gospel.

Always in the big woods when you leave familiar ground and step off alone into a new place there will be, along with the feelings of curiosity and excitement, a little nagging of dread. It is the ancient fear of the Unknown, and it is your first bond with the wilderness you are going into.

— Wendell Berry

GLOSSARY FOR
HISTORICAL SHIPS

binnacle is the built-in housing for a ship's compass.

boatswain, pronounced boh'-suhn, is the ship's officer in charge of equipment and the crew.

bollard is a large ball on a short pedestal.

bowsprit is a spar extending forward from a ship's bow (the front part of the ship), to which the forestays are fastened.

cleat is a low fastener with a horn on each side.

companionway is a set of steps leading from a ship's deck down to a cabin or lower deck.

coaming is a raised border around the hatch of a ship to keep out water.

forecastle or fo'c'sle is the forward part of a ship below the deck, traditionally used as the crew's living quarters.

fo'c'sle deck is a raised deck at the bow of a ship.

galley is the ship's kitchen.

Great Cabin is the captain's quarters.

halyard is a rope used for raising or lowering sails, spars, or yards.

holystoning the deck means to use pieces of soft sandstone to scour the decks of ships. Sailors called the stones *bibles* or *prayer books* because they scrubbed the decks on their knees.

larboard is the historical term for the left-hand side of the ship (aka *port*), looking forward. In early times merchant ships were loaded from the left side. *Lade* meant "load" and *bord* meant "side."

leeward is the side sheltered or away from the wind.

oakum, from the word *off-combing,* is loose fiber obtained by untwisting old ropes, used to caulk wooden ships.

Round House is the chartroom where the ship's progress was planned and plotted.

spar is a thick, strong pole used for a yard.

speak a ship is to hail and speak to her captain or commander.

starboard comes from *steor,* meaning "helm" or "rudder," and *bord,* meaning "side." At one time, a boat or ship had rudders tied to its side. The modern word refers to the right-hand side of a vessel, looking forward.

stern is the rearmost part of the ship.

upper deck or waist is the middle part of a British ship. This large area, lower than both the raised deck toward the bow and the even higher forecastle deck toward the stern, was where passengers could congregate if there was no maneuver requiring the area to be cleared for action.

yard is a spar that hangs horizontally across a ship's mast for a sail to hang from.

1

April 15th, 1737

It's a hard crossing, they'd been warned. Eight weeks in a wooden tub with no guarantee they'd ever get there. Anna König crouched beside a bed of roses, breathing deeply of the freshly turned loam. She had done all she could to avoid this treacherous sea journey, and yet here she was, digging up her rose to take along with her. She jabbed her shovel in the ground, mulling all the reasons this voyage was fraught with ill.

It meant leaving behind her grandparents, her home, her church in Ixheim, Germany. Her people. It would be the end of everything she'd ever known and loved.

"Some endings are really beginnings," her grandfather had said when she told him that Christian Müller, the minister, asked — no, insisted — she join the departing families. "If you don't remember anything I've ever tried to teach you, remember that."

Despite misgivings and forebodings, Anna relented. How do you say no to a minister? She was the only one who could speak and understand English. And that's why she was stabbing the earth with her shovel, digging up her most precious rose to take on the journey, hoping that the hard winter and late-to-come spring meant its roots would still be dormant. If she was going to go to this strange New World, she was going to bring this rose. And she was going. Tomorrow.

Tomorrow! The crack of doom in that one word.

Anna had begged her grandparents to join the emigrating group, but they wouldn't budge. "It's a young man's sport, that sea journey," her grandfather said, shaking his head, ending the discussion. She couldn't argue that point. The voyage was filled with risks and dangers and uncertainties, especially for the very young and very old.

Anna sat back on her heels and looked around. In a few years, who would be left in Ixheim? Who would care for her grandparents in their final days? Who would bury them and tend their graves? Tears welled, and she tried to will them away, squeezing her eyes shut.

This little valley that hugged the Rhine

River was supposed to be their home, for good, for always. Here, they had tried to live in peace, keeping to themselves in secluded hills and valleys, where they could farm the land and their sheep could graze and they could go about their daily life of work and worship without worry or hassle. This valley was dear to her, peaceful and pastoral.

Yet beneath the surface, life had started to change. A new baron held the Amish in disdain; much of the old conviviality of the village was disappearing. It was time to leave, the bishop had decided, before tensions escalated as they had in Switzerland, years ago.

Carefully, Anna wrapped the root ball of the dug-up rose in burlap. She glanced around the garden filled with her grandmother's roses. Their survival was a testament to her people's story: roots that adapted to whatever soil they were transplanted into, thorns that bespoke of the pain they bore, blossoms each spring that declared God's power to bring new life from death. As long as the roses survived, her grandmother said, so would our people. Her grandfather would scoff and call her a superstitious old woman, but Anna understood what she meant. The roses were a living witness to survival.

The sounds of hooting and hollering boys stormed into her thoughtful moment. She caught sight first of eight-year-old Felix, galloping toward her, followed by his older brother Johann. Felix frightened the chickens that scratched at the dirt in the garden, scattering them in a squawking cloud of flapping wings and molting feathers.

"A letter from Papa!" Felix shouted.

Behind him came Johann, holding his father's letter in the air, red faced and breathing hard from the exertion of climbing the hill. His eyes, bright from anticipation, fastened on Anna's face. "My father wrote there are twice as many immigrants leaving for Port Philadelphia this year as last. And last year was three times as many as the year before. He said we must make haste to join him in Penn's Woods and settle the land."

"Just think, Anna. Deer, turkey, rabbits, all easy to obtain. And with a little more effort —" he pretended to aim and shoot a rifle at an imaginary beast — "elk and wild boar to put up for winter provisions." Naturally, Johann, at age thirteen, knew everything.

But Anna, practical and skeptical and older than Johann by six years, held a different point of view. "I hear that the New World is a land of poisonous snakes, lions, tigers. And black bears and mountain lions. Gray wolves sweep down from the mountains in packs." A wolf pack frightened her most of all. When the wolves here grew desperate for food, they would attack her woollies.

Johann wasn't listening. He never listened to her objections about America. "Good water springs, lumber for building cabins."

"I've heard stories that settlers have seen red men. Many times."

Johann shook his head as he came up to Anna in the rose garden. "Friendly Indians. Curious ones. Fascinated with shiny brass kitchen kettles and knickknacks. Papa said he has found a place for us to settle." His eyes took on a faraway look and she knew he was off in his head to America to join his father. Jacob Bauer, the bishop of their church, had gone ahead to the New World last spring, to claim land and purchase warrants for those who intended to join him this year.

Anna turned to Felix and couldn't hold back a grin. A riot of curly hair peeped from beneath a tattered black felt hat, blue eyes sparkled with excitement, and a big smile showed more spaces than teeth.

The Bauer boys were like brothers to her. Felix was round and sturdy, with carrot red hair that matched his temperament. Johann, blond and thin, had never been hale and was afflicted with severe asthma. His heart and body might not be strong, that Johann, but his mind made up for it. What he carried around in that head of his was what mattered.

Now Felix was another story. Two black crows cackled from a nearby tree and he stared at them with a distant look in his eyes. "There's a crow's nest on the ship that's so high, you can see the curve of the earth."

Smiling inside, Anna said to him, "It's really that high?"

"Even higher." With a sweep of his hand Felix showed the curve of the earth. "Johann told me so."

Anna didn't know where Johann got his information. He'd had no schooling and owned no books except the Bible, but he knew all sorts of things. Solid-gold facts, he called them. She delighted in each nugget, whether true or not.

Then the twinkle in Felix's eyes faded. "It's a great pity I won't be able to find out for myself."

"The Bakers changed their mind and

aren't going, so Felix wants to stay behind too," Johann explained. "That means that Catrina Müller is the only one aboard close to Felix's age."

Felix's scowl deepened. "I'm not going if I have to be stuck on a ship with her. I'll stay here and live with the Bakers."

"I don't think you have much of a choice, Felix." *Nor do I.* Anna would never voice it aloud, but she dreaded the thought of spending the next few months in confined quarters with Catrina and her mother, Maria. Those two had a way of draining the very oxygen from the air. She set down her shovel. "Is your mother ready to go?"

Felix shrugged. "She's packing dishes into barrels."

"She must be eager to see your father."

He tilted his head. "She's humming. That's good. She wants to see Papa." Then he took off running along the narrow sheep's trail that led up the hill.

"I wish I could find a reason to go. Better yet, to stay."

"Change is coming, Anna," Johann said with annoying professorial patience. "It's in the air. We can't stay here and live like sheep in a pasture."

Anna looked up at the hillside. "I like sheep."

He crossed his arms in a stubborn pose. "I mean there is a whole new world out there. Just think of the mountains and valleys and unknown places we'll see."

"Filled with savages and the beasts. Your father has said as much in his letters."

"He also says there is land waiting for us which has never before been claimed, surveyed, or deeded. Land, Anna. We can live in safety. We can *own* land."

"Maybe there's no place that's truly safe for us."

He shook his head hard. "That's not what William Penn said. He offered a place where we can go and live in peace."

Johann didn't understand. He was moving toward someone — his father. His mother and brother would be traveling with him. Anna was moving away from those she loved. "My grandmother says it's wicked to want more than you have. She wants to just stay put and thank God."

Johann laughed. "Your grandmother is a frightened old lady who's had a hard life. Doesn't mean you should be scared of new things."

"I'm not." *Yes, I am.*

"Everything changes. That's the way of life. This Greek fellow Heraclitus said there is nothing permanent except change, and I

20

think he was right." He leaned forward and whispered in a conspiratorial voice, "Your grandmother has made Maria promise to find you a husband in the New World. She said that Ixheim has only old toothless men and young toothless boys." He lifted his voice an octave or two, warbling, to mimic her grandmother. "Anna must have Her Chance! She is pushing twenty without a man in sight."

Anna laid the rose in her basket and stood, sobered by the thought. With each passing birthday, her grandmother grew increasingly distressed. The New World, she decided, was Anna's only hope to find a like-minded bachelor.

Johann was watching her carefully, and then his eyes took on that teasing look of his. "If there's no one in the New World who passes Maria's muster, and if you don't mind holding off a few years, I suppose I could marry you."

She laughed then, and her mood shifted instantly from solemn to lighthearted, as it always did when she was around Johann. "I'll keep such a heartwarming proposal in mind."

"With fair wind and God's favor," Johann said, with his usual abundance of optimism, "we'll reach Port Philadelphia by the end of July."

When Anna pointed out that he was basing that assumption on all conditions being ideal and how rarely things ever turned out that way, he rolled his eyes in exasperation. "It's God's will. Of that my father and Christian have no doubt."

And how does anyone object to that? How in the world?

He wiggled his eyebrows and winked at her, then hurried up the hillside to join Felix, who was already on the top, to reach the shortcut that took them back to their house. Midway up the hill, Johann stopped and bent over to catch his breath. When he topped the hill, he turned and doffed his hat at her, flourishing it before him as if he were going to sweep the floor. She grinned, and then her grin faded as he disappeared down the other side of the hill and she was left with only her worries for company.

Tomorrow. Tomorrow!

Like it or not, the journey would begin. They would travel down the Rhine River to Rotterdam, board the vessel a shipping agent had arranged as passage for them, and then they'd be off to the New World.

Anna stretched her back and moved out of the shade to feel the afternoon sun on her face. The muscles in her arms and shoulders ached from spearing the shovel into the cold earth, but it was a pleasant ache. She'd always loved working outside, much more than she did the washing and cooking and keeping up of the house, the woman's work. The drudgery, she thought, and quickly sent an apology to the Lord for her ungrateful heart.

A furious honking of geese in the sky disrupted her reverie. Heading north for summer, she presumed. Her gaze traveled up the green hillside dotted with ruffs of gray wool. Her woollies, each one known to her by name. Her heart was suddenly too full for words as she let her gaze roam lovingly over the land she knew as home: over the rounded haystacks, the neat lambing sheds, the creek that ran almost the year round. The steep hills that brought an early sunset in summer and broke the wind in winter. It grieved her that she wouldn't be here this year for spring, as the lambs came and the wool was sheared and the ewes were mated and then the lambs would come again. She gazed at the hills, trying to engrave it in her memory. Where would she be next spring? She wondered what home would look like, feel like, smell like. She glanced down at her basket and gripped the leather handle, hard. At least she had her rose. If it survived, so would she.

A few hours later, Anna heard the whinny of a horse and came out of the house to see who was driving up the path. She shielded her eyes from the sun and saw Christian Müller on a wagon seat, Felix beside him.

Why would Felix be riding with their minister?

She noticed the somber look on Christian's usually cheerful face, the way Felix's small head was bowed. She crossed her arms, gripping her elbows. The wind, raw and cold, twisted her skirts around her legs. *Something's wrong.*

There came a stillness as if the whole world were holding its breath.

Let it be nothing, she entreated silently, let it be another meeting tonight to talk about the journey, or to let her know that Johann stopped to visit a friend. Let it be something silly. With every squeak of the wheels, she felt the lump in her throat grow bigger, the apprehension build.

A gust of wind swirled up the hill, flapping Anna's dress like a sheet on a clothesline, whipping the strings of her prayer cap against her neck, and she shivered.

Christian hauled back on the reins and set the brake on the wagon. Slowly, he climbed down and waited beside the wagon, bearded chin on his chest. Felix jumped off the seat and threw his arms around Anna's waist, shuddering with sobs.

Anna's gaze moved over Christian's pale face. Behind him, in the back of the wagon, was the shape of a body, covered by a gray wool blanket.

"Christian, who is it?" An icy feeling started in Anna's stomach and traveled up her spine. "C-Christian?" she whispered again, her eyes wide, her throat hot and tight. It was then she saw tears running down Christian's cheeks. The awful reality started to hit her full force and she pressed a fist to her lips. *Dear God,* she thought. *Dear God, how can this be?*

Christian turned away with his chin tucked down, then, almost lovingly, gently folded back the top of the blanket. His eyes lifted to meet hers. "The Lord has seen fit to take our young Johann from us."

2

June 26th, 1737

Bairn rounded the stern of the square-rigged ship. What a beauty she was! The *Charming Nancy* was a typical merchant vessel of her day: square-rigged and beak-bowed, with high, castle-like superstructures fore and aft that protected her cargo and crew in the worst weather. Maybe she wasn't the prettiest ship sailing the seas. No doubt she wasn't the youngest, and that did spike concern for Bairn. Even the sturdiest sail ship lasted only twenty years and the *Charming Nancy* was inching close to that age. She was worn and creaky, leaky as a sieve, and beating against the wind would be a painfully inefficient endeavor, but to him, serving as ship's carpenter, she was magnificent.

"Bairn!" A familiar voice boomed from the bow of the ship.

Bairn shielded his eyes from the sun to

see the ship's new commanding officer, Captain Charles Stedman, scowling down at him from the fo'c'sle deck. The captain tried very hard to look the part of a cultured, confident sea captain, like his much-esteemed older brother John, but never seemed to quite manage it. He was short and slender, with bushy side-whiskers, dressed elegantly with a whiskey-colored velvet vest, a tricornered black hat, and a white silk tie. "Make haste! Supervise the hold and see to it that no one is slacking!" The captain pointed to a stack of cargo that had been on the same spot on the deck since this morning.

Bairn felt heat rise up his neck, but he smiled amicably enough and tipped his hat in a feigned sign of respect. "Aye, Captain!" He had been supervising the loading of the hold — that's why he was standing at the hatch next to that very stack of cargo. But he knew the captain liked to sound off to deckhands to show he was in charge.

Bairn's gaze shifted to the first mate by the captain's side, Mr. Pocock. He shared officers' quarters with the first mate, an Englishman who was long past the prime of his life, with saggy, tired blue eyes, sun-leathered skin, and a belly that hung over the waistband of his black breeches. Mr.

Pocock had little to say unless you made the regrettable error of asking him about his gout. On that topic, he had plenty to say.

A light cross-course breeze blew in from the channel, pushing away the thin, acrid smell of tar and pitch from the docks that hung in the humid air. Bairn scrutinized the cargo that the stevedores were loading into the hold — the lowest part of the ship that stored most of the passengers' household goods, tools, and supplies, as well as the ship's supply of food, cordage, canvas, gunpowder. The capstan, a type of winch fitted with holes in which long bars were inserted, was used to hoist the cargo and other heavy loads down into the hold. By pushing on the bars, stevedores hauled in a rope wound around the capstan, moving the load up or down.

Earlier this morning, Bairn walked through the lower deck of the *Charming Nancy.* If he closed his eyes in the dark space and breathed deeply, he thought he could still smell the faint scent of wines and woolens of their recent cargo in the moist air, masking the stench of the bilge below.

Ships were ballasted with a noxious mix of sand and gravel that rattled and swished about the bilge for years, growing increasingly more foul as it absorbed the waste of life on board. The only place where the air was completely free of the smell of the bilge was the windward forecastle deck, the fo'c'sle deck, and this small space was sacred to the captain.

Bairn pitied the crew for their quarters in the fo'c'sle, below deck. Even more, he pitied the passengers who would be living in the lower deck. The stink of the bilge that pervaded the ship was strongest there. The *Charming Nancy* had spent most of her life going back and forth across the Atlantic with goods from England to trade in the colonies and vice versa, cargos that didn't care about stink. No longer.

The Rotterdam shippers had discovered that there was more money to be made shuttling Germans to the colonies of Georgia, Virginia, and New York. And now their attention had riveted to the surest of all markets, Pennsylvania.

Over the last few weeks, as the *Charming Nancy* was anchored in Rotterdam, Bairn's days were spent making repairs and adjustments to the old ship. He corrected the fitting of the bowsprit so rainwater no longer leaked into the seamen's living quarters. That should set him in good standing with the crew and make up for the more onerous task Captain Stedman had asked of him: the building of double bedsteads in the lower deck to allow for increased capacity of passengers in the ship. The poor souls would be fitted in like sardines in a tin.

"I got me a bad feeling about this trip. A real bad feeling."

Bairn spun around to face Decker. His eyes narrowed in perplexity as he studied the irritating seaman. Decker bullied the crew, caused malice and rancor, but he was a skilled craftsman and the captain had recently promoted him to carpenter's apprentice — against Bairn's objection. "Decker, you need to stop worryin' others with yer odd dreams. You sound fey. You've got the crew nervous as a scalded cat."

"It's not just my dreams. I saw Queenie under a tub this mornin'. 'Tis an omen. You know what 'at means."

To Decker, it was a portent of magnitudinous proportions: death was imminent. To Bairn, it meant the ship's black cat, Queenie, never the brightest of felines to start with, had gotten herself trapped under a tub.

Something shiny caught his eye. Decker was wearing polished black shoes with silver buckles. Bairn tilted his head. "New shoes?"

Decker clicked his heels together. "Aye.

Bought 'em off a shoemaker in Rotterdam. Seein' as how I'm an officer now, I thought I should look the part."

Bairn rolled his eyes. "Yer naught but an apprentice, Decker."

"The shoemaker said the buckles would ward off bad luck."

"Why do you nae just admit you do nae want to haul bodies across the sea and stop scarin' the deckhands. Half the crew went jobbin' with other ships once you started spoutin' off with yer crazy dreams and superstitious nonsense."

"I don't deny I'd rather tote silent cargo than tend to complainin' Germans, but 'at's only part of the reason. You know as well as I do that havin' women on board is bad luck. And the captain's tryin' to jam more bodies down here than the ship can hold."

Decker was a provoking fellow, always firing at people with hammer and tongs, but on this particular topic of overcrowding, Bairn couldn't fault him. He was helpless to do anything about it, though. "Yer a free agent, Decker. You can always sign on another ship." He knew Decker would never leave the *Charming Nancy*. The lure of the promotion was too appealing.

Decker's gaze shifted across the harbor to the tall ships that lined the docks. "Problem is, I dunno any captain out there who isn't doin' the exact same thing."

"Well, then, until you make up yer mind, see that you finish the double bedsteads."

Decker shot him a dark frown and stomped away.

Bairn inflated his cheeks and blew the air out in a gusty sigh. Decker's foreboding nettled him. While he felt a great loyalty to Captain Stedman, the overcrowding of the ships was a valid worry — not only would it strain the timbers and seams of the *Charming Nancy,* but the additional provisions needed to keep the passengers fed would add critical weight to the ship. The *St. Andrew,* the ship under Captain John Stedman's command, had already left Rotterdam with far more passengers than was safe. Bed shelves were stacked two and three deep. A man's nose would brush the bottom of the next fellow's bunk.

Opportunity drove the overcrowding, both for the passengers and the captain. Whether a man traveled in the Great Cabin or the lower deck, each had an ambition to get to the New World, where milk and honey flowed and all men could become rich.

The number of German immigrants arriving in Philadelphia had grown sevenfold in the last two years. The journey was a perilous one and many didn't survive — though that didn't stop the shipping agents and the captains from collecting their passage. Dead or alive upon arrival, each body owed its fare.

Bairn knew food and fresh water for such an enormous quantity of people would be jeopardized due to space constraints. And what would they do if they experienced delays? He'd heard macabre tales of passengers starving to death. If a ship took much more than eight weeks to cross the ocean, no doubt they would run out of provisions.

Weeks ago, when Captain Stedman had ordered the refitting of the lower deck, Bairn had cautiously objected. You had to tread carefully when you questioned the captain. His word, and mostly his ego, ruled the ship. As expected, Bairn's protest was quickly shot down. "I'll do the fashin' for me ship, lad," the captain said.

Lad. Boy. Bairn. A Scottish word for "child." That was the captain's way of reminding him of his place.

Everything in life boiled down to money, that truth Bairn had observed in his two-and-twenty years on earth, the last eleven of which were spent at sea. And he couldn't deny that it was the very thing that drove him, as well. There was nothing more important to Bairn than making money.

And yet, at least for him, something else hung in the balance with the *Charming Nancy.* Captain Stedman had strongly hinted that after this voyage he might expect a promotion to first mate, the top boatswain. A few years as first mate, then he would be ready to captain his own ship. Better still, he would have funds saved to become an investor like his benefactors, the Stedman brothers. Captain Charles often boasted that he was an investor of eleven ships. Captain John never boasted, which indicated to Bairn that he was an investor in far more.

Wouldn't life be sweet to hold that kind of wealth one day? Bairn had it all worked out: With a bit of luck and fair winds, he would be commanding a ship like the *Charming Nancy* with her hold filled with freshly sawn timber, saltpeter, iron, sugar, hempen yarn, and more — stamped and bound for England. Come spring, he would fill the ship with Germans from Rotterdam and return to Port Philadelphia. His ambition lured him onward and the cycle would begin again.

Bairn had a passionate, bone-deep desire to become wealthy. Nay, extraordinarily wealthy. And with the influx of German immigrants pouring out of Rotterdam to the New World, he was riding the top of a wave.

He saw Decker's black cat sashay over to him and curl around his boot leg, tail swishing, so he bent down to scoop her up. "Omen, me eye," he told her. "Yer naught but a curious cat."

June 27th, 1737

This Rotterdam was a poor place, and Anna longed to go home.

Weeks and weeks had passed since she had left Ixheim. Her heart still ached and her eyes filled with tears when she least expected it. In their haste to depart, there wasn't time to properly grieve Johann Bauer's unexpected passing. In Christian's eyes, it was a clear sign of more cruelty to come — aimed at the Bauer family — and confirmed that departure could not and should not be delayed.

Johann was buried the morning after his death, and the families left, in a somber mood, to meet the boat on the Rhine by high noon. Dorothea, his mother, was still in shock, barely spoke, hardly ate. She was just going through the motions of living. She stayed close to Anna, but her mind was elsewhere. Felix hadn't smiled or laughed since that pivotal afternoon in the rose garden.

The Amish group had traveled down the Rhine from Heilbronn to Rotterdam by ship, docking at each custom house so agents could board and examine their goods for taxation. Valuable time was lost — the entire month of May and part of June.

Maria Müller, Christian's wife, was outraged by the endless delays. "Twenty-six custom houses down the Rhine," she said at every meal, as if they all hadn't been there. "Twenty-six! What should have taken one week took six. Nothing but thievery, those tax collectors." Maria sniffed. "Highway robbery."

Christian tried to ward off his wife's tirade. "Remember, dear, we were helpless to do anything about it."

He knew, as they all did, that this initial complaint was Maria's prelude that led straight into the next grievance. "And as soon as we do arrive in Rotterdam, they shoo us off to stay . . . here!" She lifted a palm in the air and waved it in a circle, then heaved a loud sigh of disgust. "In squalor and filth."

Maria could be taxing, but she said things that everyone else was thinking. It *was* a disgusting place, Anna heartily agreed. An overcrowded makeshift tent city. Government officials of Rotterdam had sent them off to a holding area in the vicinity of the ruins of St. Elbrecht's chapel below Kralingen because emigrants weren't permitted to remain in the city.

"And they said *we* might bring disease." Maria rambled on. "Dirt and filth. Hmmph. As if we would bring anything but cleanliness and godliness."

And patience.

They were waiting until passage to America could be arranged between a Neulander — a recruiter — and a shipping agent. More precious time slipping through their hands. Worse, their funds were slipping away too.

Last night brought good news. The Neulander found them in the tent city to tell them he had been able to secure their passage on the vessel *Charming Nancy.* His name was Georg Schultz and he certainly didn't look the part of a man of influence. He was the fattest man Anna had ever seen, doughy and white as a dumpling, a three-hundred-pound dumpling. He was almost perfectly round. Just over five feet tall, with an oddly shaped head that seemed too small for his body and a gray beard elegantly trimmed to a point. But as soon as he spoke of the bounty of land that waited for them in America, Anna realized why Georg Schultz had a reputation for a surprisingly compelling gift of persuasion. "Land as far as the eye can see," he said, describing the scene as if it were right in front of them. "Rich, dark soil, babbling brooks with fresh clean water, virgin timber that tickles the sky, waiting for you to claim it and tame it."

Anna served as interpreter for Georg Schultz, who spoke a crisp and polished high German, and refused to lower himself to speak the peasant farmers' dialects, like that of her people. In between translations, she stirred a large kettle of stew. Georg sidled over to the kettle and took a whiff of the stew. He stood uncomfortably close to Anna, giving her a slow once-over. Her eyes narrowed and she moved a few steps away.

"In Penn's Woods," Georg said, "one might travel about a whole year without spending a penny. It's customary when one comes with his horse to a house, the traveler is asked if he wishes to have something to eat. If one wishes to stay overnight to the morrow, he and his horse are harbored free of charge." He moved closer to Anna. "He is invited to take his seat at the table and take his luck at the pot."

The breath of that man! It could peel the

varnish off a table. Anna set the wooden spoon in the kettle and stepped back yet again from Georg. "I think perhaps you are hinting for an invitation to a meal."

"A tongue as tart as a green apple, I see." Georg burst out with a laugh. "I'd be delighted." His eyes swept down her figure and returned to rest at her chest.

She spun on her heel to turn her back on him. Him and his roving eyes.

Georg moved around their temporary dwelling and frowned at the sight of the bulky household goods, the chimney backs and scythes, shovels and iron pots and frying pans, crosscut saws, axes and hatches. "So much, so much. This will cost you a fortune to transport." He pointed to Christian. "I have a suggestion that will save you money. And time." He clapped his pudgy hands. "Time and money!" He wheeled around to find Anna. "Girl! Come translate."

Anna explained what Georg had in mind and Christian's eyes lit up at the thought of saving money.

"I will trade your used goods for new ones of the same kind," Georg said. "I can get the same items in lots of dozens, tightly packed so it won't look like you have as much. You won't run the risk of the captain refusing your passage." He peered at Christian, who was looking to Anna to explain. "They can do that, you know. Refuse your passage. The captain's word is law." Georg folded his large arms over his chest. "And that would mean you must wait for another ship. Soon it will be late in the season." He glanced around the tent. "It would be a pity to lose a chance to sail with Captain Stedman."

That name meant something to Christian. His eyes went wide. "We are sailing under John Stedman?"

"Well, close," Georg said, wagging his big chins. "Captain Charles Stedman. John Stedman's brother." John Stedman had a reputation among the Palatinate Mennonites as a blue-water captain, and word had trickled to the tiny Amish church of Ixheim. Captain Stedman had safely transported hundreds of German Mennonites from the Rhine Valley to the colonies. Christian excused himself and drew into a knot with a group of men, standing shoulder to shoulder, to confer.

Anna watched Georg Schultz observe them and wondered if he looked at the men of her church and assumed they were all alike, long beards jerking, big felt hats flapping in the wind. From where she stood, they certainly looked alike, sounded alike, acted alike. But Anna could see how different they really were: Josef Gerber, a bulky, gentle man with a toddler in each arm, both towheaded, with straight-edge bangs above their nearly white eyebrows. Flat-faced Simon Miller, his hair and beard black as a crow. Lean and lanky Isaac Mast. Next to him was his gangly, sixteen-year-old son Peter, a fuzz of whiskers circling his chin to celebrate his recent wedding to Lizzie. And then there was Christian, their leader, bald and bespectacled with a long beard on his chin that was as tangled as a bird's nest. The men's heads bent together to hear Christian, shorter than all of them, and quieter too, but when he spoke, others always listened.

Yes, the men were different in many ways, but underneath they were much the same, in all the things that mattered most: faith and family and tradition.

Just then, as if they'd been given some invisible signal, there was a great nodding of heads and dipping of beards. Christian strode over to Georg Schultz to give him permission to trade off most of their household goods. Pleased, Georg Schultz promised him new goods would be waiting at the docks tomorrow to be loaded into the hold of the *Charming Nancy.*

Anna hoped Georg Schultz's word could be trusted, as they were entirely dependent on the Neulander. She thought back to warnings Jacob Bauer had written about Neulanders: they received a handsome commission on each passenger they brought to the ship, as well as free passage, so they were not always a reliable source of information.

That night, as Anna lay on her pallet, she could hear the familiar voices of Christian and a few other men as they sat by the fire, talking over the day, in good spirits now that the journey was finally getting under way. Dorothea slept peacefully beside her. Even Felix seemed cheerful tonight. Anna felt the opposite — a rush of loneliness and longing.

As she looked up at the stars, sparkly diamonds on black velvet, she tried to come up with a plan to get back home.

June 28th, 1737

Felix Bauer thought he might explode from nervous excitement. Tomorrow they would be climbing aboard a boat — a ship! — and sailing to the other side of the world.

He wished his mother and Anna were more excited about this sea journey. His mother, well, he wasn't sure she knew or even cared where she was since they had left Ixheim. And Anna tried to act like they were off on a jaunt to a neighbor's house, nothing more. But Felix saw through her. She was no Catrina Müller, putting on performances. Anna had only one or two faces, maybe three, nothing hidden, nothing exaggerated. She never once said how exciting the trip would be. She just said that going was something whose time had come. That it had to be done.

Maria Müller, Catrina's mother, had no hesitation about sharing her opinion. She didn't want to leave Ixheim and didn't mind if everybody knew her feelings. It struck Felix as funny when Maria would start out saying, "I've kept quiet long enough" and then out would come another list of worries about the journey ahead. She liked to repeat horror stories she'd heard from some of the Mennonites who were waiting in the tent city, like they were, to book passage on a ship. Esther Wenger, a Mennonite, told Maria about a ship that ran completely out of food. "They left Rotterdam with one hundred fifty on board," Maria told Christian, "and they arrived with only fifty persons alive." Felix lurked nearby, fascinated by the gruesome tale. "In the end, they had to eat rats. Rats!"

Christian's spectacles flashed her a warning, but by suppertime, everybody knew everything. The notion of running out of food was a particularly frightful one, stirring up the mothers, so Christian decided that as a safety measure, they would take additional provisions on the ship. "We will not go hungry," he reassured the anxious mothers. That afternoon, he and Josef Gerber set out to buy smoked meat, cheese, butter, peas, barley, and zwieback from the stores in Rotterdam that catered to ship passengers. Felix tagged along to carry the purchases, happy to have an excuse to get away from Catrina, who was always pestering him about one thing or another.

Christian Müller, Felix observed, had an impressive way of ignoring his wife. He would tilt his head and nod as if he was listening carefully to Maria's woes, then turn his attention to something else entirely. Felix would like to try to manage the horrible Catrina as skillfully, especially since he would be stuck with her for the next few months. Just this morning, he had stopped peeling potatoes for one moment — hardly *one* minute — because he had spotted a long line of ants and wondered where they were headed.

Catrina noticed. "Felix needs help," she

said in a loud voice.

"I do not!" Felix said, but what he was thinking was, *A pox on her!* He picked up his peeling knife, sat down again with the stupid potatoes, crossed his eyes at Catrina, and she promptly told her mother.

Catrina was born with an eyeball that was kind of lazy. Instead of looking where it should be looking, it floated off to the side. She'd tried exercises, looking this way, then that, up and down, down and up. Anna's grandmother gave her a patch to wear on her good eye to make the lazy one work, but nothing helped. Felix had perfected a way to get even with Catrina: whenever she talked to him, he would act flustered, as if he didn't know which eye to look at, which made her all the madder.

Catrina Müller was the only blight on this trip.

No. There was one more. His worry about his mother. She was quiet and sad and would eat hardly at all. And she was always tired. She would sleep the day away if Anna let her. When she was awake, there was fear in her eyes, fear of the far-off. Felix did what he could to cheer his mother up, but nothing seemed to help. Anna said that being reunited with his father was the only thing that would help his mother. But that was still a long time away.

Tonight, Felix stayed up practically all night long picturing what lay ahead. First, he considered the other side of the world: America. It was hard to have an idea of what it would be like — in his mind, the world he knew in Ixheim kept fanning out around him. So he would shift his imagination to the world nearly at hand — the sea journey. He saw himself high in the crow's nest on the ship, shielding his eyes from the sun with one hand, searching, searching, searching for the first sign of land. He spotted pirates and whales, and the captain praised his keen eyesight. He shimmied down the long poles, just like the other sailors did, and climbed the ropes like a monkey. Even better, he saw himself behind the big wheel in a ferocious storm, saving the ship from running aground.

All winter, Johann had read stories of sailing on the high seas, spinning tales and igniting his imagination of what the journey to the New World would be like. Whenever he thought of Johann, dozens of times a day, his stomach hurt. When he had something he wanted to tell Johann and had to remind himself that his brother wasn't here anymore, his head hurt. When he thought of all that Johann was missing, his heart hurt.

One thing hadn't changed. Felix would see his father at the end of this adventure. He imagined his father — a big, tall man with a long salt-and-pepper beard — waiting on the dock for their ship to sail in. Felix would spot him first, naturally, and gallop down the gangplank into his arms, stretched out wide for his son to run into them. Everything would be all right again.

Almost everything.

3

June 29th, 1737

There were so many rivers here, fast-flowing streams in a hurry to wind around the city triangle of Rotterdam and spill into the sea. Anna trailed along in the line of Amish who followed Christian Müller, and remembered that Johann had told her on a cold winter afternoon that Rotterdam was once nothing but a small fishing village. "Now it's the main access from Europe to England."

And now to America.

Anna had never been to a city. She had never been anywhere but her small German village. Now, standing on a rise that overlooked Rotterdam, looking out at the great hulls of ships in the harbor, the tall buildings that impaled the smoke and steam and heat haze, listening to the cacophony of shouting people and squeaking chains, she didn't know whether she found it beautiful or frightening. It was a much bigger world than she had thought possible.

Today, at long last, they were finally going to board the ship and set sail for the New World. Georg Schultz had been surprisingly true to his word. Yesterday, their household belongings had been placed in the hold of the ship for ballast as Christian and Josef Gerber and Isaac Mast counted everything.

The only belonging Anna cared about was her rose, wrapped carefully in burlap that she moistened with water each day. This rose would *not* be kept deep in the ship's dark hold. She kept it with her, in a basket by her side, at all times.

As they left the tent city to head toward Rotterdam's harbor, Anna noticed a group of women drenching their dirty linen in the river and slapping it against the rocks. The women, with their sleeves rolled up to reveal strong, red arms, skirts pulled high, feet bare to spare their shoes, were gossiping, cackling, singing as they washed. Anna felt a sweeping sense of loss, missing all that was familiar. Simple everyday tasks — washing clothes in the kettle with her grandmother, hanging them on a wooden clothesline, bringing the sheep down the hillside, gardening beside her grandfather — they seemed so precious to her. When would life feel familiar again? Would it ever?

"Anna? Are you all right?" Felix stood in front of her, alarm sparking in his blue eyes. "Is your leg hurting?"

She walked with a slight limp, a remnant from a childhood accident, but that wasn't the reason she had slowed to a stop without realizing it and had fallen behind. "I'm thinking too much is all." Gently she brushed the hair out of his eyes. She hardly had to reach down to do so anymore, he was getting that big. He would be nine years old come winter. "Where is your hat?"

Felix's hands flew up to his bare head. "Oh no! It must have blown off!"

"So, boy, you finally noticed," Maria Müller said, holding out Felix's black hat. A woman of considerable girth, she consistently lagged behind the others and brought up the rear of the group. Fitting, Anna thought, because she knew — why, *everyone* knew — that Maria was unhappy about leaving home. Anna took the hat from Maria and plopped it on Felix's head. She gave him a look. "You must not lose it. Your mother has no extra money to replace it."

All the Amish had barely enough money left to book their passage on a merchant ship — one thousand guilders per person.

At least Felix knew better than to fuss right then, with Maria looming, for he had a contrite look on his face without his usual commotion.

As they neared the wharves, the streets grew more congested, packed with people buying and selling, begging and thieving. Church bells clamored from every street corner, vendors bargained, dogs barked, cats slithered, shoppers stomped about on thick clogs, holding their hems up from mud puddles. Anna's nose filled with the smells of coils of sausage ropes, bins of produce, bags of spices, beeswax candles, fine perfumes, sides of raw meat. Peddlers called out their wares: turnips, spring carrots only slightly withered, salted cod, salt-cured pork, salted beef, salt! "Vissen, Vissen!" a rosy-cheeked gray-haired woman shouted with a tray of silvery dried fish, laid out like knives, hanging from her neck.

Carrying their belongings in the stifling, humid heat, the Amish walked on the market fringe toward the docks, staring up at the great hulls of ships. Soon the air brought a new scent Anna didn't recognize: a salty, briny, tangy smell. The sea. How curious!

When they reached the docks, they found a port busy with afternoon activity. Orders were shouted, drums rolled, pulleys squeaked, timbers creaked, waves lapped

51

against the pilings. Even Anna, who knew nothing about ships and sailors and sea journeys, could sense excitement in the air.

It took a number of tries with Dutch stevedores to find out where the *Charming Nancy* was docked, but the Amish eventually made their way toward the ship through a jumble of barrels, shipping crates, stacked cargo, impatient seamen.

And then they got their first glimpse of the ship that was to sail with them to America. There, at the far end of a dock, rocking gently on the waves of the harbor, was the *Charming Nancy.*

Light rain had been spattering on the deck on and off since morning, but the clouds were beginning to burn off. There was an urgency to get the voyage under way as Captain Stedman intended to sail on today's outgoing tide. Sweaty stevedores filled the hold with trunks and crates and barrels as Bairn leaned over the open hatch. It was critical that the hold be well packed, highly organized, and expertly balanced to keep the keel settled deep in the water. Additional provisions would be acquired in England; afterward, there wouldn't be room in the hold to swing a cat by the tail.

Employing nearly the full extent of his

Dutch vocabulary, Bairn shouted that the hold looked good and to keep going. Like he did in every port, he had picked up enough foreign language to communicate what needed to be said to the stevedores. He climbed the ladder to the lower deck, where the passengers would stay. If all went well, this would be the last time he would be in this part of the ship until it reached Port Philadelphia. He, as ship's carpenter, along with the first mate and the captain, would never venture down below except for an emergency. The captain's Great Cabin and the officers' quarters might be small, but they were in the stern of the ship where fresh air came in through the windows, providing relief from the pervasive stench of the lower deck and bilge, and they were protected from crashing waves.

Bairn climbed the companionway stairs to the upper deck. He heard a strange squeal — an animal in distress — and bolted over to the railing. He watched in disbelief as he saw a stevedore try to lead a large pig up the gangplank with a rope around its neck. The pig wasn't cooperating. It eased back on its haunches and then down on its forelegs, refusing to budge off the dock, squealing unhappily. Bairn gripped the rail and leaned over the edge, watching the scene unfold with amusement. The stevedore tried to pick the pig up, but two hundred pounds of hog was too much for even the goliath strength of the man. The pig buried its head under its front legs. The stevedore pushed the pig from behind and Bairn started chuckling. When the stevedore tried rolling the pig up the gangplank, he burst out laughing.

If he wasn't in a hurry to get this ship loaded and ready to sail the channel, he could have stood there all afternoon, enjoying the sight. Instead, he went to the galley and took a handful of oats from the crock, then went down the gangplank. The stevedore had worked himself to a frenzy. Bairn held one hand up to stop him from his wrestling match with the pig. He took the rope leash from the stevedore and spread oats up the gangplank. Like a docile dog on a lead, the pig followed the oats trail straight up the gangplank. When it reached the deck, Bairn tied the pig's rope to a bollard. The stevedore ambled up the gangplank with an embarrassed look on his red face.

"Y'need to think the way a pig thinks t'get it t'do what you want it t'do."

The stevedore didn't comprehend what Bairn was saying, but he understood that he meant him no disrespect. He shrugged, then grinned, and Bairn smiled with him.

"Bairn! Get the captain and get down here!"

He spun around to locate the voice and saw the recruiter, Georg Schultz. If there was anyone who could set his teeth on edge, it was Schultz. To most, Schultz appeared to be a carefree fellow: a cockalorum, a jolly little man who drank for the pleasure of it. Bairn knew those small eyes bespoke a cunning shrewdness; he knew that every action Schultz took was motivated by money. He was a cagey character who was able to import a steady stream of innocent Germans, vetting them with visions of a land of milk and honey just waiting to be enjoyed on the other side of the ocean. Ultimately bilking them out of their hard-earned savings. Along the way he alienated more than a few people, but Schultz managed to keep the ship captains happy by filling the lower decks with passengers.

Down on the dock, Schultz was waving frantically to Bairn. Beside him was a long line of bonneted and bearded people in dark, somber clothing, milling silently about on the dock, peering up at the ship. They were known on the docks as the Peculiar People. He scrutinized the faces, wondering what they were thinking as they waited to board. Did they feel fearful? Anxious? Certainly, they must be judgmental of the profane deckhands. But he read no hostility, no contempt, little anxiety, mostly simple curiosity.

Why should it matter? The passengers meant nothing to him.

Yet try as he did to ignore it, Bairn experienced the stirrings of uneasiness in his midsection, as he always did when he came across these odd people — a prickling, a plucking in his chest.

Waiting, waiting, waiting. Anna kept one eye on Dorothea and the other on Felix as they stood on the dock, absolutely sure that one or the other would end up in the dark water and neither of them knew how to swim. Felix had an abundance of curiosity and a dearth of common sense, and Dorothea was still muddled in a fog. Never emotionally sturdy, the death of Johann took her over the edge.

Felix's stomach grumbled loudly. "How much longer? I'm getting hungry." His stomach was a bottomless pit.

"It shouldn't be too much longer," Anna said. Her heart ached in a sweet way as she watched relief ease his face. As she saw him bend down to throw a pebble at a seagull, she wished for the hundredth time that Johann were with him. Felix seemed so lonely. The only other child close to his age was Catrina Müller, and she was a sore trial to him.

And suddenly Georg Schultz appeared in front of her. Again the hackling feeling. He wanted her to interpret as he spoke to Christian. "Guilders, Christian," Anna relayed. "He wants you to prepay the freight. Full freight for each adult, half freight for each child from age four to fifteen. No charge for those under four."

Alarm flickered through Christian's eyes. "I wasn't anticipating a charge for children. We spent more than expected when we bought extra provisions in Rotterdam yesterday. If we pay now, we will have nothing left." He rubbed his forehead. "What can be done?"

Think, Anna. Think. She looked Georg Schultz in the eye. "We will pay half-freight now, and the remainder when we arrive safely in Philadelphia. We want to ensure that we will be well cared for."

Georg Schultz pointed to her and growled low in his throat, "Kommst du mit."

She followed him up the gangplank and noticed an official-looking figure standing at the top of the gangplank, watching her approach with sharp, penetrating eyes. For a split second he reminded her of Felix's father, bishop Jacob Bauer — treetop tall, muscular, wide-beamed shoulders. Then the moment passed and she saw how very different from the bishop he really was. Jacob was plain and humble and holy. There was nothing plain nor humble nor holy about this man.

This man was dressed impeccably in a sturdy, long-sleeved coat that hugged his ribs, a crisp white linen shirt, tight-fitting breeches that tucked into polished knee-high black boots. Sun-streaked, amber-gold hair threaded with red, kept long and held back in the traditional seaman's queue. High cheekbones framed by side whiskers, boxy jaw, and cold slate-gray eyes. His skin was nut-brown from days in the sun, or perhaps from his heritage. While he appeared young, his seaman's stance, so solid, so self-confident, and his style of dress sent a simple message: that he was in charge, and that he was all business.

Georg Schultz, intimidated by no one, barely came to the middle of his chest. "Bairn, where is the captain?"

The man propped his shoulders against the polished oak and crossed his arms over his broad chest, as though preparing for a

58

long chat. "He's in the Great Cabin. Not t'be disturbed. What do you want, Schultz?" Behind him, sailors hurried from one end of the deck to the other, exchanging words, issuing orders. Now and then, the man would bark an order to the sailors who hurried past him in a rich Scottish burr. This man, Anna thought, had the kind of authority that shut you up fast if you were a young sailor inclined to challenge something he had just said.

He glanced at her then, the hard line of his jaw softening just a little, looking down at her with an inscrutable gaze, making her feel even smaller and more awkward.

Had he noticed she was taking a survey of his person? Her neck heated, and she lowered her gaze yet still felt his intense scrutiny. Why was he staring at her? Perhaps there was something on her face. Her skin itched by suggestion, and she brushed self-conscious fingers across her cheeks.

He straightened to his full height. Goodness, he was tall. The tallest man she'd ever seen. He spoke English with a distinctive accent that she couldn't quite place, shortening words and lilting the end of a sentence. Northern England, perhaps, mixed in with the Scottish. Her grandfather would have been able to pinpoint it.

Georg Schultz pointed a thumb at Anna. "She says they won't pay full fare until we reach Philadelphia. Only half fare for now."

A frown settled over the man's features, and he hooked his thumbs in his waistcoat pockets as he studied Anna. "The captain won't like hearin' that the passengers cannae pay passage."

"I didn't say we *couldn't.* We will pay. You can be assured of that." She looked down, afraid he'd read the truth in her eyes, more than she was ready to reveal. She felt no such assurance that the Amish would be solvent by the end of the journey, not after how their coffers had been diminished down the Rhine. But if they ended up in a desperate situation, she felt sure that Jacob Bauer would find a way to provide passage once they reached America.

He was still staring at her, she suddenly realized, though with a bemused look on his face. "You speak English quite well."

Georg Schultz answered for her, folding his pudgy arms over his chest. "The only one of this batch of Peculiars who can speak it."

"How did y'learn?"

"My grandfather. He served in the military in Switzerland."

"A man of yer . . . people . . . knew both

plow and sword?"

She knew he had barely stopped himself from saying the word Peculiar. She'd heard the dockworkers mutter the disparagement. "My grandfather had no choice but to serve. And he was clever at learning languages."

"And taught them to his family."

"Yes." Anna's grandfather was convinced that their people must be wise to the ways of the world, wise as serpents and innocent as doves, especially in the skill of communication. No one in Ixheim shared his conviction, but he was adamant that his granddaughter would speak, read, and write English, German, French.

"Then what is yer reasonin' to only pay half fare?"

"We want to be sure we will be treated well. Good food and clean water."

The man gave her a skeptical glance. "Lassie, if yer people cannae pay passage, the ship 'twill become a market. Buyers in Port Philadelphia will find out how much each person owes. Those who cannae pay their debts are called 'redemptioners.' They haggle with the buyers fer so many years labor t'pay off the debt. The redemptioner belongs to the buyer until that debt is paid off. *Belongs,* like a slave. It happens. Quite a lot. To men, women. To children too."

The muscles in Anna's midsection tensed. She bit her lip. Her expression must have registered the sting of his words, for he softened.

"Even if a person doesn't survive the journey, the passage will be owed. 'Tis unfortunate, but it happens more often than y'might imagine."

Their eyes met, locked, held. His gaze was like granite. "I understand."

"Yer basket," he said. "It should go down in the hold. To save room. You'll want every spare inch down in the lower deck."

"No," Anna said.

"All nonessentials belong in the hold." He bent over to take the basket, but Anna's grip on it tightened.

"No," Anna repeated. "This basket *is* essential." She stared at his calloused hand that covered hers, refusing to let go, then peered up at the man, so incredibly tall, it put a crick in her neck. Up close he was larger than life and even more intimidating. For a moment she couldn't blink, breathe, or move.

He released his grip on the basket. "What's in it, then?"

She tried to speak, but it was as if those stormy dark eyes had fused the words to her throat. She finally swallowed hard, his bold gaze and the scent of sandalwood from his clothing doing funny things to her stomach.

He angled her a glance with the barest of smiles. "Now, I know you can talk, because you've already bargained yer way across the ocean."

She coughed, clearing the knot of awkwardness from her throat as she tightened her grip on her basket. "A rose. It is precious to me." Her lips compressed into a straight line and one hand was on her hip. It was the look and stance she used when someone thought she was too young to know what she was doing, which happened rather a lot back in Ixheim.

"A rose?" A shadow of something passed through his eyes, then vanished like vapor, making her think she'd imagined it. Next he surprised Anna with his terse, dismissive words. "I'll inform the captain of yer predicament." He turned and strode down the ship's deck.

As Anna followed down the gangplank behind Georg Schultz, her thoughts remained with that tall, arrogant man in the fancy frock. She snapped a glance over her shoulder. "If he's not the captain, then who is he?"

"He's the ship's carpenter. A boatswain." Georg Schultz held up three thick fingers. "Third in command."

At the bottom of the gangplank, Anna explained the arrangement to Christian and waited as he pulled out a leather pouch. The money was counted and handed to Georg Schultz. When the ship's carpenter shouted down to load the passengers, they lined up behind the large group of Mennonites to walk up the gangplank. The mighty Mennonites, was how Anna thought of them. There were so many of them! Twice, perhaps thrice as many as there were Amish. Tensions between the Mennonites and the followers of Jacob Amman were thorny at best. How would they survive living together in such close quarters? Anna gazed at the ship as she took her place in line, sticking closely to Dorothea, who held Felix's hand in a death grip.

If all went well, this ship would be home for the next two months. If all did not go well, it could be longer. Maria liked to remind everyone of another of Esther Wenger's horrifying tales: a ship's passage that took nine months. Nine months! Three-quarters of a year. The thought made Anna shudder. But then she'd also heard Maria speak of a journey that took only four weeks. She was counting on the latter — a swift passage, blessed by God.

Once on the ship, they were led straight down the companionway into the lower deck. Anna's eyes stung with the sour stink and took more than a moment to adjust to the dim lighting. She helped Dorothea climb down the last few steps as Felix disappeared to explore the lower deck. Christian went quickly ahead in the cavernous space, pointing out sleeping shelves, nooks and crannies where families could claim space near the bow of the ship because the mighty Mennonites had claimed all available space in the stern. It was quickly apparent that passengers outnumbered beds.

The beds bore little resemblance to the kind found in Anna's home in Ixheim. These were wooden bunks, six feet long, three feet high, open at both ends. They were set in rows, side by side, and stacked to the ceiling. No more than two persons were supposed to be assigned to one bunk — according to Esther Wenger, who told Maria — but Georg Schulz insisted that each family was only allowed one bunk. Georg, first down the companionway, took the largest one, nearest the stern of the ship and closest to a hatch. For the Gerbers and the Müllers and the Masts and others, one family per bunk would mean crowding four or five or six into one bed. Anna looked toward the stern and saw a Mennonite family of ten settling in. Ten in one bed!

Maria was directing traffic. "You, Josef, you take your family over there. Conrad — you take your brood and go over there. You'll be cozy as a yolk in an egg." Her eyes swept the area until she found what she was looking for: a corner berth, the roomiest area for trunks and packages to be stored.

"And here is where Christian and I will sleep," she continued. "Anna, you and Dorothea and Felix should use pallets and sleep over there." She pointed to the gun deck, where a cannon was pointed through a square hole. "The air will be good for Felix. Growing boys need fresh air. Yes, you'll be most comfortable there."

"Of course, Maria," Anna said. *I sincerely doubt it, Maria,* she thought. As she placed her basket on the ground, she peered out the small opening at the open sea. How wet and cold could this area get when a storm blew in?

Catrina stood in front of Anna with her hands on her hips, though at the age of ten she had no hips to speak of. "Where did Felix go to?" She pursed her thin lips together. "Being a boy, and a most bothersome one at that, he'll need to be watched every moment so that he doesn't go straight into the sea and end up as food for the fishes." That was Catrina all over: huffy and prone to hysterics, always first with the alarm whether it was valid or not.

Dorothea and Anna exchanged a glance. Never far from Dorothea's mind was the fear that Felix could fall overboard. Any number of disasters could befall a boy on a boat. Especially a boy who does not think.

"Catrina, thank you for your concern," Anna said, "but you don't need to trouble yourself over Felix's whereabouts. His mother and I keep a careful eye on him at all times."

"I try to set a good example for the children." Catrina drew herself up importantly and sniffed. "Somebody has to."

"But . . . where is Felix, Anna?" Dorothea looked around the lower deck anxiously.

Oh no. Where did that boy go? Then Anna spotted a shock of red hair over by a cannon portal, examining the cannon balls, stacked in a pyramid. She pointed him out to Dorothea and watched her visibly relax.

As soon as Anna spread out their pallets and laid quilts down, Dorothea sat and held her quilt and rocked back and forth, staring out the small portal opening of the cannon, a forlorn figure. Anna hoped she would improve in spirits by the time they reached Port Philadelphia, or Jacob Bauer would be in for a shock to see the condition of his wife. It was just like last time, after Dorothea received the news that her oldest son Hans had passed. In her grief, she had become a hollow ghost of a person.

Anna still wasn't convinced of the wisdom of including Dorothea in this journey; she was still so fragile in her sorrowing over Johann, but Christian made the decision to bring her. "Jacob is expecting to see Felix and Dorothea," he said. "He's been there for a year now, purchasing land for each of us. It would be worse to have the family remain separated."

But he did agree that Dorothea needed minding, not to mention Felix who minded no one — and those caretaking chores were assigned to Anna.

Anna thought about the last conversation she had with her grandfather. "I'll be back," she told him.

"Girl, there's no turning back in life. But don't you worry. The Lord is watching over us."

Her grandmother told her it was bad luck to look back, that if you looked back it meant you'd never return. So as Anna walked down the muddy path to meet Christian and the others, she didn't look back. Tears streamed down her face, but she didn't look back. She was *going* to return.

Anna checked on Felix, who was hanging over the rails of the pig stall trying to pat the pig. The poor pig. It looked as bewildered and lost as everyone else, but at least Felix had found something to amuse himself. She thought there might be a little extra space near the pig and chickens to try to hold English classes for Felix and the Müller girls and anyone else who might be interested. She had brought a few books with her for that purpose. Learning English was one thing she could do to help prepare them for their new life. Though Felix was interested in everything *but* his lessons.

She had hoped there might be some Mennonite boys close to Felix's age, but there were just a few school-age girls and he wanted nothing to do with girls. The rest were toddlers. So many toddlers! Too many for a peaceful journey.

Maria was fussing over how to fit her trunk under the bunk, so Anna went to help her and then returned to Dorothea. Surely more cramped, uncomfortable quarters couldn't be found. The dark, damp lower deck was only five feet high. She pitied the men who would spend their days hunched over. By the time they reached Port Philadelphia, their backs would resemble question marks.

Wooden crates, boxes, sacks, bundles of food crammed the narrow aisle. Somewhere up front, a small child wailed relentlessly. And the lower deck was filthy. They would need to spend these first few days cleaning and scrubbing. At least, Anna thought, there would be something to do.

She'd heard the carpenter say that when the tide turned in their favor, it would be time to depart. Removing his hat, Christian bowed his head and fell down to his knees on the deck, as did everyone present, including the Mennonites. He offered up one of the most heartfelt prayers Anna ever heard him pray, fervently asking the Lord for blessings on this journey.

Longing for home filled Anna's heart. She felt an overwhelming need to know they'd be safe, that the next haven would indeed be welcoming, but there were few guarantees.

At sunset, the sky turned a miraculous color of pink and gold, shining off the water. She peeked out the small window and hoped it meant God's blessing on them.

Soon, the *Charming Nancy* sailed into the

channel with the lights of Rotterdam blazing brightly behind them. It was a whole world, this ship, and they would sail to America in its very bowels.

4

June 30th, 1737

Felix Bauer woke up feeling great. He had a cast-iron stomach, unlike his mother and Anna and nearly everyone else who lay retching in their bunks, moaning piteously, laid low by seasickness. He was sorry they were ailing, truly he was.

Christian thought the channel crossing should take only a day, two at the most, but a strong storm blew gales from the west, causing the ship to roll and pitch and fight against the winds. Felix didn't mind the topsy-turvy motion of the ship, but he did have a complaint: the food. It was awful. Worse than awful. Everything was boiled and mushy. Even the vegetables were boiled to death, served in a great bowl big enough to be passed around the lower deck. Catrina said that was the English way, but he didn't know how she would know that. Still, he ate everything he could and tried to have more but was denied by Maria Müller. "That's more than enough for you, Hans Felix Bauer!" she would squawk at him, like a mad hen. He left each meal nearly as hungry as he had started it. He would have to talk to Anna and his mother about it if they ever stopped moaning from seasickness. So meanwhile he had a look around.

Particularly intriguing to him were the large cannons that were placed at portals around the lower deck. He tried to lift one of the heavy cannon balls set near the base of the cannon in a small triangle but nearly dropped it on his bare toes. He wished he could ask someone how a cannon worked. He considered asking Christian about it, but then he saw him stretched out in his bunk, head lolled back, snoring at the top of his lungs.

The passengers had been sternly warned to stay in the lower deck and not come to the upper deck, dangerous with all the ropes and activity of the sailors. Felix explored the entire lower deck; he was shooed away by a dour-looking Mennonite grandmother in the stern, so he mostly poked around the bow where the pig stayed, and four chickens in a cage made of twigs and twine. The windlass, a type of winch used for raising the anchor, was in the bow. It was all interesting and new and exciting, for about five minutes.

Then he came across the crew's sleeping quarters in the bow of the ship. The room was dark and Felix poked around until he was startled by a loud snore. First one, then another. Sailors were sleeping in hammocks, hung from the beams by large hooks, and he had practically walked right into one. He might be curious, but he wasn't stupid. He backed up slowly and hurried out.

Felix peered up the hatch to the bright sunshine on the upper deck. Briefly, he considered the warning that they were not to venture onto the deck without permission. He decided that the warning applied to those who didn't understand the ways of a ship — someone like Catrina, who would get in the way and be a nuisance. He, on the other hand, was keenly interested in the sea. Hadn't he and Johann studied books about ship faring? Well, Johann might have done the actual studying part, but he told Felix all kinds of things he had read.

Thinking about Johann made Felix sad, so he fixed his mind on one bright spot: because everyone had grown seasick, he was able to escape all adult constraints. No mother to flutter around him like a finch in a field of grain, no Anna fussing at him to sit still for English lessons. He was eight years old and he'd had enough schooling to last his lifetime. He was free to explore the ship at will and that meant above deck. He was particularly eager to get away from the eye-watering stink of the lower deck. Even the sailors covered their noses with a cloth when they walked through the lower deck to their sleeping quarters. He crept up the companionway stairs, felt the warmth of the sun hit the top of his head. He peered around and found another world entirely.

Suddenly, his underarms were grabbed and he was held upside down over the hatch, as someone gave him a vicious shake. He couldn't understand what the sailor was saying, but he figured he was about to get tossed down the hatch, headfirst. A small dog appeared in his line of vision, upside down, and peered at him curiously.

"Decker!"

A pair of black boots appeared in Felix's field of vision. The owner of the boots shouted in English to the sailor, who held Felix upside down by the ankles. The sailor tossed Felix on the deck like he was a bag of flour, right by the black boots. Slowly, Felix opened his eyes to face the owner of the black boots, and wondered what kind of trouble he was in. Instead of a stern look, the man's eyes held amusement, though he motioned to Felix to go below. As Felix slowly got to his feet, he decided that man might be the tallest man he had ever seen. Taller even than his father.

Waiting for him by the top of the companionway stairs was the sailor who held Felix by the ankles. Felix groaned. He had seen this squinty-eyed sailor before, as ugly as he was mean.

Squinty-Eye was hard not to notice. A large scar ran down one side of his face, causing one eye to pinch together. When he walked, his knees made a *click-clack* sound. He would click-clack through the lower deck on his way to his sleeping quarters, laughing and mocking and scolding the passengers who were sick. Last night, he even kicked the bucket out from underneath Maria Müller, so that she vomited all over her sleeping shelf. Then he pushed Felix out of the way, as if he was nothing but a buzzing fly, and click-clacked on by.

Carefully, Felix descended down the companionway ladder, keeping as far away from the sailor as he could. Squinty-Eye's face grew tight and narrow, with his eyeballs shooting around from side to side. It was almost too scary to watch. About three steps down, Squinty-Eye reached down and popped him square in the ear. Hard!

Getting hit when you're not expecting it can really shake you up. Felix's legs started wobbling like they were made out of his mother's chilled lamb stock, his eyes started leaking water, his nose started running. All he could do was sit on the next-to-the-last step and hold his sore ear as tears jumped out of his eyes. His throat wouldn't quit jerking up and down and making weird noises.

Suddenly Catrina was right in front of him. "What's going on? What'd you do?"

Scowling at her, he blew past her and went to sit near his mother. For now, he would stay in the lower deck, but he'd had a taste of another world — and he was going back to it.

By the second day of crossing the channel, Felix had become adept at keeping out of sight. He had slipped up onto the upper deck and hid behind the capstan. He looked up, squinting against the glare of the sun. The sky was so wide and empty and blue it hurt to look at it. Up here, the wind was blowing strong, and he had to anchor down his hat by jamming it hard over his ears. Unfortunately, a sailor spotted him from the rigging and shouted down at him. Felix barely made it down the companionway before Squinty-Eye could make a grab for him and toss him down the open hatch. He knew he had to be more careful . . . and that was when he started to become aware of the stroking of the ship's bells.

By paying attention to the bells, Felix learned the rhythm of the ship. One seaman had the duty of watching the hourglass and turning it when the sand had run out. When the seaman turned the glass, he struck the bell as a signal: Once at the end of the first half hour of a four-hour watch, twice after the first hour, three times after an hour and a half, four times after two hours had passed, until eight bells marked the end of the four-hour watch. The process was repeated for each succeeding watch. Whenever the bells sounded, all sailors stopped in their tracks and strained to listen.

Felix learned when to stay out of sight as lookouts were being relieved, and he discovered when he could safely prowl around because the seamen were distracted with their duties. He grew fascinated by the tangle of ropes that raised and lowered the sails. The lines attached to the triangle sheets reminded him of intricate spiderwebs that he used to find back in his barn in Ixheim. Once or twice, he ventured from his hiding places to peer over the railing. The channel water swept flat and blue to the far edge of the world. England.

If Felix could remember to leave his telltale black felt hat down below, and if he stayed in the shadows up above, making himself as small as possible, crouching low, quiet as a mouse, he was almost invisible and could stay hidden for hours. He was captivated by the goings-on above deck. He could tell the difference between the officers and the seamen. The seamen dressed in sloppy, loose clothing. Most were barefoot. There were two officers — the tall young one who wore long black boots and a short old man with gray hair and droopy eyes. Still no sign of the captain. Johann had said the captain would be wearing a tricornered hat. Felix had seen a lot of kerchiefs and plenty of wool skull caps, but no tricornered hats.

On the third day of the channel crossing, Felix was determined to explore the Great Cabin, so he looked up and down the deck, spotted no one, and made a mad dash for the stern. He nearly had his hand on the door handle of the Great Cabin when he heard voices inside.

Felix took off full speed for the lower deck. He didn't see the three sailors until he'd nearly run right into them. He slowed to a stop, his knees loose, his belly quaking, his heart thumping wildly in his chest. One sailor uttered a soft curse. Felix lifted his eyes and saw a young seaman he'd heard called Johnny Reed, not much older than Peter Mast. He had a hawklike face, gaunt and high nosed. And thin. So thin he looked put together out of sticks. He wore a stocking cap over his straggly hair. The other sailor had droopy eyes and a jiggly Adam's apple — first mate Mr. Pocock. And the third sailor was . . . Squinty-Eye. Next to him was his awful dog with its tongue hanging out.

Felix watched now, his eyes wide and dry, his breath scraping through his throat. He gave himself up for dead, sure he was doomed. He'd been seen, and you dared never be.

"Well, now, what do we 'ave 'ere," Squinty-Eye said. He spewed a thick glob of spit onto Felix's bare toes. "Could be we need to give this little Peculiar a swimming lesson. Drop 'im overboard and see if 'e can outswim the sharks."

Felix whirled and broke into an all-out run, just ahead of Squinty-Eye's slap. He scrambled down the deck, his feet moving faster than his thoughts. He ran awkwardly, with his coat flapping and his thin arms splayed out from his sides, not stopping until he reached the top of the companionway. He took the stairs two at a time, blowing past Catrina, who stood at the bottom with a chicken in her arms. She stared at him as he flew by. At least one eye did.

He dove into the pallet where his mother sat, idly mending, and pulled the blanket over his head. He was sure he could hear Squinty-Eye's mocking laughter through the cracks in the deck planks.

July 2nd, 1737

Anna's stomach seized up like a fist. She had no idea that seasickness could lay a person so low, day after day. The entire lower deck, save the noisy Mennonite toddlers, were laid low, prostrate on bunks and floor pallets. But how could they have known? None of them had sailed before.

She'd eaten little since the ship had left Rotterdam and now, tossed about the channel, her stomach had gone from queasy to rebellious to violently ill. Not eating made it worse. She knew that. She must eat.

"I need air," she said to no one in particular. She knelt by the cannon portal and leaned out as far as she could, grateful that Maria had inadvertently appointed them to a place with something like a window. Sea

81

spray slapped her face and she gulped in the cold, fresh air. Her throat burned, but she was done retching for now.

She hoped.

"Anna."

Anna spun around to find Lizzie Mast standing in front of her, clutching her middle. Lizzie was a tiny slip of a girl, barely sixteen. She had married Peter Mast, also sixteen. "Is something wrong?"

"Is this normal?" She took Anna's hand in hers and held it over her abdomen.

Anna nodded. "It's a tightening. It's normal. They're practice for the real thing. You'll feel these many times in the next few months." She stepped back as though struck. "Lizzie, my grandmother said you told her the baby would be due in late autumn, yes?"

Lizzie kept her eyes down. "Sometime in fall. An autumn baby." She crossed the deck to return to her sleeping shelf and curled up like an overcooked shrimp.

Anna's mind was moving slow from the seasickness . . . but she started to count out the months. If Lizzie was due in late fall, then she shouldn't be experiencing those tightenings for a while longer.

She started across the deck to go question Lizzie, but the ship lurched and she went flying onto the cannon. Her knees sagged and she felt ill again — twisted stomach, spinning head, a brain that had lost its ability to string two thoughts together.

July 3rd, 1737
Four days at sea and Felix had yet to lay eyes on the captain. He'd heard his voice up above, yelling orders in what Anna said was a thick Scottish burr. Wouldn't Anna's grandfather love to hear the way he rolled his *r*'s? He could mimic any accent, her grandfather.

This morning, when Felix was hiding on the upper deck, he finally caught a glimpse of the captain and he wasn't at all what Felix expected. He was a small man, with enormous muttonchop whiskers, dressed up in fancy clothes. He looked more like the Baron of Ixheim heading off to a party than a sea captain.

But then Felix saw him pick up a speaking trumpet and gaze out over the seamen for a moment, saying nothing, letting his attitude silence them. It reminded Felix of the way his father would begin a Sunday sermon — in silence, until all eyes were focused and minds were quieted. Felix had overheard Josef Gerber say that his father could control the church with one glance.

That's what it seemed as if the captain was doing right now — controlling the entire ship with his glance.

Through the speaking trumpet, the captain barked out orders in a deep baritone voice that was surprising in a man so short, and he used it to good effect, bellowing out commands with absolute authority. He shouted quite a lot, that captain, and sailors quivered at his command. Felix would like to have that kind of respect from others one day.

When he saw the captain head toward the forecastle deck, Felix scurried down to the opposite end of the ship to the Great Cabin and waited until the helmsman was distracted before he slipped inside.

The captain's quarters was a small bowed room, with a built-in bunk on one side and a table fastened to one wall. It was the only private space Felix had found on this ship. He peered out through the small windows at the channel. It was a different view from the stern and Felix squinted, the way he'd seen seamen squint against the sun or at the churned-up frothy water left in the ship's wake, as if it was telling them something. He was thinking that maybe he was becoming as savvy about a seaman's life as any sailor ever was.

Felix turned from the window and noticed a shelf of books built into the bulkhead and held in place by a wooden bar. One book caught his attention and he opened it to see if there were illustrations. He wondered if the captain would notice if he borrowed a book for Anna now and then. She liked to read, like Johann did, though that got him into trouble in the end. Terrible trouble.

If Felix did borrow a book from the captain, and if Anna asked him where he'd found it, he would have to make his lie short and simple, to keep her from worrying. Johann often pointed out that Felix always got caught in lies when he tried to spin too much straw on them.

Suddenly, the ship's bell sounded and he realized he'd lost track of time and the Great Cabin was no place to tarry. He hadn't thought this through. He hadn't thought at all. Heavy footsteps drew near and he whirled around, desperate for a place to hide in this tiny room. He threw himself onto the captain's tiny bunk and pulled the curtain, letting out a shaky breath. Pure panic, and not a good place to be. He held no illusions that the captain wouldn't accept a boy from the lower deck in his private space, or let him borrow a book without asking permission. Just like the Baron of Ix-heim.

The door to the Great Cabin opened and footsteps crossed the coaming. Then Felix heard the scrape of a wooden chair against the floor and a squeak of a hinge. Through a crack in the curtain, he peeked through and let out a shaky breath, relieved to see that the man who was in the Great Cabin wasn't the captain but that tall officer. He wasn't dressed sloppy like the other seamen, and he wasn't barefoot like they were. He wore long, shiny black boots, up to his knees. The officer opened the wooden box that sat on the captain's table and pulled out some funny-looking tools. He started working with the tools, then, absorbed, he sat down on the chair.

Felix wondered what those tools were used for. His father had all kinds of tools but nothing like those.

Thinking of his father caused his thoughts to drift back to his brother Johann and a sweeping sadness rushed over him. Anna said that Johann was in a better place and they shouldn't wish him back, but Felix was fairly sure that Johann would rather be here, with them right now, than be taken away from them. He wondered what his father would have to say when he heard about

Johann, once they reached Port Philadelphia.

Would his father hate the baron as much as Felix hated him? The baron was the reason his father left for the colonies so abruptly last year. The baron was the reason Johann was dead. He remembered the conversations his parents had that night before his father left for the New World, in quiet voices he probably wasn't supposed to be hearing. His father had said that if he didn't go now, the baron would find a way to kill him and make it seem legal. He was that evil, his father said, and Felix knew now that he was right. The baron couldn't catch Jacob Bauer so he had caught Johann. And it was all legal, just like Papa had predicted.

All Felix had to do was think about what the baron did to Johann and the sadness would rise up in his throat to choke him. He looked through the crack in the curtain again, his eyes suddenly blurring. Anna had told him that grief and sorrow had a way of piling up inside a person until there was nothing but to cry them all back out again. But Anna was a girl, and it was all right for her to cry. Men, like his father — they didn't cry. Sometimes if he just held his breath and concentrated hard, he could almost see Johann. Almost see him waving to Felix in the hills, beckoning him to join him.

Felix tried to swallow down the wad of tears that was building in his throat. It just hurt so much to think about his brother being gone forever. He squeezed his eyes shut. *Don't you cry, Felix Bauer. Don't you dare cry.*

He heard the rustle of paper and looked again through the crack of the curtain, blinking hard against the tears. Felix was so close to the officer that he could smell the scent of his clothes, wood spice and tar and smoke. The unusual smells helped to push thoughts of Johann to the back of his mind and bring Felix back to the present.

He stared at the officer, fascinated, wondering what he was doing. Felix was already learning the proper term for each part of the ship. He could barely hold back from climbing the tangle of ropes like the barefooted sailors did. He imagined himself like a bird, scanning the great vista of water from high above, watching America grow closer and closer over the curve of the earth. From down near the cook's kitchen, he could hear the ship's bells strike another afternoon half hour away. He nestled further in the captain's down-filled mattress and watched the officer turn pages in a book. Felix thought he could stay here for hours, days even, happy as a clam.

And then his stomach rumbled a loud, hungry, echoing growl.

5

July 3rd, 1737

Bairn wasn't alone.

The captain had sent him into the Great Cabin to fetch the sextant to make a noontime bearing, and he took a moment to look through the logbook to check coordinates. He found himself reading through the entries of the last few days:

June 29, 1737
Set off from Rotterdam. Freight: 132 qualifying men, German Palatinates recruited by newlander Georg Schultz.

Georg Schultz. How he despised that man.

Bairn sat motionless. For the first time in a very long time, memory threatened to push back, and sweat broke on his forehead. He refused to remember. He would *not.*

Just as he was pondering how much he abhorred Georg Schultz, how that little man always found a way to tweak him, to remind him of what he held over Bairn's head, an odd sound emerged from the captain's bunk. He straightened, lifted his head, turned around, and saw something move behind the curtain. Queenie, the ship's cat, perhaps? He yanked the curtain open and there . . . was a red-headed German boy from the lower deck.

Bairn laid a hand on the boy's shoulder and the boy recoiled at his touch, jerked back. He grasped the boy's shoulder and held tight. "Do y'realize where you are?"

The boy's face skewed up with fear. He couldn't understand him.

"You should not be here. You could be flogged." He made a whipping motion with his hand and the boy understood that. His blue eyes welled in utter terror. Bairn softened; he hadn't meant to frighten the laddie.

"Was iss dei Naame?" *What is your name?*

"Felix. Mei Naame iss Felix." *My name is Felix.*

"Kumme." Bairn pulled the curtain open and took a step toward the door. *Come with me.*

When the boy recovered from his shock, he scrambled out of the bunk. "Kannscht

91

du mei Schprooch?" *Do you know my language?*

Bairn shrugged. "Wennich." *Enough.* Mostly forgotten. "Kannscht du Englisch schwetze?" *Can you speak English?*

Felix nodded vigorously. "I learn . . . schteik." *Fast.*

Where was Felix? Anna had looked all through the lower deck and couldn't find any sign of him. Keeping her voice calmer than she felt, she asked Dorothea if she had seen Felix go by.

They all felt ill. Maria was wretched, Barbara Gerber looked pea-green, Lizzie Mast lay moaning on her bunk, but Dorothea seemed to fare the worst. Ghostly pale, she hadn't been able to keep anything down for days. Her expression of bleak dismay intensified to one of alarm, but before she could begin to panic, Anna rushed on. "I'm sure I saw him down near the animals." She skirted around the narrow path toward the front of the ship.

Anna frightened the chickens by swinging their cages to peer around them. They clucked and fussed at her, but she found no red-haired boy hiding behind them.

Where was Felix?

She was struck in the face with the pungent smells of chicken and pig, odors that were so much a part of her life that she seldom noticed them in Ixheim but mixed with the pervasive smell of sick people sent her stomach rolling again. As hard as she tried to keep her mind occupied, she couldn't stop her stomach from rebelling to the constant roll and pitch of the sea.

She almost felt like she was drowning in this dark, fetid air, as if she couldn't breathe. What an *awful* stench! She had to get upstairs, away from the gloomy lower deck and passengers in utter misery, had to fill her lungs with fresh air, and by now she was fairly confident Felix was up there, prowling around. She could imagine him tumbling overboard when one of those big sails swung around. She had warned him countless times to stay below and out of danger.

But that is not the reasoning a boy follows.

As she made her way to the companionway, the ship twisted itself into the trough of a wave and her stomach twisted in the opposite direction. She groaned. The bow slammed onto the water and her stomach clenched. Another roll of nausea rose up and she ran up the stairs as quickly as she could. She took her first full breath of sea air and it filled her lungs, the sunlight and fresh wind revived her. Ah, relief!

A sailor, washing the decks with a bucket of seawater, eyed her and tossed the bucket right at Anna so she took in a mouthful of dirty salt water. She coughed, choked, tripped, and as she stumbled, a firm hand gripped her at the elbow.

The scent of sandalwood enveloped her and a low voice spoke into her ear. "Are you all right?"

"Oh heaven help me," she said. "I think I'm going to be sick." She took an unsteady step forward, away from the hand that cupped her elbow and rushed to reach the railing. She gripped the railing and leaned over as far as she dared, sea spray slapping her face.

Two large hands gripped Anna's waist and held her steady.

"Nee. Fattgeh." Her voice sounded like a mewling kitten's cry.

"Go away?" The deep voice sounded amused. "Go away and let y'tumble on yer head into the sea?"

"Don't help me." She kept her eyes closed so she didn't have to look at that horrible sailor, see contempt or mockery for her weakness.

But the sailor ignored her and his calloused hand held her head as she choked and gasped, heaving dry heaves. There was nothing left in her stomach to toss up, but the gentle hand continued to hold her head until the dry heaves stopped.

"There, lassie, let it pass."

Her throat burned, but she was done for now. She straightened up, burning with shame, her face scarlet. She could feel it. She wasn't sure which was worse, heaving over a ship's railing or having a brute of a sailor try to bring her comfort. With the back of her hand, she wiped her mouth and realized that the sailor's calloused hand belonged to the ship's carpenter, not the beast who threw the bucket of salt water at her.

" 'Tis nothin' but a case of the mal de mer, n'more. Come along with me and the boy while I fetch you some ginger root to help."

From around the waist of the ship's carpenter popped a mop of curly red hair. Felix.

The carpenter held up a hand. "Before you start giving him a tongue lashin', follow me." He tilted his head toward the front of the ship. "Come along then."

As she followed him, she saw a sight at the bow of the ship that stopped her in her tracks. She stared at the sight with dropped jaw; so startled, she forgot she was seasick.

The carpenter spun around to see what was keeping her, then grinned at her obvious embarrassment. A sailor stood on an open platform with holes cut in it, lashed to the bow of the ship. He was relieving himself directly into the channel, rinsing off with a bucket of salt water, for all the world to see. "That, m' lassie, is known as a head."

The *Charming Nancy* twisted down the side of a wave, and Anna flew forward. The ship's carpenter caught her shoulders before she struck the railing. Everything around Anna started to spin. Spinning. Spinning, spinning. Then darkening —

"She's gone all pasty colored," she heard Felix cry out.

Anna's knees sagged. *I must not faint. I must not faint.* She grasped onto the forearms of the ship's carpenter as her stomach flipped and churned. He put a hand firmly on her shoulder to guide her as they walked forward on the shifting deck.

On any ordinary day, Anna would have been mortified to allow a stranger to help her, to touch her, but this was not an ordinary day. With Felix following closely behind, the carpenter helped her into a small rectangular room not much bigger than a closet. A short bald man was mixing bread dough in a large bowl and looked up in surprise at his visitors. A clay pipe stuck out of the corner of his mouth. He wore an apron covered with food and charcoal smudges and . . . was that blood? Anna's stomach clenched again.

"That's Cook and this is the galley," the carpenter said. "The ship's kitchen."

"Galley," Felix quietly repeated to himself. "Cook and galley."

The ship dipped and twisted. Anna took long, deep breaths, and tried to think about the green hills of Ixheim after a spring rain. "I think . . . I think I need to sit down." Before she sagged in the ship carpenter's hold or was sick down the front of his expensive shirt. "Please." The single word nearly choked her.

He helped her to a barrel along the wall. "Here you go."

Anna sat carefully upon the barrel's lid and braced herself with both hands on the side. She took some deep breaths, willing her stomach to stop cramping. Slowly, she lifted her head and looked around the room, then her gaze landed on the ship's carpenter. A black cat appeared and twined around his boots.

"There you be, Queenie," Cook said. "I

haven't seen you for days."

Absentmindedly, the carpenter said, "She's been trapped under a tub, Decker said."

"Queenie?" Felix asked.

"Aye, that's her name. She's the ship's cat."

Anna looked up. "I thought cats were afraid of water."

"They are," Cook said. "But every ship needs a cat."

"Why?"

"To catch rats." One side of his mouth lifted and the clay pipe bobbed as he spoke. "Prodigious rats."

Anna barely stifled a gag.

The carpenter kept rummaging through cupboards. "Cook, have you ginger root? The lassie needs some t'settle her stomach. She's as sick as a poisoned pup."

"Aye," the cook said. He jutted his chin toward a basket and went back to punching and kneading the dough.

"Judas Iscariot!" Felix shouted, pointing to the bowl of bread dough.

Anna clapped her hand over Felix's mouth, astounded by his outburst of profanity, then her eyes went wide with shock. The cook was missing a hand. When she saw the reddened scarred stump as he pounded the dough, her stomach twisted and turned again.

The cook waved his stump in the air in the direction of the ship's carpenter and laughed. "Fine handiwork of Bairn's." Then he calmly went back to kneading the dough.

"Had t'be done," Bairn said, matter-of-factly, still poking through the cupboards. "I only lopped it off because it had gone gangrene on you."

She slid another glance at the carpenter — Bairn. What kind of name was that for a man who had the courage to cut off a man's gangrened hand? He was too tall to stand upright in the low-ceilinged cabin. And he appeared strong enough to lift her in one arm and Felix in the other. His face revealed nothing of what he was truly made of, whether good or evil, a man who kept himself closely guarded. And yet those eyes of his . . . there was something compelling to her about them. She couldn't make herself look away.

Bairn took a small knife from Cook's work counter and sliced some ginger root. "Chew on this. 'Twill help."

When he handed her the ginger, their fingers met and then their eyes. The spicy scent tickled her nose and she caught a look of mirth flit through Bairn's eyes. Here and then gone. Shyly, she lowered her chin and nibbled on the ginger root.

Bairn reached behind Felix to pull a tin off a shelf. He opened the tin and offered cookies to Felix. "Take two, they're small. Cook is a stingy man."

Cook snorted. "I was more generous before you lopped me hand off."

"If I hadn't taken yer hand, you would've died fer sure." He turned to Anna. "The ship's carpenter often doubles as the ship's surgeon."

"Same tools!" The cook made a slicing motion with his one hand, like he was chopping wood with an axe.

Anna's stomach rose and fell.

"Aye, same tools," Bairn said, "but I take more care with both wood and bones than he'd have you believe."

Mesmerized, Felix's head bobbed from one direction to the other, listening to the cook's sloppy English and then the carpenter's crisp turn of phrase. Anna wasn't sure how much Felix could understand of this conversation between the cook and the carpenter — he never seemed to pay attention during her English lessons — but the casual description of a gangrenous hand made her stomach twirl like it was being tightened in a vice.

Chewing the ginger rapidly, Anna tried to get her mind off her nausea and took stock of the compact space of the tiny kitchen. Under the hot furnace rested a platform of bricks, no doubt to keep the heat from burning right through the wooden deck. Every inch of space was claimed, but used in clever ways. Cupboards had been customized to fit the narrow room, including a narrow corner cupboard. Spices were lined in rows of shelving with a wooden dowel to keep them in place. She doubted Cook would have to take more than a few steps to gather ingredients.

"Anna, how does a cook manage with one hand?" Felix whispered in their dialect.

Bairn must have figured out what was on Felix's mind because he answered before Anna could ask. "Cook used t'be a seaman until the accident that took his hand. The sea is all he ken. Becoming a cook was the only job he could do with one hand. You'd be surprised at what a man can adapt to when he has no choice." After Anna finished translating Bairn's words to Felix, a grin slowly spread over the carpenter's face. "But one hand or two, I am thinkin' he would still serve us rotting slop."

Cook pointed a sharp knife at him. "Rotting slop, my eye."

101

Bairn turned to Anna. "The captain is waitin' for the sextant t'do the noontime bearings. He'll be bellowin' soon if I do nae get to him. It'd be wise t'get below decks before the stroke of the bells fer a watch change."

Warmed and warned, Anna stood to leave. "Thank you for the ginger. Come, Felix." His blue eyes, round as silver dollars, stayed riveted on the carpenter.

"What's yer name?"

"Anna."

"I'm Bairn. Have you ginger root down below?"

"I might. I'll look through my chest." Her grandmother had given her a box of remedies, but Anna hadn't paid much attention. She should have thought to look through the box for a seasickness remedy — it would be the same as for stomach ailments. What she really should have done, she realized now, was to have paid closer attention to her grandmother's methods for healing.

"If you do nae have any, send Felix to find me."

Cook spun around from the stove. "You'll not be raiding me galley!"

Bairn winked at Felix. "It's all in the askin'." He turned to Cook. "You can always get more in Plymouth."

"Plymouth?" Cook scowled. "No wonder we haven't reached Cowes by now. Plymouth will be days away yet in this wind."

"Aye, but the captain prefers to water the ship with the sweet waters of Dartmoor in Plymouth."

"That, and he doesn't want his crew to be tempted to jump ship for higher wages in Cowes."

Bairn nodded.

Anna's unsettled stomach was finally easing a bit, enough for her to pose an objection. "But why? Why must you stop in England at all?" She wanted to get this sea voyage over with and behind her.

Bairn and Cook exchanged a look of amusement. "To stock up on supplies."

"Why couldn't they have bought supplies in Rotterdam?" There were all kinds of merchants milling through the dock area, clamoring at them to buy, buy, buy.

"To comply with law. T'buy provisions for the ocean voyage there, rather than at Rotterdam, boosts the English economy." Bairn took a step to the door and turned back to Anna. "The layover should only last a few days."

A few days! Anna's heart sank. The delays were adding up.

Bairn was watching her. "I wish I could spare you the mal de mer, but ye'll find some relief when we dock at Plymouth. Most everyone gains sea legs. Sooner or later."

Cook let out a guffaw. "If you think this little tempest in a teapot is bad, just wait until we're in open sea and ride out a hurricane."

"Pay him no mind." Bairn dismissed Cook with a wave of his hand. "Believe me, I ken how y'feel."

Cook coughed out a rusty laugh. "Bairn was a famous vomiter."

A stain of color spread across Bairn's sharp cheekbones. " 'Tis true. Years of service is no guarantee against the mal de mer. My solution was to forsake the bunk and sleep in a hammock. Hammocks remain stable while the ship moves, whereas bunks buck and plunge with the ship."

"He's right, girlie," Cook said. "Hammocks are the way to go. It protects most seamen against seasickness."

Bairn looked at her. "Are you sleepin' in a bunk?"

"On a pallet, on the ground."

Bairn shook his head, looking woeful. "The worst place of all is t'be on the floor of the ship. Sleep in a hammock. I put plenty of hooks along the crossbeams. And there are extra hammocks available. They're in a barrel in the bow."

"I'll try it tonight." At this point, she would try anything.

"And keep a closer eye on that one." Bairn tipped his head in Felix's direction, who was occupied by lifting the lid on each barrel to see what was inside. "I found him in the captain's cabin." He leaned slightly toward Anna and whispered so Cook didn't overhear. "Takin' a nap in the captain's *bunk.*"

Anna shot a hard glance at Felix, bristling with things she felt like saying to him, things he needed to hear, but he was oblivious to her. That boy was oblivious to most everything.

Bairn walked with them to the upper deck. " 'Tis goin' to come onto rain soon."

Anna looked up and saw only blue sky. "Why do you say that?"

He gestured toward the horizon. A bank of gray clouds inked the line between sea and sky.

She moaned and Bairn grinned — but not in a mocking way.

This ship's carpenter, he wasn't what she expected him to be. His gray eyes met hers with a gentle compassion that surprised her.

She couldn't look away from his eyes. They were gray. Not blue-gray. Not hazel-gray. Pure gray like polished pewter. They pierced into her eyes from beneath straight dark brows and tanned skin that contrasted with his sun-streaked hair. A strange feeling arose — something familiar, something appealing. Slowly, she adjusted her stance, balanced on her own feet, and backed away, then hurried to join Felix at the stairs.

At the top of the companionway, she chanced a glance back and found Bairn staring at the bottom of her dress with a curious look on his face. She looked down and realized she was barefoot. He had been looking at her ankles and she felt her face go scarlet once again.

He tilted his head as if he wanted to say something, but then the ship bell clanged and he moved away, tipping his head once more.

Felix waited for her on the next step, his eyes glued on Bairn as he strode down the deck.

"Felix, you foolish, foolish boy. How could you have dared to go into the captain's bunk?"

"Well, I won't do it again," he said in a puny voice.

But he would. She knew he would. She

could read his mind.

Anna paused, reluctant to go below, and watched the sea, watched sailors climb up and down the rigging as if it were child's play. The idea of climbing that high left her dizzy. The sway of the ropes was more nausea-invoking to her than the rolling of the deck. She couldn't look up at them anymore.

Not so for Felix. "Amazing, isn't it?"

"Amazing," she echoed faintly, though her tone wasn't the same as his.

"Being up there must feel like flying."

She took a deep breath of salty air, dreading the thought of going back down into the stale, putrid air of the lower deck.

"What do you think of Bairn?"

What did she think of him? She didn't know. She had no idea how to act with this man. She was accustomed to older men, like Christian and Josef and her grandfather, and young boys, like Peter and Johann and Felix. But she hadn't been around many men her age, and certainly not someone like him. "What kind of name is Bairn for a ship's officer?"

"It's Scottish for *boy,* he said."

Aha! She knew Felix understood more English than he let on.

He lifted his head. "He's nice, isn't he?"

Nice? Yes, in a way, Bairn was surprisingly kind to them. But his eyes were distant and a little mysterious. A bit sad too. "He's not one of us, Felix. He's a stranger, an outsider. He doesn't follow the straight and narrow path. You ought not to be talking to him." She raised an eyebrow at him. "Nor should you be sneaking into places you don't belong. The captain's quarters, of all places! You should be ashamed. Next time, Bairn may not be as friendly to you."

Anna resisted the urge to pinch her nose as she reached the bottom step of the companionway. With more than a little relief, she realized that her stomach wasn't bothering her nearly as much as it was before she went above deck. She wasn't sure if it was the fresh sea air, the ginger, or just the benefit that came from thinking of something other than seasickness. She went straight to her chest to search her grand-mother's remedy box for ginger root and smiled when she found it. She sliced it up to pass out to those who were sickest.

Lizzie lay on her pallet, green as a spring gourd, utterly miserable.

"Chew this, Lizzie. It will help." Anna knelt down beside her and tried to distract her. "Your babe will be the first of our church to be born in the New World."

"Or on this horrible ship."

Anna's head jerked up. "What?"

Lizzie's face crumpled. "Oh, Anna. I lied. I was with child when Peter and I were wed. I'm . . . six months along." Her voice dropped to a whisper. "Maybe seven."

Anna's heart pounded so hard it threatened to bruise her ribs from the inside. She couldn't breathe.

"If Christian had found out, he would put us under the Bann. He wouldn't have let us join the group for the crossing."

"If he had found out, his only concern would be to make sure your baby has a chance to survive!"

"Hush . . . keep your voice down."

"How could you have dared to step foot on a ship?"

"I thought we would have reached Port Philadelphia by now. I never expected all those delays down the Rhine, then more in Rotterdam."

Anna let out a sigh. She, too, had been astounded at how slow a start this journey was getting.

"Anna . . . you have to promise to help me."

"Me? Help? I've never delivered a baby."

"Your grandmother has." Her eyes skirted across the aisle to where Maria sat, watching them, craning her neck and straining her ears to try to listen to them. "You've watched her. You know about doctoring."

It was true that Anna had assisted her grandmother, but she only did what her grandmother told her to do. She never thought about it, about what was happening next or what to look out for or why. Her grandmother had the gift for healing and Anna didn't. Nor did she want it. Whenever a baby was about to arrive, her grandmother would send her out to get hot water and Anna gladly vanished. "But I'm —"

"You're all I've got."

Maria walked slowly by, arms crossed, ears peeled. Anna dropped her head and sliced off another piece of ginger. She waited until Maria was out of listening range, then whispered, "Lizzie, Maria has more experience. She's *had* children."

"No! Not Maria. You know what she's like with those strange words and rituals."

Maria fancied herself to be a Braucher, one who used folk magic — prayers, rituals, and spells — to heal common ailments.

"What about Barbara? She's had twins. And there are a few other women. Even the Mennonites. Goodness, they've got all those toddlers! They must know a great deal about giving birth."

"No. Please, Anna. Promise me you'll be the one to help me."

Anna looked into Lizzie's pleading eyes. A child having a child. She mustered up a weak smile. "Perhaps your baby will wait to arrive until we reach Port Philadelphia." Perhaps. But she doubted it. She sighed. "How far along are you?"

"Seven months."

"Truly?"

"Maybe more."

Anna rose to her feet, smoothed her hands over her skirt, a habit she had picked up from her grandmother when giving instructions, and said, "Then, when the time comes, we must make do with what we have."

But the truth was, Anna had nothing to make do with. No experience, no knowledge, no tools. The worrisome thoughts came too fast, tumbling one after the other. She walked anxiously around the lower deck, wondering where in the world a baby could be delivered. And what if something went wrong? Things often went wrong, even for her grandmother.

She found a hammock in a barrel and attached it to hooks on the beams of the ship. Felix saw and copied her, as did Catrina. Soon, hammocks were getting hung all around the lower deck. Anna found a book in her chest and sat by the cannon portal for light, looking out at the wind-ruffled water of the channel.

Conditions were far from ideal — barely tolerable to endure a sea journey and certainly not to have a baby. Daylight showed through the wide gaps in the planks above them, and rain shuddered through those same gaps. To bathe, they had to go behind a makeshift curtain and rinse themselves with salt water, which made their skin feel dry and itchy. The same method to relieve themselves. The lower deck was equipped with "easing-chairs" or commodes. The most prized berths were farthest from these, in the stern of the ship, and closest to the hatches, which gave some ventilation. Now she understood why the mighty Mennonites had hurried to be first up the gangplank and into the companionway. They had more knowledge of these sea passages than the Amish and were far savvier. The front of the ship, where the Amish and the animals were assigned, took the brunt as the ship's bow sliced into the waves. There were cockroaches, lice, fleas, and rats. And now a baby was to be born.

No, conditions were not at all ideal.

Then a spark ignited in Anna's mind. This

bleak situation might have a silver lining. If she were to tell the captain — whom she had yet to see but had heard barking orders from above — if she were to tell him that there was a woman on board who was due to deliver, the captain would no doubt put Lizzie and Peter out when they reached Plymouth. Out of concern for Lizzie — all genuine — Anna would volunteer to accompany them on a return ship to Rotterdam. She could be home in Ixheim, having dinner with her grandparents by . . . let's see, the end of August?

A small smile tugged at the corner of Anna's lips. Things were looking decidedly better.

6

July 4th, 1737

The ship was surrounded by utter darkness. Bairn couldn't hear anything at all except for the gentle murmur of the sails as they luffed in the breeze. Standing on the bowsprit in the middle of the night, he was alone in a realm of silence.

It was as if the ship was sailing off to another place, as if a black pathway pulled the ship among the stars. And it was beautiful.

The sea gave Bairn a measure of stability and order that the outside world had seemed to lack. The *Charming Nancy* was home to him now and he felt like her caretaker. And in a way, he was.

As ship's carpenter, he considered himself to be the ship's physician. It was his job to know her weaknesses, her strengths, her history, her injuries, her scars. It was up to him to know how much ill weather she could face, how much her seasoned timbers could bear, what tonnage her belly could comfortably carry, the age and wear of her skins.

He heard the bells ring for a watch change and knew morning would come soon. He should return to his quarters to try to get some sleep, though sleep was eluding him of late. Whenever he closed his eyes, flashes of memory popped before him. Flashes of his father in his red coat. Flashes of his mother pulling bread out of the oven. His father reaching over to spread the red coat over Bairn. And then . . . flashes of sickness and tears and death. He would startle awake, heart pounding, gasping for air. What he had tried for years to forget pursued him like a wild dog, nipping at his heels.

As he walked into the officers' quarters, Mr. Pocock, the first mate, came hobbling out, favoring his sore gouty foot, yawning. "Onto watch." It was rare to be alone and uninterrupted, so Bairn lit a lantern, set it on the floor, and crouched down to pull out his sea chest. All that he owned in the world was in this chest. He opened the lid and reached to the bottom to pull out the coat. He sat on the floor, his back against Mr. Pocock's wooden bunk, and held the coat against his chest. Made of a fine red wool, lovingly woven on his mother's loom. It was his father's coat, the only possession he had left from his family. His most treasured item. He breathed in deeply, one more time, then folded the coat and placed it carefully back in his sea chest, covered it up with his clothes, and shoved the chest under his bunk. He lay down on his back in the upper bunk, resting his head in his hands.

He'd felt the dark anguish of old take hold, stirred up by the passengers down below. Watching them, hearing them, observing the happy interaction of the families. Their presence provoked his disquiet, bringing it all back, unearthing the past he'd long buried.

Bairn tried to tell himself that it was only old grief rolling over, that it would soon go to sleep again, but he knew it was more. Knew it by the strange uneasiness he'd felt at unexpected times, knew it by the dreams that kept jabbing at him, knew it by the way he tensed up whenever he caught sight of the Peculiars.

His mind traveled back to the visit yesterday afternoon with the red-haired German boy. As he started toward his carpentry shop, he noticed Felix hiding behind the capstan. He motioned to him to follow along and the laddie responded with gusto, all but bounding behind him.

Afternoon light had poured into the shop from a tiny window at the back wall. The air was thick with the sweet-sharp scent of wood and pitch and oakum. Drifts of sawdust and curls of wood shavings lay on the floor, tools hung neatly on the wall. Bairn loved this little room; his personal space on a crowded vessel. Craftsmanship required thought, and thought required a quiet environment. It was his custom to linger in the shop long after he was done for the day.

Bairn pointed to an upturned nail keg for the boy to sit on. He quickly realized the boy understood more English than he would have expected. Felix was a bright and clever laddie, though his pronunciation of English was truly horrific. Bairn was cautious about correcting him because he didn't want the laddie to stop trying, but Felix didn't seem to mind the corrections. Just the opposite, he seemed eager to learn the language. Bairn explained the various tools he used. He showed Felix the wood planes, their handles burnished by years of use, their blades so sharp and precise they could shave off curls of wood as thin as paper. He handed him tools that he'd purchased over the years in different seaports, explaining how each tool served a unique function but all were indispensable. Each one gave him precise control over fine details.

Working with wood resonated with Bairn in an elusive but elemental way — it satisfied him down to his core, and gave him peace. Partly it was the pleasure that he derived from solving problems — working out angles and planes when a project wouldn't lie cleanly. Partly it was because he felt closest to his father when he was in this shop. He had learned carpentry at his father's side.

And partly it was the wood itself. He liked the way wood spoke to him as he worked with it, murmuring and squeaking and whispering, almost as if it was alive. When he split apart a piece of pine or cedar or oak, it perfumed the air with its spicy sweet smell.

On this rainy afternoon, the room grew stuffy and warm. Bairn took off his jacket and rolled up his sleeves. Felix's eyes went wide when he saw the ink drawing pricked on Bairn's upper arm. "Done with India ink," he said. "It can never be washed off."

"It is a girl," Felix said.

"Aye." Bairn squeezed his muscles to make it look as if the girl was dancing. "Not one of me prouder moments. But a good reminder of how stupid a man can be when he's had a wee bit too much from a brown bottle."

Felix's eyes went wider still, and it occurred to Bairn that he shouldn't have shown him the tattoo. No doubt the boy had never seen the likes of such wickedness and debauchery. Then Decker's voice rang out from the half-deck, calling for Bairn, and Felix had disappeared out the door in a flash.

Bairn yawned, hearing the ship's bell strike four in the morning. He should try to get some sleep before dawn, so he blew out the lamp and closed his eyes. His wished he could shut down his mind as easily as the lamp's flame.

He wondered if the boy would tell his sister about his tattoo and hoped he wouldn't. Then he wondered why he should care what Anna thought of him.

It was easier when the lower deck held only cotton and linens, wine and woolens.

July 5th, 1737
Georg Schultz unnerved Anna. This morning, after she had bathed and changed into a clean dress behind a curtain, she emerged from behind the curtain and there he was,

arms folded, leaning against the beam. The morning sun, she discovered, was streaming through the cannon portals to illuminate the gauzy curtain, creating a shadowy outline of her figure. He had been watching her bathe and change clothes.

After supper, Felix needed a haircut, so Anna cut his, and then cut the hair of the three-year-old Gerber twins. She wrapped an old sheet around the boys to catch hair. When she was done, she took the sheet over to the pig's pen to shake it out. With one snap of the cloth, she was alone, and with the next, Georg Schultz stood beside her. She caught her breath with a sound. He seemed to be everywhere at once.

"Hello, Anna," he said. "Did I surprise you?"

She frowned at him. "Yes, you did."

He looked at the scissors in her hands. If he thought she was going to cut into that greasy nest of hair on him, he was going to have to think again. Nevertheless, he kept staring at her. She brushed past him and quickly returned to Dorothea over by the cannon.

Dorothea lifted her dull eyes to Anna's. "Is that stout man bothering you?"

Yes. "No."

"He bothers me," Dorothea said. "There's

something about him that is frightening."

Anna put the scissors back into her trunk and sat down on the pallet next to Dorothea. "Would you tell me a story?"

Dorothea closed her eyes for such a long time that Anna thought she might have fallen asleep. But then she opened them and began to speak. "Did I tell you how our families came to be in the Palatinate?"

"Tell it again." Dorothea's stories alternated between too long or too intimate, and were very repetitive. Anna's grandfather said that once was all he needed, but Anna always listened anyway. To her, the tales were worth hearing again, and it seemed Dorothea needed to tell them to someone. They were harsh recollections of her childhood in Switzerland, when the Täuffers, the name given to those who believed in adult baptism, were hunted and chased out of their homeland.

When Anna first heard Dorothea's stories, she had been surprised and astonished, then she had grown a bit inured to their dramatic sequence. Now, after leaving their isolated village, after the long weeks in that horrible tent city, after the pail of seawater thrown into her face by that sailor with the small dog, the stories held new meaning for her.

"My family was living in Bern, Switzerland, on a beautiful mountain." Dorothea's voice started out fragile, brittle, and much attenuated, as if rusty from lack of use. "We farmed land that no one else could farm, and we were very happy there. But a new mayor was elected to the Canton, a Catholic, Mayor Willading. He hated the Täuffers and wanted to rid Canton Bern of them. First, he forbade the Täuffers to meet to worship. Then they started to arrest the church leaders. My father was one of them. Families went up the mountain to hide in the Alphüt, where the hay was stored. The mayor demanded that all hay storage huts were to be searched for any hidden Täuffers. If a farmer turned them in, he would be given a reward of 30 Kreuzer. My father was betrayed by a poor man whom he had once fed. Early one morning, eight officers arrived at the door. Father had told us to hide under a stack of hay while he went off with the officers, but an officer started to thrust his sword into the stack and my father stopped him. We were discovered and sent off to prison."

"How awful to think they even arrested children."

She nodded. "First they planned to execute the Täuffers, but the Council chose instead to deport us to America. They confiscated our home, our belongings, everything . . . and just sent us off on large rafts down the Rhine. Just like that. We lost everything." She gazed at the wooden floor planks as if she could visualize the Rhine journey. "My father would say: Man soll sick nicht zum land binden." *One is not to become attached to the land.*

Anna noticed that Dorothea's voice had grown stronger in the telling of the story. "What happened then?"

"We were told to never return to our beloved Switzerland. If we did, we would face death. We were sent up the Rhine to Amsterdam, and then to America."

"To Philadelphia?"

"No. To North Carolina. But my father planned an escape before the ship left Amsterdam. He didn't want to leave Europe, so we fled in the night, on foot, until we reached Ixheim and found some refugees who helped us. We relied on the goodness of strangers along the way, sought refuge at farms and other places. And then we came to —"

"My grandparents' farm."

"Yes." A corner of Dorothea's mouth lifted. The first near-smile she'd offered up in weeks. "They helped us get assigned land by their noble person. Their landlord."

"The baron."

"Yes. The good baron, the old one. Not his son."

"God was watching over you."

Dorothea gave a slight nod. "Had we gone to America, we might have faced a terrible fate. A year later, over one hundred of the colonists were killed in a vicious Indian attack in New Bern. Our friends in America were killed."

Anna covered Dorothea's hands with hers. "And somehow, the church continued to grow."

"Yes. It flourished as a rose among thorns."

Keep talking, Dorothea. Don't stop. "So you met Jacob in Ixheim?" Anna urged. She didn't want Dorothea to slip back into her melancholia.

Dorothea looked up at Anna, eyes as clear as day. A gentle smile suddenly broke through her malaise, lighting a soft glow in her eyes. "Yes. We met each other that very first week and fell in love soon after."

Today, Anna listened to Dorothea in a way she hadn't before. As she spoke of Jacob, her husband, Anna noticed that her face relaxed and her eyes grew clear. It was the first time that Anna realized how much Dorothea loved Jacob and how safe she felt when he was near.

"And a year later, we had our beautiful baby boy, Hans. You remember him, Anna."

"I remember." She would never forget Hans Bauer.

"We were happy in Ixheim. We wished for more children, but we knew not to question God. After many years, Johann was born to us. And not much longer after that, Jacob felt God calling him to lead the church to the New World."

Anna could recite the rest of the story, word for word. Jacob Bauer had come across a real estate tract written by a man named William Penn, a Quaker. The king had given Penn a large land holding in America — 45,000 square miles — to satisfy a debt to his father. Penn was selling off land to those who sought to worship in peace. This, Jacob felt, was the answer needed for the little Amish church of Ixheim. He was eager to take advantage of Penn's offer before the land became settled. He left for the New World in 1726 with the church's blessing, their money to purchase land, and his eleven-year-old son, Hans. The plan was for many in the church to follow the next year. But a severe epidemic of smallpox went through the ship and both Hans and Jacob succumbed. When Jacob recovered from delirium, he discovered his son had died and all his money had been stolen. Brokenhearted, Jacob booked passage on the next returning ship. He arrived in Ixheim in late November, without land, without money, without his son.

"There were those who criticized Jacob for returning. Some felt he should have stayed, for the church's sake. To get started in the New World." Dorothea's hands twisted and turned the edges of her apron, as if she could still feel the pain from that time. "He did it for me, out of love. He knew he couldn't tell me about my boy's death in a letter. Just like I must tell him about Johann in person. Some things are not meant for letters."

Even Anna remembered the stir that was caused when he had returned to Ixheim, empty-handed. He was a man who was always in forward motion. She remembered her grandparents' disapproval that he had not stayed in Penn's Woods and sent for Dorothea and little Johann. Instead, he returned to grieve with his wife. In time, they were blessed with another son, whom Dorothea named Hans — as was the custom — to honor the son who died on the voyage, but he was called by his middle name, Felix.

Anna, only nine at the time, felt the impact of Hans's death. Living next door to the Bauers, she had seen Hans daily, though he generally ignored her. At the time, the two years between them made him effectively an eon older than her. She was too young for him to pay much notice to.

On long summer nights, Anna and Johann would help Hans round up the sheep to put in the pen. But on the day Hans left with his father, she was stuck at home, as she had broken her leg after a fall and was confined to bed while it healed. Hans had left a dug-up rose under her window, a goodbye gift. She planted the rose in her grandparents' garden and it thrived, growing strong and sturdy, giving off delicate pink flowers each spring. She glanced over at her basket with the leather handle. *That* rose.

"You know the rest of this story."

"Tell me anyway."

"It wasn't long before Jacob's restless nature stirred again. He wanted to set out for the New World, but I wouldn't let him leave. A new minister had settled in Ixheim, Christian Müller, and he was also eager to move to the New World. He intervened and persuaded me to let Jacob go. I finally relented, but only on the condition that

Johann did not leave with Jacob." She covered her face with her hands. "The Lord giveth, and the Lord taketh away."

Anna rubbed circles on Dorothea's back, and softly said, "Blessed be the name of the Lord."

Suddenly Maria stood in front of them, arms folded over her ample chest, intruding on this thoughtful moment. "Anna, I've been giving some thought to your situation."

"My situation?" They were all in the same situation!

"What are you now, two and twenty?"

"Nineteen."

"Exactly. You're not getting any younger. See those crow's-feet around your eyes?"

Anna's hand automatically went to her eyes.

"Oh honestly, Maria," Dorothea said, rolling her eyes to the ceiling.

Maria ignored her. "It's time for you to marry."

Anna's gaze swept the lower deck. "But there's no one I want to marry."

Maria's face filled with pity. "I know, I know. You've met so few men in your little life." She raised a finger in the air. "By this time next year, we will have found your intended. I can feel it in my bones. I know

128

these things." She leaned forward. "It wouldn't hurt to brush your hair now and then. You must start to think ahead, Anna, as I do." She started up the aisle of the lower deck toward the stern, looking over the few eligible Mennonite bachelors as if she were shopping for ripe fruit. Ironic, Anna thought, because she often complained that these Mennonites were far too worldly for her liking.

Anna shook her head, hoping the thought would quickly leave Maria's mind as so many other thoughts did. Dorothea said she was thirsty — the food Cook provided was liberally dosed with salt and everyone was always thirsty — so Anna rose from the pallet to fill up a cup and glimpsed her reflection on the water's surface of the open barrel. Was that really her? She saw a face that was too harsh, too careworn for a woman not even twenty, with all those worry lines and her hair drooping off her face. She looked nothing like the young girl her grandfather once called pretty as a posy.

Later that night, near midnight, Anna awoke with a start. A chill moved through her. Someone was standing near the end of her hammock.

Suddenly in a burst of noise that made Anna let out her breath with relief, a small dog emerged from the seamen's quarters and started to bark and snarl. Now they were all awake. Felix called the dog off, and whoever was at the edge of Anna's hammock moved quickly away into the shadows. In just a few minutes, everyone was snoring again. Not Anna, though.

"Doggie," she whispered. "Come here, old boy."

The dog slipped near her hammock and looked up at her. Then his tail began to wag. She tapped her lap, and the dog jumped up on her hammock. It was the dog that belonged to that mocking sailor. She petted and scratched behind his ears and the dog curled up, lay down, and went to sleep.

Anna tried not to think about who was at the edge of her hammock, but it was like trying not to think about a cricket chirping. The more you don't think about it, the louder it gets.

7

July 8th, 1737

In the dark of the night, Bairn could see a glimmer of lighthouses on the southern coast of England. In just a few hours, the *Charming Nancy* would proceed around the Cornish coast and put into the port of Plymouth, and it was a sight he could hardly wait to see. Even more so, he could hardly wait to go ashore. He had already applied to the captain. The work of going ashore, placing orders, and handing over cash was done by Captain Stedman and whichever of the officers or tradesmen he trusted most. In the case of the crew of the *Charming Nancy,* that meant only two men: Mr. Pocock and Bairn. Happily, Mr. Pocock's gout caused him such suffering that he chose not to apply to go ashore.

Scarcely two hours later, Bairn stood on the fo'c'sle deck, relaying the first mate's orders through the speaking trumpet to the sailors on the upper deck and half deck. There was a terrific flap and slither of canvas as mainsails came down to reduce the ship's speed. Water that was breaking against the hull gentled as the ship slid into more sheltered waters, and finally Bairn gave the order to release the massive anchor cable. They floated slowly until a slight tug brought the *Charming Nancy* to rest. The anchor had dropped.

Dawn was barely visible on the horizon as Bairn gazed out on the Sound. The *Charming Nancy* was one of a mass of vessels crammed into Plymouth Sound. This was one of the busiest ports in England and was full of working craft: fishing fleets, pilot boats, private merchantmen. And then there were the Royal Navy ships: His Majesty's men-of-war. Plymouth was the last provisioning stop for vessels sailing south to Africa or the Indies or the Azores, for those sailing west for America or Newfoundland. The quantity of shipping in port, and the clumsiness of a large ship under sail, meant sailing across the Sound to pick up supplies was impracticable, so the captain would send delivery boats back and forth to fetch supplies.

In the heat of July, with the air still, Plymouth Sound smelled like one vast privy.

"Bairn!"

He whirled around to face Mr. Pocock.

"The captain wants to see you."

"Did he say why?"

Mr. Pocock shrugged, but averted his eyes.

It was an intimidating thing to be summoned into the Great Cabin. It didn't happen often and it left an impression when it did. On this occasion, the captain was attired in his best breeches, preparing to go ashore. He pointed to the chair for Bairn to sit down on while he stood, a customary practice for him because of their height differences. He leveled his eyes at Bairn and told him that his application to go ashore was denied. "You are in charge of repairs to the ship while Mr. Pocock and I secure provisions. I want Decker to build additional pens for animals."

Bairn's grip tightened on his hat, fingers crushing the brim, but he worked to keep his face impassive to mask the acute disappointment he felt. He had been sorely looking forward to time ashore in Plymouth. He wanted to make sure the provisions would be adequate for the journey, and if there was a little extra time, he might look up a sweet, well-endowed maid he had met in a pub a few months back — Rosie, or was it Sally? He couldn't remember — but he thought he might pay a call on her.

Instead of the comforts of a woman, he would be stuck on the ship, minding twenty hapless sailors, not to mention hundreds of Peculiars down below.

"No seaman is to leave the ship unless you have sent him to pick up provisions." The captain snapped his fingers. "There and back."

Now *that* piece of information Bairn had expected. Jobbing seamen looking for better wages did not hang around. The captain couldn't afford to lose another seaman on the voyage — he was already critically short on crew.

Bairn decided to test the waters to change the captain's mind. "With Mr. Pocock ailin' so from the gout, I thought perhaps I might accompany you, as I did last time."

"Nae this time, Bairn. Mr. Pocock will see a doctor while we're in port."

"Mayhap I should come along, then." Bairn pressed on. "Sir, we have nae had to lay up provisions for so many before. 'Tis a significant amount of passengers down below." As carpenter, he was responsible for ensuring food was properly preserved. He had an interest in ensuring that all goods coming on board were properly casked — if they were not, he would get the blame when the food went rotten and water went brackish, as often happened despite his best attempts. If it wasn't the humidity on the ship that bred mold, it was the weevils that wormed their way into every closed container. "I was about t'give Decker instructions to finish holystonin' the deck."

Captain Stedman straightened his collar. "Decker's nae ready fer additional responsibilities."

Blast it all! That's what Bairn had told the captain when Decker had sought the position of carpenter's mate. Decker would never be ready. He wasn't trustworthy. The last time Decker had applied to go ashore, the captain granted him leave and he ended up causing trouble in a late-night pub that served cheap liquor. He was arrested, and the captain faced a fee of several pounds to get him out. Bairn thought the captain should leave him incarcerated, but Decker was an experienced seaman and had skills the ship needed.

The captain patted Bairn on his back. "Dinnae look so forlorn, Bairn. 'Twill give you practice of managin' a motley crew when you become first mate." Then the captain stopped talking and simply pointed to the door. Dismissed.

That was the second time in recent weeks

that the captain had hinted a promotion lay at the end of this voyage. While that was a good sign, Bairn came out of the Great Cabin shaken and disappointed, trying to ignore a cluster of seamen who were watching him from the decks.

A few moments later, the captain emerged from the Great Cabin holding his satchel and met Mr. Pocock at the side of the ship where the longboats were being lowered.

"Wait! Wait for me!" Georg Schultz clamored to the top of the companionway and made his way around the sailors working on the deck on their hands and knees, bumping into them without apology. In one hand was a leather bag, in the other was his cloak. "I'd like to go ashore with you, Captain. I have some business to attend to." He set down his satchel, dropped his cloak on top, then hiked his pants up over his large belly.

Off to find a Pharo Bank, Bairn thought with disdain, knowing Georg Schultz as he did. A fool's way to spend money. Bairn's income came too hard to risk it on a hand of cards, even in the unlikely event that it was honestly dealt.

Captain Stedman frowned. "Mr. Schultz, if yer nae back when we set sail, we leave without you."

"Captain," Bairn said, "when do you plan

to shove off fer America?"

The captain peered up at the early morning sky. "Within a few days, Lord willin'. Assumin' we get a prosperous wind." The air was absolutely still. The only sound was the cry of gulls.

Blocks squealed and the captain's barge was lowered into the water. Bairn watched the three men scale the rope ladder down into the longboat and sail toward the docks of Plymouth. The captain stood at the prow, adjusting his tricorn hat, with the rowers behind him, feet widespread as the longboat listed a bit as Schultz settled into a middle seat.

The first and possibly most important task of a ship's company newly arrived in port was to arrange for the watering of the ship — filling the casks with fresh water for the sea journey. Meanwhile, Captain Stedman would be pacing the government abattoirs in Stonehouse Creek for beef, bickering over the price of meat at cattle markets in Plymouth Hoe, and visiting agents for the Tamar Valley market gardeners to negotiate the price of greens. All things Bairn should be doing, while Mr. Pocock searched the shores for a cure for his gout.

Bairn turned his attention to ordering a few deckhands to bring the empty water casks. They rolled them along the deck and lowered them over the side into the longboats, then made their way to Plymouth for filling. Bairn watched the second longboat head toward shore with empty casks and tried to shrug off the feeling of gloom that descended.

In the quiet, Anna heard something like thunder above deck. She lay there, still sleepy, and fuzzily tried to figure out what the ship's noises were revealing. She heard loud squeaks and groans of a turning chain, then a sharp jolt as the ship came to a steady quiver and there was silence, broken only by the slap of water against her side and the pad of the seamen's feet on deck.

After the initial shock of being at sea, her mal de mer had begun to ease up, thanks to the suggestion of using a hammock made by the ship's carpenter — Bairn. As she felt less miserable, her awareness of her surroundings grew.

She started to realize that the *Charming Nancy* had a language of her own: constantly talking, murmuring, whispering. Soft, gentle, soothing sounds, unlike the harsh noises made up above by cursing seamen. Timbers groaned, bells rang, masts creaked, sails flapped, as if the ship were an enormous living creature. It was an epiphany for Anna, to feel connected, protective even, of this aging old vessel that was doing her best to see the little church over the deep waters.

On this July morning, Anna lay in her hammock, already sweating in the summer heat. She leaned over and reached for the top of her chest to get a handkerchief and a small bottle of lavender water. She sprinkled some onto a piece of thin linen and pressed it over her nose. It helped, she had found, to mask the smell. To her surprise, she might just miss this old wooden Lady, but not enough to pass up a chance to get off the ship in Plymouth and get right back on one that was heading to Rotterdam. She swung the hammock by pushing a foot against the wall. She was actually enjoying a little quiet despite the sweltering humidity of the morning, so hot she felt as if she was slowly melting.

It was all too peaceful to last.

Anna yanked the handkerchief off her face. Had they finally reached Plymouth? She barely finished the thought in her mind as an eleven-gun salute from the harbor startled everyone awake. Wonder and worry made her jump from the hammock and run to the portal by the cannon for her first glimpse of Plymouth.

The captain! She had to speak to him at once.

Bairn walked along the deck, supervising the seamen who scoured the deck with soft sandstone. Now anchored in Plymouth harbor while the captain secured provisions, the ship would undergo make-and-mend days: torn sails patched, leaks caulked, a mast repaired.

He heard his name called and turned to see Anna standing at the top of the companionway. He walked toward her to see what she wanted.

"May I have a word with you?" She turned and hurried down the companionway.

He followed her down but stopped on the second-to-last step, blinking against the sudden darkness after the bright sunlight. Rank smells assaulted him: stale sweat, vomit-soaked floorboards, chamber pots. He held the neck of his waistcoat to his nose. It was not only the smells that made his heart quake, but the hacking coughs that filled the lower deck. He tried not to gag. Decker had complained bitterly of the stench of the lower deck, but he assumed it was an exaggeration because he despised the Peculiars.

If this was the result of a few rainy and

140

windy days on the channel, how would the Peculiars survive a trip across the Atlantic? "I'd prefer to talk on the upper deck." He hurried back up the stairs and took in deep breaths of salty sea air. He remembered Anna and turned to lend a hand to help her over the coaming.

She had a pleased look on her face, like a cat that swallowed a canary.

"Is there something y'need?"

"Yes. I need to speak to the captain."

"I beg yer pardon?" Passengers did *not* ask to speak to the captain. *Especially* female passengers.

"There's a matter I need to speak to him about. Before we leave Plymouth."

Only a few feet away, Decker listened to them, his gaze tempered with frank suspicion. Bairn moved Anna away from Decker and close to the railing, over in the sunshine. Her eyes closed as the sun hit her face, as if she was soaking it up. "He's already left t'go ashore. If you tell me, I'll relay it to him when he returns."

She frowned, disappointed at that news. "No. It's a private concern."

He eyed her with a telling intensity. "I *am* the ship's surgeon." Not that the title meant anything. He really didn't know much of anything about sickness and illness other than using his tools to lop off gangrened limbs. And it was only that one time, with Cook, out of desperation.

She hesitated, heat touching her cheeks. "I doubt you'd have experience with this particular concern. It's a rather delicate nature."

"I'll try to remember t'let him know." He gave her a brusque nod and gazed out at a seabird as it dove into the water and emerged with a fish in its beak.

"There's something else."

He turned his eyes to her once again.

"The people in my church — we need to be allowed up here on this —"

"Upper deck."

"— for a daily walk and fresh air. For sunshine." She turned her face to the sky, like a flower, and smiled softly, as the sun washed over her skin.

"Passengers aren't allowed up on deck. 'Tis too dangerous for them."

"It's dangerous down below too." Anna stiffened her back. "You saw for yourself what conditions are like down there."

Aha. So that was why she wanted to talk to him down below. Clever lassie. "They should have a respite fer a spell while we're anchored."

"People are already sick —" she held up a

142

hand to stop him from interrupting her —
"not just the mal de mer. They have coughs
and colds."

"Why are they sick?"

"Because this old boat is as leaky as a
colander! Water pours through the gaps in
the ceiling."

Bairn's chin lifted a notch. "What?"

"It reminds me of the earthen dikes of
Holland."

Bairn's eye grazed the deck. In the wet
crossing of the channel, the oakum must
have worked itself loose between the planks.

"And then the hatches."

"What about them?"

"Water pours in the hatches whenever it
rains."

Bairn should have made sure the hatches
were covered with canvas, though that
would have meant less circulation of air too.
"Perhaps some of your least hardy ones will
want to disembark here and return to Rotterdam."

She looked as if that was exactly what she
would like to do, but couldn't. "Christian
— our minister — would never allow that."

"He might when you tell him you'll be
facin' much more severe weather on the
Atlantic."

"Christian would say that our lives are in

God's hands."

Decker walked up to join them. "We'll see what he says after we throw the first dead body overboard and watch the sharks feed on it."

Bairn jerked his head up. "Decker! Mind yer business and get back to work."

Decker fleered at Anna and spun around. The seaman seemed to have stunned her silent. A glimmer of remorse for her sake went through Bairn, though he didn't know why he should feel any empathy for her. The Peculiars chose to make this trip. "Yer people should've just stayed put, back on the Rhine. You'd be safer there."

"The bishop believed that God was leading our church to the New World."

"So you uproot yer lives because one man thinks he heard a word from the Almighty?"

"Yes. No. It wasn't just one man. Others agreed too. We are seeking a way of life, a shared set of values."

"And that's what America means to all of ye?"

"That, and we can own land. We can't own land in Germany."

Bairn scoffed. "Land."

"Land to pass on to children. And to children's children." She lifted her chin. "Speaking of children. Are you in agreement

144

that each passenger may take a turn above each day?"

" 'Tis impossible."

"Why? We need fresh air."

"Perhaps if you cleaned the lower deck, it would help."

Her mouth fell open and her back stiffened like a rod, mightily dignified. "We do clean! Every day. There are a great many people down there! And children. They need fresh air, exercise, sunshine, and light. Everything needs light to grow and be healthy. Every living thing. Why, even mushrooms respond to light."

Now it was Bairn's turn to be stunned silent. "Mushrooms?" *Mushrooms!*

She met and held his gaze. "Yes."

He was astounded by this female's audacity. She barely reached his chest and yet she spoke to him like she was captain of the vessel and he was naught but a lowly deckhand. Audacious, but he admired her pluck too. "Perhaps while we're docked in Plymouth, you could take a turn around deck durin' the day. But not durin' a watch change."

"Thank you."

He took a step away, but she called him back.

"And another thing." She cleared her throat delicately. "While we're docked here, we will be washing our clothes down below. I'd prefer to dry our clothes up here, on the boat's —"

"Ship. It's a *ship*. A boat fits on a ship."

She spread her arm out in a half circle. "— on this top part."

"The upper deck," he said, annoyed. "Have you nae been on a vessel before?"

"No. Unless you consider a flimsy raft on a sheep's pond."

Something floated through Bairn's mind, a wispy echo of three children laughing on a hot summer day. For a moment the memory was so sharp it took his breath away. Then he pushed it off to the furthest corner of his mind, as he always did. Such memories disturbed him. "Have y'much to wash?"

"Yes. And clothes take days to dry below. But they could be dry in a few hours up here on the . . . upper deck."

He frowned and turned back to see the captain's longboat near the shore. "Fine. But mind that you only hang some things on the larboard side where naught can be seen from the waterfront." She looked at him confused. He pointed to the left side of the ship. "It would not do fer the captain t'see ladies' unmentionables flappin' in the wind off his precious ship."

146

Anna's eyes went wide and a blush pinkened her cheeks. Then a slow smile started at the corners of her lips — lovely lips, he happened to notice — before it spread across her face. "I'll keep that in mind."

The smile on this bonnie lassie — it bloomed like a rose, simple and elegant. The effect rendered him speechless.

She took a step or two, then turned back to him. "Have you lived your entire life on a ship?"

He hesitated, giving him pause with regard to his choice of words. "Nay. Not me entire life. But most of it." He was no more than a boy, a scrawny waif on the run, when the Captains John and Charles Stedman took him under their wing. He went back and forth between their vessels depending on who needed an extra hand. First as a cabin boy, then a deckhand, working his way up to ship's carpenter. The Stedman brothers saw that Bairn was determined to better himself, and that he had an ability to comprehend even the complicated mathematics of navigation. He advanced quickly, thanks to their tutelage.

"A ship makes for an odd childhood."

"The sea has been good and fair t'me." Better than most people.

Her gaze shifted to the harbor. "So that is Plymouth?"

Bairn walked to the railing and she followed him over. "Aye, started as naught but a pokelogan." Her eyes lit with amusement and he found himself studying them — wide blue eyes so deep and dark and guileless, a man could lose himself in their depths.

"A what?"

"Two rivers flowed together t'make Plymouth Sound. This is where the pilgrims first sailed to the New World. That's the Mount Edgecumbe estate."

"Where?"

He pointed to a large chateau. "See the battery of guns along the fringe of the estate? They're pointed seaward toward France."

"Why are they pointed at France?"

"Because the English hate the French. And vice versa." He pointed to the distant hills. " 'Tis where Sir John Hawkins lived. He started the Atlantic Slave Trade."

Anna gave him a sharp look. "And one day he will have to answer to God for that."

Bairn stifled a grin. "Aye, and he'll be dressed with golden buckles on his boots."

She looked shocked. "The love of money is the root of all evil."

"And the root of all happiness."

"God measures a man's life by more than his accumulation of wealth." She tilted her head curiously. "Don't you believe in a just God?"

"If there is a God, I believe He is an angry tyrant."

"If I believed that, then I would try to avoid Him at all costs."

He met her gaze. "Indeed," he said, letting a broad smile escape.

She tilted her head thoughtfully, and her face softened. "Somehow, I don't believe you."

"You think it's impossible for a man to not believe in God?"

"I think everybody believes in something."

"I do. I believe that a man's destiny is up t'him. And I believe a man must grab whatever happiness he can in life, because it isn't goin' to last."

"But that is an entirely profane and secular view of life."

He grinned, amused and impressed. He wasn't accustomed to women with a bright noggin on their shoulders. She wasn't amused and seemed quite serious about the topic, which only made him all the more amused. Nonetheless, he made himself meet her steady gaze.

"What if you're wrong? What if there is

something more? Something beyond us. God's Word says He sees all things, knows all things. Nothing we do is hidden from His eyes." A soft pity filled the woman's eyes, stinging Bairn's pride.

His collar started to feel hot, tight. What had started as a droll conversation had quickly turned into an uncomfortable one.

"Perhaps you should join us for church on Sunday . . ."

He held up a hand to stop her. "Do y'realize that you've now given me more orders in one turn of the glass than the captain does in a full day?"

She tilted her head to one side, as if she was trying to think back to what she had said to him to make him possibly think she ordered him about.

He had never seen such extraordinary eyes. They sparkled with pinpoints of darker blue behind a fringe of dark lashes. He found himself going soft like a candle left too close to a fire. It was a strange feeling for him.

"Anna?"

They both turned their heads to see Christian Müller standing at the top of the companionway, watching them with a curious look on his face. Anna walked over to him and he spoke to her in a low voice in their peasant dialect. She turned to Bairn. "He wants to know how long we will be anchored in Plymouth."

Bairn shrugged. "Hard to say. The captain needs to provision the ship and that can take a few days, at the very least." Probably longer, but he didn't want to discourage them. They had no idea what they would be facing in the next few months, none at all. He wasn't even sure he knew. He thought back with longing for the past ocean crossings when a ship held nothing but cargo in the lower deck.

He watched Anna as she descended the ladder down into the lower deck. She was quite a lovely girl, lovely cheeks, lovely lips. Quick of mind too. Especially for a Peculiar. Unusually so for a Peculiar.

Decker came up behind him. "You're not the only one on this ship who wants some o' that."

"Decker, have you no sense of decency?"

"Not when it comes to Peculiars."

"Why must you be such an arrogant fellow? Why do you despise them so? They've done naught to you."

"Pious prigs. Uppity. They think they're better than me."

"They are."

Decker's head snapped up at that, and his

thin lips pulled into a tight line. For a moment Bairn wondered if he should keep Decker at tasks far removed from the passengers. Poor devils. It wasn't bad enough they had to be confined to the lower deck, they had to endure ill treatment above deck.

But then the ship called to Bairn, dismissing all thoughts of a bonnie lassie below deck, stirring his senses with a blend of oakum and pitch, scents from the vessel that awaited his attention.

He spotted the top of redheaded Felix scooting behind the sailors as they were holystoning the deck and decided not to stop him from exploring. How much trouble could he get into when the ship was anchored and the captain was ashore? After all, a boy is only a boy once.

8

July 8th, 1737

Felix wormed his way through the knot of sailors on the deck and found a spot on the forecastle where he could hide unobserved. Better still, Bairn had left his spyglass on the forecastle deck while he was talking to Anna, and Felix thought he might not mind if he borrowed it.

It was the first look at an English port that Felix ever had, might ever have, and he was intrigued by simple details — the swarm of ships in the sound, the crumbling old buildings on the shoreline, the scantily dressed women who waved and called out to sailors. He saw men at work on the docks stop to drink from a flask, in no apparent hurry to complete their tasks, and he wondered what made them so thirsty. He thought of how he would have described the sight to Johann and found that it didn't hurt quite as much to think of his brother as if he were still alive, as if he could still talk to him. As if he wasn't cut off from him forever.

And maybe he could. Anna said she thought that heaven was like a curtain, not a wall.

Suddenly, someone seized Felix and stuffed him into an empty wooden barrel with holes in the top and sides. His head popped through the hole on the top of the barrel and he found Squinty-Eye laughing at him, his awful, ugly dog by his side. For the evil seaman, it was a great joke. Not to Felix.

" 'At's what you deserve for venturing onto the fo'c'sle deck!"

Felix tried to pretend he wasn't as thoroughly humiliated as he was, but the wooden barrel was heavy — its whole weight rested on his shoulders and he couldn't sit or stand. When he became too uncomfortable to stand it any longer, he begged Squinty-Eye to release him, promising to never go onto the forecastle deck again, and the barrel was removed.

Felix took off for the lower deck, mouth and eyes open wide, legs pumping hard, one arm flailing and the other holding down his hat. But even as he flew down the companionway, he knew he would break his promise to Squinty-Eye by the stroke of the next bell.

His father had always taught him that there was a solution to every problem. But he had also told Felix that sometimes the solution wasn't where people would ordinarily expect it to be, that you might have to look in unexpected places and think in new and creative ways to find the answers you were looking for.

Felix just had to find a better place to hide.

The only time Anna had felt dry in the past week had been in the galley. The passengers did their best to keep the lower deck clean, but they had to use seawater, so everything felt sticky, stiff, grainy, grimy. And always damp.

As soon as the longboats left for shore and the upper deck was quiet again, a deckhand named Johnny Reed came down to the lower deck and told them a fire had been lit on deck for passengers' laundry. Anna tried to coax Dorothea to go above deck with a few other women who felt well enough to help, to get a little sunshine and fresh air, but she said she was too tired and needed to rest.

Anna filled the cauldron with salt water from a wooden tub and set it to boil. Barbara Gerber, Maria and Catrina Müller, and Esther Wenger and a few other Mennonite women brought up heaps of dirty clothes. With nothing in the way of soap, the clothes would be boiled and the dirt beaten out of them. As soon as the water boiled, the women went back down below to gather more laundry while Anna rolled up her sleeves and set to work for the biggest laundry day they'd had since leaving Rotterdam's tent city. She added her dresses into the cauldron, one at a time, finding it amusing to see how dresses rose to the surface, waved their empty sleeves, then vanished beneath the steaming water.

An eerie feeling came over her, a sense that she was being watched. She turned to find the sailor named Decker standing close by, staring at her.

"That's just what it will be like for you Peculiars. Half of you will go under before this journey is over. Down, down, down to a watery grave." He stirred his finger just like she was stirring the cauldron.

Anna jerked back and whirled around to the cauldron, hot color flooding her cheeks. She hadn't drawn an easy breath around those sailors, especially this one that Felix called Squinty-Eye. He had a nose like a crow's beak and a whittled brown face, a long scar dividing a cheek, and his black button eyes were sneering at her as if he expected her to be the first one overboard.

She watched him saunter past Maria, with her arms full of laundry, elbowing her out of his way. Indignant, Maria was about to elbow him back, but Barbara pulled her back and whispered in her ear. Anna didn't have to hear her to know what she was saying: Love thy enemy.

When Anna saw Felix dash by, she pulled him aside. Somehow it seemed that boy was either just coming or just going. It was hard for him to settle. "He's nobody to trifle with, that Decker. I've seen the sailors tremble around him." Bairn was the only one who seemed able to manage Decker.

Anna went back to scrubbing clothes, longing for the fresh water of Ixheim. Her skin crawled and itched after days of saltwater cleansings, but at least her dress hung loosely. The men had rashes from their tight breeches, stiff from salt water. She wanted to get the clothes beaten and hung on the deck before the sun reached midday. Before Bairn changed his mind about letting her use the upper deck as a clothesline. The top deck trembled as the women thwacked its timbers with shirts, shifts, sheets, even hammocks. Rivulets of filthy water trickled down the sides. Before long, the rails and rigging of the ship were festooned with drying clothes, and there was still more laundry to wash.

Anna picked up a wooden bucket to get more water to boil and wondered where Felix had disappeared to. She hadn't seen him in a while, so she headed toward the companionway, thinking he might have gone below deck to check on his mother.

Near the top of the stairs was Bairn, kneeling on the deck with a pot of reeking tar and a brush. In one hand was a tool that looked like a hatchet. He was driving something that looked like untwisted rope in the seam between two planks. Crouched beside him, holding a basket of that fuzzy fiber, was Felix.

"Lookin' for anyone in particular?" Bairn said as he noticed her, slowly rising to his feet.

He towered above her, his feet planted in a wide stance. Unlike the other times she had seen him, he wore no hat, no coat, no neckerchief adorned the collar of his white linen shirt. Simply a pair of suspenders looped over the shirt's full, dropped shoulders. He was shockingly handsome in a roguish, careless way, shirtsleeves rolled up to his elbows, tousled hair looking like windblown straw. Why, he almost looked like a farmer.

Bairn saw the wooden bucket in her arms and reached for it. A warmth from working in the hot sun rose from his clothes. A spicy scent of sandalwood and pitch and . . . something familiar that tickled her nose with its pungency. The smell of horse.

Anna wrinkled her nose and looked at the fuzzy fiber in the basket near Felix. Lumps of hairy fluff. "What is that?"

" 'Tis oakum. It swells up when it gets wet."

"Is it made of horse hair?"

Those stern lips suddenly lifted in a slight smile. "Very good. Aye, horse hair, among other things." He lifted the wooden bucket. "Do y'need it refilled?"

"Yes. I was going to find Felix to fill it."

"Decker," Bairn called over her head.

She turned to see the squinty-eyed sailor leaning against the railing as he repaired a tear on a sail.

"Fill the bucket with seawater."

Anna saw disdain flicker across Decker's eyes. She looked back at Bairn. "I don't mind doing it."

"Decker doesn't mind, either. Do you, Decker?"

Decker did mind. He wasn't about to object to the ship's carpenter, though. Decker went to the side and grabbed a rope attached to a pulley. Hand over hand, he lowered the bucket and scooped up water.

Anna turned back to Bairn. "What are you doing?"

"I'm teachin' the laddie how t'wield an adze."

"A what?"

"An adze. A . . . mallet. I use this mallet to drive oakum down between the seams. Like . . . caulkin'."

"Is Felix getting in your way?"

"Nay, not on a make-and-mend day." He leaned toward Anna. " 'Tis best t'keep boys busy."

Felix shrugged, but his eyes were shining. He looked like he'd just been handed the moon. He was thoroughly happy to be scooped up alongside Bairn. Too happy, if you asked Anna.

Decker slapped the wooden tub by Anna's feet before returning back to caulking the deck.

"Felix — take it to Maria by the cauldron. She's waiting for it. And then go downstairs to bring up another basket of clothes. And bring my rose basket too." The rose could get some needed sunshine today.

As the boy opened his mouth to object, she cut him off. "You can go back to work with Bairn after you have helped me."

Suddenly, they heard Bairn shout out, "Decker!"

Anna turned to see her freshly washed shirts and dresses and pants floating on top of the sea. Far from the railing, Decker was patching a sail, pulling a needle and long thread through the cloth, an innocent look on his face.

Bairn marched over to the railing, a thunderstorm brewing on his face. "Decker, get the boat hook, fetch all the clothin' back up, and then you will rewash everythin' and set it t'dry. Go down to the hold and fetch fresh water to wash."

Decker narrowed his eyes, causing that one eye to look even squintier. "The captain won't like it if you use fresh water."

"The captain isn't here, is he?"

Decker stared back at him, a showdown, and finally stomped off to get the boat hook to snatch up the clothes. He snared all the clothing with one sweep of the boat hook and dropped the sopping wet clothes on Anna's feet.

Bairn was there in an instant. "For that, Decker, you will clean the slime from the scuppers and scrub the deck from prow to stern."

"No, please." Anna felt her face flush red.

"We fight fire with water, not with more fire."

Bairn's gaze at Decker held firm. "Indeed. You'll end up gettin' another bucket of salt water tossed in yer face."

"I'm sure it won't happen again."

Decker shook the stringy hair from his eyes and muttered "Witch!" under his breath.

Bairn's expression darkened. "Decker, before you get to the scuppers and the scrubbin' of the deck, you will slush down the mast."

Decker glared at Bairn and stalked past him to the galley.

"What does that mean — to slush down the mast?"

" 'Tis an utterly foul duty." Bairn pointed to the main mast. "He'll use a pot of drippings from the galley and climb to the masthead. Then he'll work his way down the masthead rubbin' the fat into the wood with his hands."

"To discipline him?"

"Nay. 'Tis a necessary chore. It preserves the wood and helps the tackle run up and down the mast more easily. It's like greasing a pole. And 'tis a particularly useful task to hand out to a smart-mouthed seaman like Decker."

Decker returned from the galley with the pot of stinking grease. He climbed up the riggings and made his way over to the masthead. On the deck, far below Decker, Anna and Felix gathered the wet clothes into a basket.

A loud sound like a cracked chicken bone came from above, then a scream. High above on the jumble of ropes, Decker had lost his footing and fell, ripping an awning from its moorings and knocking a spar loose. Bairn flung up his arms to protect Anna and Felix and push them out of the way as Decker hit the deck. The spar crashed down, slamming down on Decker's head. For a moment, there was only silence and the call of the seagulls.

"Are you all right?" Bairn said to Anna.

Anna looked at Felix, whose eyes were round with shock. "Yes, we're fine."

Bairn bolted over to pull the spar off Decker. Blood was streaming from an ear.

Anna recognized the stillness of death in the sailor's prone form. "Is he . . . ?"

Bairn put his head to Decker's chest to hear his heartbeat and looked up, eyes wide, face drained of color. "Aye," he said, in a voice barely loud enough to be heard. "Aye. He's gone."

Johnny Reed pointed a finger at Anna.

"She did it. She said he wouldn't mock her again. Decker was right. He said she was a witch. She's fey."

Cook pushed his way to the forefront. He looked at Decker, then at Anna, then back to Decker. "Nay, she's not fey. The breath of God came down and smote him."

But the seamen all stepped away from Anna.

9

July 8th, 1737

Bairn held the funeral for Decker at sunset
when shadows grew dusky instead of sharp,
on the leeward side, as was the ship's
custom. Gulls scolded from a sky streaked
with red and gold as the sailors pressed in a
wide, deep circle around the body. Decker
was laid out in an old sailcloth with a heavy
stone placed at his feet, then the cloth was
wrapped snug around him, secured by ropes
tied around his neck, his body, his ankles.
Someone had thought to put his pair of
boots with silver buckles on his feet. Decker
had been proud of those boots.

Anna and Felix stood in the back with
other passengers who had come to attend
the service. Bairn caught sight of her over
the heads of the sailors, and he noticed the
eyes of several sailors drift toward her. The
rumor that she was a witch had quickly traveled through the ship. Superstitions were

part of the seaman's life and they were eager to see the witch from the lower deck with the golden hair and fine figure, an uncommonly beautiful woman.

As the highest ranking officer on board, Bairn led the service, his first funeral. He had considered sending a message to the captain in hopes he would return, but that could take days. Having a dead body aboard ship was considered bad luck. Decker had created enough mischief when he was alive. Bairn didn't want to allow rumblings of bad luck on the *Charming Nancy* to fester and risk losing more deckhands. He imitated what he had seen the captain do on many occasions: he stood in the traditional pose of funeral respect — feet straddled, the palm of one hand clasping the back of the other resting at his lower abdomen. He read Psalm 23 from the Bible and rolled richly over the *r*'s as Captain Stedman did. There was a moment of silence — broken only by a tapping sound that came across the scrubbed deck, drawing near. Decker's dog came to pay his respects. He skulked toward the body, sniffed, then worked his way through the crowd until he found Felix, and sat down beside him. The laddie pretended not to notice. Then Bairn gave a nod and a sailor sewed the shroud around Decker's body, with the last stitch put through Decker's nose — a seafaring custom to ensure that the dead was truly dead. Then a handful of seamen picked up the shroud and tossed it overboard to a watery grave.

Felix ran to the railing and Anna reached out a hand to grab his shirt collar and pull him back.

"Let him see, girlie," Cook said, rubbing his jaw. Doomishly, he added, "Will be the first of many to be cast into the black deep before this journey is over."

Anna looked at him, shocked. "God's will is for no one to perish."

Cook only shrugged. "Who's to know what is behind the inscrutable will of God?"

"Cook, that's enough." Bairn's tone was brusque. When Anna turned to him, he said, "Why would you come to watch this?" He motioned to the line of Germans, funneling down the companionway to the lower deck. "Why would any of you come?"

She looked up at him as if the answer was obvious. "We prayed for God to have mercy on his soul."

He felt a sudden sinking in his chest. "That's nae what I thought you'd say."

"What did you expect me to say?"

"Something pious, I expect."

"Pious? Like what?"

He cast about for a way to explain. "Something smug like the spirit of God is more powerful than the spirit of wickedness." His voice was quiet as he dipped his head toward her. He didn't even know where that thought had come from. "Why would you show respect to a man who cursed you and mocked you?"

"I wished him no ill will. I forgave Decker for his insults." She lifted an upturned palm in the direction of the Germans. "We all did." She called to Felix, leaning over the railing, and the two of them followed the rest of the passengers back down the stairs.

A knot of pride shifted in his throat and he gulped it down whole, suddenly ashamed of his naïveté. He gazed at her receding back with quiet amazement.

Later that evening, Bairn stood at the ship's bow, bracing the rails as he leaned over to look at the dark channel waters. The moon was but a thumbnail, the stars a mere smattering, the night was now truly dark except for yellow lanterns from vessels that bobbed in the channel. Crew members were gathered around the deck in clusters of three or four, playing cards or rolling dice. Johnny Reed curled up in the bowsprit to read a book by the glow of the lantern.

The ship would soon be shipshape for the

sea crossing. Everything was in order, everything except the churning in Bairn's gut. He simmered in silence, still raw over Decker's untimely death. Accidents happened, he knew that. It wasn't Bairn's first funeral at sea and it surely wouldn't be the last. But he wondered if it could have been avoided, if he had provoked the belligerent seaman to such anger that he acted carelessly while climbing the ratlines.

Provoked. Decker was the one who provoked.

And then there was Anna. She had her own way of provoking a man. What would she think of Decker's death? Could it have been avoided? More likely, she would say that Decker's time had come. She would believe that the Almighty played a role in those decisions.

Belief. He knew better.

Why, then, did Anna tell him she didn't believe his unbelief? Her comment disquieted him and he didn't know why.

Yes he did.

No he didn't.

The old weight of anxiety and self-doubt settled on Bairn again. After all he had been through, he still remained utterly vulnerable, bereft, even in the one place he had started to feel more or less at home.

He raised his fist toward heaven. *When will You leave me alone? What have I ever done to You?*

He dropped his fist. It was pointless. There was no use arguing with Someone who wouldn't argue back. He'd never gotten much satisfaction from a God who didn't seem to speak or see or hear. Or feel.

Then it occurred to him that he was talking to God and he had just told Anna he didn't believe in God. He sighed and leaned his forearms on the railing.

Why should he feel so drawn, so curious about her? He didn't know why he bothered to think of her at all. He didn't need a woman telling him what to do or what to believe. He didn't need a woman looking him straight in the eyes or telling him he was wrong about nearly everything.

He did not need a woman. And he definitely didn't want one like pious Anna. So innocent to the ways of the world, pathetically innocent. Like all the Peculiars. In this world but not of it. Bound by faith that appeared gentle and yet was so severe.

He tried to put away all thoughts of Anna and went to his quarters. But he couldn't put away the sadness that overcame him, the unnamed longings. He had another vivid dream . . .

His mother was in the front room, sitting in the bentwood rocker his father had made when they were first married. The room had not changed; the basket of mending was by the window where the afternoon light was best. The rocker was near the fireplace for warmth, a child was curled up by his mother's feet, napping. The curtains on the window were as crisp and white as if they had been washed and ironed and starched that morning.

Bairn was not lost, his father was not dead.

When he startled awake from the deep dream, heart pounding, his face was wet with tears.

July 9th, 1737

The whole sky was on fire. Felix hid in the bowsprit to watch the sun dip lower and lower in the west, filling the sky with flames of red and orange and gold. Squinty-Eye's awful dog had found him and had settled somewhere near his feet. He ruffled its ears to keep the awful dog quiet.

His father would appreciate this sunset. On most summer nights in Ixheim, he and his father would watch the sun set behind the hills. "Going, going, gone," his father would say as the last bit of sun slipped away. Felix wondered what a sunset would look like in Penn's Woods. The very sound of the place made it seem like nothing but trees.

Tonight, on the bow of the *Charming Nancy,* Felix watched Johnny Reed sprinkle salt on a fishing net — salted in, he'd heard sailors call it, to bring good luck — and toss it over the side. The net caught a fish that was so big and bulky that it took three sailors to reel it in. Felix popped his head up to watch them wrestle the thrashing fish up onto the deck. They wouldn't have seen him even if he'd been sending up flares — not with their keen interest in Johnny Reed's catch. All the sailors gathered round the fish — as big as a man. Cook even came out of the galley with a butcher knife, with his cat following behind him.

" 'Tis a shark," Bairn said.

"Shark stew for dinner," Cook said, sounding pleased. He handed Johnny Reed the knife to do the honors of butchering the fish.

Johnny took that knife and opened it up, then screamed like a girl and dropped the knife so that it speared its point into the deck. "Don't look!" he shrieked, covering his eyes.

The seamen looked at once, curious, peering inside the fish's belly, then something terrible overcame them and they staggered backward.

"What's inside?" Cook asked. "What is it?"

"Not a what but a . . ." Bairn bit the end off his sentence and seemed to gulp it down. Then he tried again. "It's a man. Swallowed whole like Jonah's whale."

Cook stretched the opening of the fish. "You're right. He still has his boots on." He looked up at Bairn. "Silver buckles on the boots."

"Oh no," Johnny squealed. "Don't say it."

"Aye. 'Tis Decker," Cook said, matter of factly.

Johnny leapt up like he'd sat on an anthill. He bolted to the railing to vomit over the side of the ship. Oh my, he was sick. It went on forever.

"That sight," Bairn said, peering into the fish, " 'tis beyond anything I've ever seen."

"It's a sign!" Johnny Reed said in his high-pitched voice. "There's a witch aboard. Doncha see? Decker's tryin' t'warn us. From the hereafter!"

The dog jumped up and barked. Felix ducked his head down.

"The only sign is that even a fish couldn't stomach Decker," Bairn said, disgusted.

"Aye," Cook said, humor in his voice. "No more vomiting, gentlemen. 'Tis a grave matter." He cackled in laughter, until Bairn silenced him with a look.

"Johnny, go get another sailcloth and two rocks." Bairn put a hand to the back of his neck. "We'll try to bury Decker again."

Felix was curious to see Decker's body inside the fish, but seamen kept running to the side to throw up over the rail and he was worried that if he moved, he'd be spotted. The bowsprit was the best hiding spot of all. The stupid cat found him, though, and jumped up to the bowsprit to poke around, which made the awful dog start to bark. Fortunately, no one was paying any attention to the cat or the dog or the bowsprit.

If only Johann were here, Felix thought for the hundred and first time. Anna would squirm and his mother would faint and his father would frown that he took delight in the tale, but Johann would've appreciated such a gruesome story about the squinty-eyed sailor swallowed whole like Jonah in the whale. Maybe he'd wait for the right time and use it to shock Catrina silent.

After Decker's body splashed into the water and sunk, the other sailors milled about on the upper deck, talking about witches and fishes. Bairn stood alone at the bow of the ship, looking west to the dying sun. The moon was coming up full over the harbor. Felix considered making his presence known, but decided against it after observing the somber look on Bairn's face. Just as he was about to make a run for the companionway stairs, he thought he heard Bairn quietly say, "Going, gone."

July 10th, 1737
Bairn woke in the morning to a suffocating mist. Fog had settled in. He covered his face with his hands in despair. Temperatures had risen high enough without the added smothering of a blanket of fog, without any hint of wind. No supplies other than casked water had arrived yet from Plymouth harbor, and Bairn had no expectation that the captain would return to the ship until there was a favorable wind.

He splashed water on his face and pulled at his neckerchief, longing for a vast blue ocean and its briny spray, when his only concern would be which direction the wind was blowing.

Outside, he pulled off his boots and grasped the ratlines, then began to climb. Within moments, the deck lay underneath him like a gray blanket. So dense had grown the fog that he had to feel for each handhold, each line onto which he set his feet, and carefully test the rope before he shifted his weight to it. He could see naught in any direction.

He slid down a backstay to the half-deck, wincing as a splinter impaled his palm. Blast it all! He stood there, holding his palm with his other hand, watching the barely drifting fog, frustrated.

Managing the crew in this kind of stand-still weather was a challenge. Boredom was deadly on a ship. The men grew ugly at about the same rate as spoiled fish. Bairn kept hearing murmurs among the deck-hands that Anna was a witch. Each time she ventured above deck, the sailors darted away from her as if she had the pox. One sailor was whittling on a stick of wood and sliced his thumb. He held up his piece of wood in Anna's direction. "She did it! She knew what I was making."

Bairn grabbed the wood from him. It was a carving of a naked woman. He tossed it overboard. "Then why dinnae you whittle somethin' less offensive to a lassie?"

The sailor let out a howl as his wooden carving disappeared into the sea. "That's all I know how to make!"

Another time, Anna had come to peg laundry onto a yard. High above, a seaman on the rigging stopped to watch her and dropped a tool. It landed on Johnny Reed's head, causing a welt. "It's her doing!" the seaman shouted.

"It's yer own doin', you fool," Bairn shouted back. "Instead of watchin' her walk, hold on to yer tools."

As firm as he was about the topic, the men wouldn't listen to reason. They were sure Anna was a witch and was casting spells on them. This afternoon, she bent down to pick up Queenie, and Johnny Reed screamed like a banshee, then held up his fingers in a cross, as if he was warding her off. Bairn saw the strain in her features, the confused hurt in her eyes . . . but it wasn't all bad to have the seamen fearful of her. He remembered Decker's comment that there were others on this ship who were watching Anna.

But then Bairn would remind himself that it shouldn't matter to him how the seamen treated her. She was nothing to him. Just a passenger below deck. He would retreat to the Round House to fill his mind with plotting the ship's chart across the Atlantic, providing a blessed distraction.

And yet, there was something about her that he couldn't get out of his mind. Those large blue eyes, perhaps, or her ripe, lush mouth — a mouth that any man would call tempting. He couldn't blame the sailors for staring at her. He shook his head, trying to clear it, determined to make every effort to avoid her as much as possible.

Once again, he wished he could have gone ashore to Plymouth. *That* would have taken care of his longing for female company.

July 12th, 1737

For two foggy days, Bairn kept the seamen as busy as possible with mend-and-wear tasks — every hole had been patched, every deck scrubbed. The sleeping shelves of the lower deck had been brought above to scour and wash, sails had been mended, masts repaired, hammocks washed and dried. Tasks were running out. They couldn't stand much more of this uselessness.

Added to the friction was the growing kerfuffle over having a witch on board. Johnny Reed came to him in a panic this afternoon, after Anna had brought her basket above deck and unwrapped the bundle. "It's a flower!" Johnny said, eyes spinning with fear as he burst into Bairn's carpentry shop. "You know what it means to have flowers on board!"

Aye, Bairn knew. Flowers were for funerals. To have a flower on board was a portent of death.

"The girl's a Jonah, Bairn. You've got to get her off this ship."

Bairn rolled his eyes.

Johnny closed the door and lowered his voice. "Bairn, there's talk among the men of jumping ship before the captain returns."

Bairn was afraid of something like this. He'd seen the men clump together in tight circles, murmuring to each other. Yesterday, as a precaution, he had dispatched the two longboats to the shore and told those four seamen to wait for the captain to return. Few of the sailors could actually swim, so he wasn't too concerned about losing the entire crew. Still, it was no way to start an ocean voyage. "Johnny, do what you can t'keep heads calm. She's nae a witch."

But Johnny's superstitions were unbendable. Illogical, but that never mattered to sailors. Bairn rubbed his forehead. A mariner's life was rife with superstitions. Superstitions gave seamen some sense that they had control over their circumstances, though a sea voyage was an endeavor based on chance. A great irony, Bairn believed. What the sea wants, the sea will have.

Bairn went to find Anna and found her wrapping up a sad-looking plant in burlap. "That's yer flower?"

"Yes."

"It looks half dead."

"I know. That's why I wanted to give it some fresh air." She looked up at the sky. "It needs sunshine."

"Perhaps . . ." He leaned against the railing. "Perhaps you would nae mind tossing it overboard."

She froze. "Do what?"

"The thing is . . . havin' a flower on board frightens the sailors. They think it portends a funeral."

She frowned and continued wrapping the sad-looking plant in the burlap. "This stays with me."

"The men want you put off the ship."

He expected that piece of information to shock her, to make her hand over that plant. Instead, she lifted her head with a look of delight. The smile on that girl — it melted his perturbation like butter in the hot sun. "So be it." She jumped up. "I'll go pack. You'll need to explain everything to Christian."

"Not so fast. I'm hopin' the men will come 'round to reason before it comes to that."

Her smile faded. "I'd rather be put off the ship than part with this rose."

He remembered how stubbornly she clung to that basket when she'd first come on

180

board. "Why is it so important to you?"

Gently, she placed the burlap bundle into the basket. "It was given to me by someone special." As she walked toward the companionway, the sailors scattered. Like a female Moses parting the Red Sea, Bairn thought.

A rose. A hazy memory tickled the edges of Bairn's mind. He once knew a girl who loved roses; he hadn't thought of her in years. The girl, with other memories, had long ago been shoved to the recesses of his mind. Too painful.

A scuffle between Cook and a sailor snapped Bairn's attention to the present. Added to the friction on the ship was Cook's terrible cooking. At best, he was an indifferent cook. The last few days, the food was inedible.

Earlier this morning, after he'd been unable to identify the food on his plate, Bairn couldn't take it any longer. He had marched to the galley with a plate of mushy, salty beige slop. "I've endured plenty of meals of sour beer and the bitter taste of weevils in a ship's biscuit. But this? This isn't fit fer swine! It's so sour it makes me teeth rattle in their sockets."

Cook scowled at him. "Get me fresh supplies."

"They'll be here soon enough."

"When? We should've sailed days ago! We're going to head straight into hurricane season."

"Do you think I dinnae ken that? But what can I do in this gloom? The captain is waiting fer fair wind." He stopped himself. This was no way to talk to Cook, his friend. "What's the matter with you? You seem blue-deviled today. Is it the fog or somethin' more?"

Cook rubbed his jaw.

"Is yer tooth acting up again?" No wonder they'd been eating slop! Whenever Cook's bad tooth flared up, his cooking — never stellar to begin with — faltered. They all suffered when Cook suffered. "I'll pull it fer you."

"Stay away from me! You'll leave me toothless like you left me without a hand."

"Cook, you ken you would've died had I not taken yer hand."

"Anna can fix."

Bairn and Cook spun around to find Felix at the doorway of the galley.

Cook's sparse eyebrows lifted. "Does it require yanking?" He made a jerking motion with his one hand.

Felix smiled a toothy smile. "No."

"Go get her, laddie," Bairn said. "Anything to keep Cook from killin' us with his cookin'."

Anna returned with Felix, listened to Cook's complaint, and made a remedy of garlic paste to apply to Cook's sore tooth, along with a hot compress.

By midday, Cook's pain had lessened dramatically and Anna was immediately elevated in his eyes. Even more surprising, Cook welcomed Anna and Felix into his galley. No one was ever allowed into Cook's galley except the officers.

July 13th, 1737

The crew had been spooked by the rose incident yesterday, but after observing Cook's changed countenance and greatly improved cooking that evening, the seamen decided Anna might — just might — not be a witch after all, but a healer.

This afternoon, one or two off-duty sailors gathered around her, tentatively, asking questions about their complaints. Then a few more. One of them found a wooden crate for her to sit on and they sat on the deck at her feet, pummeling her with questions. Stiff joints? Rheumatism, she diagnosed. Try hot compresses, she suggested. Boils? Cut a thick slice of onion and place it over the boil. Wrap the area with a cloth. Change the poultice every three to four hours until the boil comes to a head and drains.

Bairn watched the doctoring session from the railing, amused, impressed, but also wanting to make sure the seamen treated Anna well. She had no idea how tempting she was, especially to a crew starved for female companionship. The male attention she was garnering was not a thing to trifle with, not to an innocent like her.

"Show her your hand, Bairn," Cook said.

Bairn still hadn't been able to get the splinter out of his palm. The flesh around the wound was raw and puckered at the edges, fresh blood seeped through. "I'm sufferin' enough."

Anna walked up to him. "I try to bring suffering to no one, least of all the helpless and the sick."

"I'm neither," he said.

"Let me decide that."

He held out his hand to her. She ripped off a piece of clean bandage and dabbed at the seeping wound.

"Yer bringin' sufferin' to me now, the way you're proddin' me like I was a sheep in a bog."

She ignored him and dabbed at the wound, dabbed and dabbed and the splinter eased out. When it was completely out, she

184

showed Bairn the sliver of wood that had been impaled in his hand. Her eyes lifted to his, and she smiled. A small smile that quivered as it curved across her face. A small smile that stirred his heart.

Anna was feeling kindly about the *Charming Nancy* tonight, despite the heat, the troublesome delays, the worries about supplies not arriving, the petty bickering between the Amish and the Mennonites. Maria Müller and Esther Wenger's friendship, tenuous at best, had cooled after Esther remarked that Jacob Amman was a hardheaded radical. Such a comment about the founder of the Amish church, Maria felt, was unforgiveable.

Everyone was suffering in the fog, above and below deck. The heat was intense, the air was stifling, heavy, the humidity intolerable. Late this afternoon, Maria pulled out her leather trunk from under her sleeping shelf and let out a bloodcurdling scream. "What's happening?!" she cried.

Felix, most curious and quickest, was first by her side. "It's just dusty." The trunk was covered with a film of white.

"Not dust, Felix. It's mold," Christian said, trying to calm his frantic wife as she scrubbed the trunk with a rag. "It's the dampness."

Felix dug in his pocket and pulled out his pocketknife. "So that's why my pocketknife keeps getting rusty."

Tonight, as Anna and Dorothea and Felix shared a meal of moldy zwieback and salted meat, a rat the size of a barn cat had run up and grabbed Felix's hat. Felix took off after that rat while everyone near them watched with amusement. The rat ran up and down the aisle of the lower deck, Felix ran up and down, the rat ran back and forth, Felix ran back and forth. Finally the rat dropped the hat at one end of the deck. While Felix bent down to get it, the rat doubled back, picked up the hunk of toast by Felix's hammock, and ran the other way.

Dorothea laughed so hard her face turned red. "Why, that rat knew just what he wanted and figured out how to get it."

It felt wonderful to hear Dorothea's laugh. Anna found herself admiring the rat, until it occurred to her that things had to be pretty dull for a person to admire a rat.

"Enough talk of problems," Christian had reminded everyone during evening devotions. "We shall focus on God's goodness. Nothing good or bad happens to us but what first passes through the Father's hand."

As Anna lay in her hammock that night,

she thought of the blessings of the day. Felix and the cunning rat. Dorothea's laughter. A respite from seasickness. The lower deck, though dank and musty and damp and moldy, smelled infinitely better than it had a week ago.

Her cheerfulness had to do with helping ease Cook's toothache, she supposed. For the first time since leaving home she felt as if she were here for a reason. The sailors no longer thought Anna to be a witch who had conjured up Decker's death. Now they believed her to be a healer, and while she didn't feel qualified for such a label, she longed to be useful. As she had sat on the wooden crate this afternoon, she treated sailors' cuts and boils and blisters and mouth sores and eye infections, trying to remember remedies her grandmother had used back in Ixheim. The seamen became less hostile and afraid; they began to laugh as she treated them, and they thanked her when she had finished. They didn't need to, though, for their gratitude was plain. For the rest of the afternoon and evening, they showed kindness to the passengers — tolerating their presence above deck, filling tubs of water for them, nodding and smiling as they tried to understand each other. It was a relief for the witch rumors to abate, although she had held a thin hope that she might be put off the ship because of them. And it wouldn't be her fault! Surely Christian would understand. Alas, that hope had dissipated with the rumors.

What did Bairn think of her healing? After all, he was the ship's surgeon, but he didn't seem to take offense that the crew sought her out. He stood by the railing as she treated the sailors, watching and listening, but not with malice in those gray eyes. Those eyes — she had to force herself to look away from them. Why? She found him full of contradictions and was never quite sure what he was thinking, though she wished she knew. A hundred questions about him sprang to her mind, longing for answers. There was something mysterious and distant about Bairn and he fascinated her, though she knew it was wrong to think about a stranger, a worldly man. And he was all that. He admitted as much. Yet the more time she spent in his presence, the more baffling he grew and the more drawn she felt to him.

Then there was the fog — both a blessing and a curse. As long as there was fog, the *Charming Nancy* wouldn't be leaving Plymouth. The fog was a curse because they were running through their victuals. But it was also a blessing because it meant Georg Schultz wasn't on board.

Anna gave thanks for this night and the smelly, damp, leaky boat and for what lay ahead. And she prayed she hadn't done any harm to the seamen.

But she still intended to talk to the captain about returning to Rotterdam the moment he set foot on the ship.

10

July 14th, 1737

Bairn spotted Felix hiding behind the windlass and strode over to him. "I've been searchin' fer you. What are you up to now, laddie?"

"Nix." *Nothing.* Felix gave him a wide-eyed, innocent look that didn't fool Bairn for a moment. "Vas ist das?"

"It's a windlass. It's a type of winch used to raise the anchor."

Felix pointed to another winch. "Net das?"

"Nay. That's a capstan. We use it to hoist cargo and other heavy loads. Methinks you ken English better than you let on. The more y'try speakin' it, the better it'll go for you in the New World." He nodded his head toward the fo'c'sle deck, inviting Felix to ascend the ladder. He wanted to move them away from the clump of seamen who were gathered in a circle to mend sailcloth.

Bairn showed Felix the wheel. "Yer at the

helm of the ship." He put his hands on the spokes of the wheel. "Come, take possession of the wheel." He made way for him to stand before him at the wheel.

Felix slipped into place and grabbed the wheel. "How can it . . . verk?"

Bairn was pleased to hear the boy use his halting English. "The wheel is attached to a rudder, far below us in the hold."

"I see it."

"What? Have you been prowlin' down in the hold too?"

"Yuscht eemol." Felix bit his lip. *Only once.*

"I'll wager you've been down more than once." He grinned. He couldn't fault him; he would've done the same thing as a laddie. Why, in fact, he had.

"Do captain stand at vheel all day? All night?"

"Nay. He gives orders to helmsmen who take turns at watch, day and night."

"Night too?"

"Aye. When we put out to sea, the wheel is difficult to control. It takes constant mindin'. Not unlike some boys I ken."

Felix grinned, revealing missing teeth. It pleased Bairn to see the laddie smile so readily. Boys should have reasons to smile.

"How do you . . . the vheel . . . how do

191

you . . ." He motioned with his hands as if turning a wheel.

"Guide the ship?"

Felix nodded. "To America."

Bairn pointed to a box behind him. "Do you see that box? 'Tis called a binnacle. It houses the compass. In the Great Cabin — which is where I first found you sleepin' in the captain's bed — there's the chronometer. We use mathematics to determine longitude and latitude. The captain tells us whitherward, and we set the course." He looked up. "And then there's the sun and stars, as well. That's the mariner's ancient way to set a course."

Felix gripped the wheel as solemnly as if he were a helmsman during a severe storm.

The ship's bell rang to mark the time of watch. "I must go. And you should get below so your family isn't worried about you."

With a fallen face, Felix reluctantly started toward the ladder.

"Felix, I noticed Anna has a limp. Is she hurt?"

"One leg is . . ." He held up his hands at different lengths.

"Shorter than the other?"

Felix nodded.

"Was she born that way?"

"Nee." Felix held his fists together and snapped them like a twig. "It breaks and does not . . ." He searched for the right word. "Fix."

"Heal. You mean her leg dinnae heal properly." An idea brewed in Bairn's mind. "Supposin' you help me with somethin'. A secret."

Felix grinned like he was ready to receive a gift. He hurried back to Bairn's side, deeply interested. "Vat?"

"Would you be able to bring me her shoes?"

"Shoes? You vant Anna's shoes?"

"Aye. She goes barefoot most of the time. All you Peculiars do —" He stopped himself, realizing he had just maligned the boy's people. "Like the sailors." Most sailors went barefoot aboard the ship, as it was easier to climb in the rigging of the ship without clumsy shoes.

Felix looked down at his bare toes and wiggled them.

"Could you do that? Bring me her shoes?"

"I go. I look."

" 'Tis our secret!" Bairn reminded him. "If you can get above deck without bein' seen, leave them in me shop."

He watched the flop of curly red hair descend down the companionway to the lower deck. There was something about that boy that touched Bairn, though he couldn't pinpoint the reason other than Felix reminded him of himself at that age. Curious about everything related to the ship and the sea.

Later that evening, he found Anna's shoes on his workbench, courtesy of a sly laddie. They were humble shoes, made of sheepskin, well worn. He hung a lantern from an iron hook; the light cast a broad beam over his workbench. He spent time carving a heel, sanding it, nailing it carefully into the sole, adjusting it, and then he remained in the deserted carpentry shop for near an hour, staring out the empty doorway, a lantern in his hand, considering Anna. Wondering why he bothered to fix her shoe.

Anna lay on the hammock, trying to distract herself from the loud snores that rose above the hiss of waves breaking against the hull, but the smells of chamber pots that needed to be emptied overpowered her will. The entire vessel seemed to sleep except for the sounds of someone who paced the deck above.

The longer she lay awake with the heavy dank odors of crowded humanity, the more she felt desperate to get upstairs and fill her lungs with fresh air. Quietly, she slipped out of the hammock and crept to the companionway to climb the steps. She pushed the hatch up and took a bracing breath; the sea air caressed her face, cleansing, refreshing, healing.

"Who goes there?" A lantern shone in her face.

" 'Tis Anna."

Bairn lowered the lantern. "I should have known. Yer above deck lately as much as young Felix. Is somethin' wrong?"

"No. I just . . . couldn't sleep and needed fresh air."

"Aye, I can believe that." He took her hand and led her up the final tread onto the deck.

She drew her hand free.

"Hold on to somethin'." He settled her hand into the crook of his elbow and led her to the railing. She peered over the side. The moon shone on the water's dark surface. They stood side by side, quietly, for a long moment. "Wait here a minute, Anna. Keep yer hands on the railin'."

He strode toward the back of the ship and disappeared for a moment, then reemerged. He held something behind his back. "I noticed you have a limp."

Anna flinched and looked away. She could

feel her face heat up. She'd grown so accustomed to a limp that she rarely thought about it.

His tone softened. "I didn't mean to embarrass you. I adjusted yer shoes to even out yer gait." He held out her shoes to him. The right shoe had a platform that raised it over an inch. "I can adjust the heel if it dinnae feel quite right. I had to make a guess."

She looked at the shoes, not quite understanding.

"It's something I've done fer other sailors. If you dinnae fix that limp now, you'll end up with a crooked back when yer old and gray."

"I . . . I don't know what to say."

"Naught but a small thank-you for helpin' the sailors with their ailments."

She was grateful for the dark of night because her face was a tempest of emotions. She was touched by his action, and puzzled by it too. "How did you find my shoes?"

"That red-haired brother of yours."

A smile lifted Anna's lips. "Felix isn't my brother."

Now it was Bairn's turn to be surprised. "He's not your brother? You dote on him. You seem t'make it yer business to keep the boy away from sin and foolishness."

"So true. That boy is a full-time job."

"Why aren't his folks dotin' on him?"

"His father is waiting for everyone in Port Philadelphia. And his mother . . . They had a death in the family right before we left for Rotterdam and she . . . she's grieving still. I'm used to keeping watch over Felix. I've known him since he was born."

"Well, that makes more sense. You dinnae resemble each other at all." His gaze swept over Anna, making her blush. "My mother has red hair like Felix's. In a certain light, it looks like fire."

"Does she live in Scotland?"

"Nay. Not Scotland."

"But your accent . . ."

"Acquired from servin' the captains fer nigh on eleven years."

"You still have family, then?"

"I . . . ken not." Even the mere murmur of his voice sounded heavy, burdened, infinitely sad.

"You still haven't told me where you call home," she said, truly curious. She felt a need to put him in some familiar place, though familiar to her would mean the hills and valleys of Germany. But she couldn't imagine him in Ixheim, plowing a field or tossing hay to a band of ewes.

He pulled his attention from the sea and looked at her. "I don't call anywhere home."

His gaze had wandered to the sea beyond; he seemed to have forgotten her. A stillness had come over him.

"Everyone," she said softly, "is somebody's son."

The plane of his arresting face softened as he studied her through somber eyes. "Mayhap the sea is my home, my family."

"The sea?"

"Aye. The sea has been good and fair t'me."

"But the sea can't love you back."

Before she could ask another question, a bell rang and Bairn stiffened. "The ship's bell is ringin' for a watch change. You should go below. Would not be good to give the deckhands any more reason to gossip about the lassie from the lower deck." He walked her to the top of the companionway and nodded, leaving her there.

She found Bairn full of contradictions. He was not a plain and humble man. He was a wayward soul. He was not one of them. He claimed not to believe in God and to only believe in himself. He was not many things, but she had discovered he was one thing: he was kind.

As Bairn eased onto his bunk, he thought of how Cook would tweak him if he knew he had spent time tonight adjusting a heel on a shoe for a Peculiar girl.

One moment, Bairn found Anna something of an annoyance and the next, a sweet innocent he felt inclined to protect. What was it about her that drew him? She had a loveliness about her, and clearly, a rare strength of character. She certainly wasn't what one would expect of a Peculiar: timid and trembling. Or a pub girl: bawdy and bold.

He only knew he was developing some feelings for the girl, which surprised and alarmed him. He was no fool; he knew he mustn't entertain thoughts of her. He must keep his wits about him. They came from different worlds and would return to different worlds and he wasn't about to jeopardize his promotion to first mate by toying with a girl from the lower deck, no matter her appeal.

It was that thought that finally pushed him on toward sleep — thinking about why he ought to stop thinking about Anna. He slept soundly for five long hours, the longest he'd slept in weeks, and woke to feelings of comfort and a cozy warmth that he remembered from years long past.

■ ■ ■ ■

July 15th, 1737

To Felix's great dismay, Anna decided that it was time to start teaching English. He'd gone to all the school he ever meant to. Even more disappointing was that he and Catrina were the only students.

Anna had found an old table and set it near the hatch to get some air, then gave Catrina and Felix slates and chalk to copy down words. Then to string the words into sentences. While Felix was laboring over the writing: *The dog sits in the sun,* Catrina labored over her own sentence. She jabbed Felix in the ribs. He looked at her slate and read: *Why doesn't your mother get out of bed?*

He wrote back to in-everybody's-business Catrina Müller: *Which eye should I look at to answer your question?*

Naturally, Catrina ran off to show her mother what Felix had written.

The truth was that he didn't know how to answer her. He had no idea when his mother was going to stop feeling so tired.

Last night, know-it-all Maria gave his mother a talking to, telling her that over-grieving was a complaint to the Lord. Felix did not like Maria Müller, with her face like a disapproving prune and the extra starched prayer cap on her fuzzy hair. She thought she was so superior, just like Catrina did.

His mother only lifted her sad eyes and said, "Maria, if you ever bury a child, and I pray you never will, then come and tell me how I should feel."

He knew his mother was grieving over Johann, and he understood that all her grieving had doubled back over his oldest brother, Hans, the brother he never knew but was named for — Hans Felix Bauer. But what he didn't know was when she would be herself again. She'd gotten so skinny and pale, he barely knew her. He worried about her, but he couldn't stand being near her — her sadness made him feel smothered, as if he couldn't breathe — and that thought made his insides twist with guilt. It was one of the reasons he tried to go up top as much as he could. It helped him take a break from his mother's sadness down below.

Happily, Bairn welcomed him above deck. Felix would tag along behind the carpenter, listening, soaking up everything he could about a seaman's life. He could understand more and more of the crew's stories. Yarns, Cook called them. The sailors could tell him all sorts of interesting things and sailing trivia, but no one could tell him when his mother would get out of bed.

He thought he might ask Anna about his mother, though he didn't know exactly what he would ask her. Something made him believe Anna would know and that she wouldn't make him feel bad for asking. She certainly wouldn't have given him Catrina's one-eyed "Oh, you poor motherless boy" pity look. Or Maria's snooty "Don't you know?" Anna would give him the plain, pure, teacherly truth.

While Catrina and her eye went off to complain to her mother, Felix leaned across the table to Anna. "Is my mother ever going to be well?"

Anna seemed like she was thinking whether or not she should tell him something. She was looking straight at him, and even though it was hard, he looked right back at her.

Felix tried to appear intelligent, and he thought it worked because finally Anna said, "Life can be very hard sometimes, and when it's been hard for your mother, she suffers from something called melancholy. It's like her heart burst. She has a difficult time coping with sad things, like Johann's passing." She waited to make sure he understood her. He nodded.

"It's like she has a wound, and it's taking a long time to heal. But you can't see this wound. It's deep inside."

He loved it when Anna talked to him like he was grown-up. He didn't really understand half of what she meant, but it felt good to be talked to like that.

"Before you were born, when your oldest brother died on that ship, she suffered for a long time. It wasn't until you were born that she started to feel happy again."

"Do you think she won't be happy again unless she has another baby?"

"I think seeing your father will help her feel a lot better. In the meantime, we need to be patient and understanding." Anna smiled. "Soon, the ship will leave Plymouth Sound and sail to America. Soon, Felix."

July 16th, 1737
Bairn yanked off his boots and stretched out on his bunk. At six foot five inches, he was accustomed to having his feet hang off the edge and scrunching around before getting comfortable. The creaking of a ship's timbers had always been a soothing sound to his ears. Tonight, the sounds alarmed him, causing him to revisit the repairs he had made to her. Was she shipshape? Ready for the ocean crossing?

He never used to fret over a vessel's seaworthiness, not when the lower deck was filled with goods. His thoughts drifted to Anna, wondering if she had fallen asleep yet and if she preferred using a hammock. And then he thought about the tiny springing curls that framed her neck beneath her cap. He thought of her lips, softly parted, of how the fog swirled around the two of them and how the moonlight cast a hazy glow about her. As if she were a celestial being, an angel.

The sea can't love you back, Anna had said. That was true. The sea has her wanton way with those who love her, but in his mind, she was a safer bet.

An old familiar ache filled him then and he forced his mind off a certain Peculiar down below and onto other things, anything else to ward off his melancholia. At last, he fell asleep. Next he knew, he heard the ship's bells signal five o'clock and breathed deeply of the tannic air. His eyes flew open. The air had a different scent. He bolted off his bunk and rushed up the ladder to reach the main deck.

Outside, a mild breeze ruffled his hair. He turned a practiced eye out to the water. The fog might be lifting, at last. Hallelujah! The overcast wouldn't linger, nor would the gloomy mood that hung on him.

By midmorning, seams began to open in the cloud cover. The still waters of the channel slowly shifted from gray to green to blue.

That afternoon, delivery boats started to arrive with provisions from the captain's purchases in Plymouth. All was in a flurry as the seamen readied the hold. The capstan was once again squeaking in use as crates and barrels were lowered into the hold in rapid sequence. This was a busy time for Bairn, he was responsible to the captain for the storage and distribution of provisions. The *Charming Nancy* nearly bulged with excess: barrels of hardtack, salted meat, beer, sacks of flour, oats, malt, gunpowder, and scores of wooden boxes containing amber bottles of liquors.

By the time the sun had set for the day, the *Charming Nancy* had completed its cargo and was fully wooded and watered. Cook was happy to have a full larder, the crew was unusually cheerful.

Now, they were just waiting for the captain to return. The captain and the wind.

Before leaving Rotterdam, the animal pens in the bow of the lower deck had been filled with passenger trunks, other than a small area for the pig and chickens. This afternoon, Bairn had told Felix to let the passengers know they would need to move their trunks to their sleeping berths so that more livestock could come aboard.

When Felix heard that more animals would be arriving, he darted above deck to his favorite hiding place on the bowsprit. From where he crouched in the shadows, he was able to peer over the railing and see the delivery boats sail toward the *Charming Nancy* from across Plymouth Sound, filled with animals in pens. Two more pigs, a goat and her kid, and cages of chickens. He was disappointed to see so many chickens. How many chickens did the New World need?

The delivery boats came alongside the *Charming Nancy,* the smaller animals were passed up, then the pigs were forced into a canvas sling and hoisted on board, where a rope was slung around their necks and they were hauled forward. Seamen sweated and the deck steamed with pig muck. Felix wondered if those pigs had any idea how special they were — sailing off to another land. Most pigs lived and died in the same farmer's pen.

As Felix saw the chicken cages get passed up to the sailors, he could think of nothing else but a home-cooked chicken dinner by his mother. He remembered how his father would go out in the yard and grab a chicken by its neck, wring its neck off with his left hand while whistling a tune, pluck it, clean it, and take it to his mother to cook. He thought he might persuade Anna to ask Cook to make them a chicken dinner one night.

Better still, he might mention a chicken dinner to Maria. She complained bitterly about Cook's food and she had a talent for badgering people to get what she wanted.

Felix licked his lips; he could practically taste that chicken. Food was seldom far from his thoughts.

The *Charming Nancy* had become familiar to Felix over this last week while the ship was anchored at Plymouth Sound. He knew his way from the lower deck to the 'tween deck to the fo'c'sle. He had poked through every cupboard in Cook's galley and discovered where Bairn and Mr. Pocock messed and where they slept and where they charted the ship's path. He had watched work being done to the hull and masts; he had seen large sheets of canvas get laid out on the dockside and later knotted to the masts and spars; he had seen cables and shrouds attached and tested as the ship was rigged. He had grown familiar with the feel of timbers beneath his bare feet and the hideous smell of the ship's bilge. He knew what was meant by aft and forward and leeward, which was the mizzen mast and which the main, which was a halyard and which a sheet. He had come to know the *Charming Nancy* like he had known his father's farm in Ixheim.

But Bairn had told him that sailing a ship in the open sea was different from a ship in port, and Felix couldn't wait for the journey to begin. He glanced up to see a sailor slide down a backstay. He aimed to try it himself, the first chance he could finagle without being seen.

Felix Bauer was having the time of his life.

11

July 17th, 1737

It was a fine, clear day in Plymouth. A few cottony white clouds drifted across a pale blue sky, moved along by just enough of a breeze to keep things pleasantly cool. Because of tidal conditions, the ship would not set sail until after eight o'clock, just after sundown. Bairn knew that Captain Stedman would arrive soon, seeing as a fair wind had finally blown in, but it was also the Sabbath. Captain Steadman was a God-fearing Presbyterian, at least on Sundays. He would not put his crew to work on the Sabbath unless it couldn't be avoided.

By midmorning, a steady flow of warm air from the south had ruffled the blue surface of the channel.

Restless, Bairn paced the deck until he heard a strange wailing sound, as if a dog was howling and in terrible pain. He drew close to the hatch in the stern of the ship to hear what was going on in the lower deck, and realized that the mournful sound was music. The Peculiars were singing. He glanced around the deck to make sure no seaman was nearby, then crouched down to peer through the lattice top of the hatch and saw the Peculiars gathered in the center of the lower deck, sitting on the deck floor, men on one side, women on the other.

Bairn sat down, one knee bent, one leg straightened out, and listened to the hymn singing, which went on and on and on. The same tuneless, sorrowful hymn, a sound that resonated. An old song, but where would they hear new ones? They were a fusty people.

He spotted Anna sitting among the women and noted the unmistakable joy on her face. She leaned her head to one side, pondering something. Her face was so lovely, so delicately structured, that it gave him a stomachache. What made a man feel that stomach-churning agony for one woman and not another?

When the singing was finally over, Christian Müller rose to his feet and began to preach from the Bible. Bairn had thought Christian to be a mild-mannered man, henpecked by his domineering wife, but as he spoke, he grew more and more animated.

Bairn strained to listen, forging words and sentences together to grasp Christian's meaning.

"Each one of us will face a watershed moment that will define all others in a life. The moment that puts our humanity to a test. When that moment arrives, we each need to ask ourselves, which path will it be? Will we follow God's ways or will we choose man's ways?"

And what, Bairn wondered, would be the difference? If there was a God — and he wasn't convinced of that, though he wasn't entirely convinced there wasn't — wouldn't they want the same things? Would God not want man to work hard and prosper? That was Bairn's holy endeavor. That was the only thing that mattered to him — growing rich. Was that so wrong? Anna seemed to think so.

He didn't have time to ponder the theological puzzle for long because Cook came out of the galley with a bucket of slop to toss overboard. Bairn jumped to his feet.

"And why do you look like a boy caught with his hand in the biscuit tin?"

Bairn shrugged. "Just bored. There is naught to do but watch weather and water."

Cook's eyes traveled to the hatch. He was no fool. "It's that girl. She's got you cowed."

Bairn brushed off his pants. "I don't know what yer talkin' about."

"I've seen the way you watch her when you think no one's looking."

Bairn took another tack. "She's a sight better lookin' than watchin' ye."

Cook laughed, then coughed, nearly spitting out his pipe. "Ain't that the truth." He dumped the potato peelings over the side of the ship and seagulls immediately flew in for the pickings. "I can't wait to get under way. Sick of this waitin'."

"Aye."

Cook looked down at the hatch. "As soon as we get them Peculiars dumped off in Philadelphia and head back to England, the better. I'd much rather have a hold filled with goods to trade than a load of holy rollers."

"You sound like Decker. What do y'have against them?"

"Can't understand their jabbering in that gutteral tongue," Cook shrugged. "And they don't appreciate me cooking."

Nor did Bairn. "After spendin' weeks down in that vile-smellin' lower deck, don't you think you'd be complainin' about anythin' and everythin'?"

Cook laughed. "They don't know what they're in for. These last few weeks have been a tea party compared to what's comin'." He gazed up at the sky, noticing the halo around the sun — a sign of rain to come. The wind was picking up, and a few gray clouds had appeared in the sky. "We're in for a humdinger, or I miss my guess."

"They'll find out soon enough. If Captain Stedman is like his brother, we'll be sailin' tonight on the outgoin' tide. The wind shall soon be blowin' a gale." Bairn could feel its breath. The air smelled storm-damp.

They both knew the weather from years of watching it. The sea rolled in a long, low swell, lifting the *Charming Nancy*, then carefully easing her down again. A gust of wind whipped Bairn's queue, lifting it off his neck.

Wind. Glorious, glorious wind.

Bairn strode toward the fo'c'sle just as the deck lurched beneath his feet. He climbed up the ratlines to inspect the gathering clouds. He swung onto the forestay and slid to the deck in seconds to begin his inspection of the deck, checking every cleat and line and mast and yard and spar. No one needed a loose spar in a high wind. And he suspected a high wind by the way the surface of the water was whipping up.

As the tide would turn and Plymouth Sound would begin to gradually drain, he knew the time had come. Tonight, the *Charming Nancy* would sail out under top-sails into the Atlantic.

Anna woke in the night from a deep sleep, startled by the sound of footfalls racing above her, by orders getting shouted out.

"Winch that cutter aboard, then up anchor."

It was the captain's voice, directing the men on watch. "Mr. Pocock, set course for the Atlantic. This storm is going to get worse, and we need to be out of the channel before daybreak or we'll be here 'til kingdom come."

She blinked, disoriented, trying to collect her thoughts and remember where she was. She put her head back on the hammock, listening to the sounds above her. She heard the flapping sound of sails as they unfurled. She heard the creak of a chain being lifted. And then, movement. Her eyes flew open. The boat was setting sail and she hadn't spoken to the captain yet. Her plan! She had to tell the captain that she wanted to be put off the ship so she could return to Rotterdam from Plymouth with Lizzie.

She jumped from her hammock and hurried to the companionway. When she reached the top, she pushed the hatch up and slipped onto the deck, shivering as needlelike rain pelted her. She shielded her eyes and watched the activity going on above decks. Sailors were running, climbing up ratlines, their feet instinctively knowing where to find footing. Everywhere seamen moved about the ship. Those who did not have their feet planted firmly on deck hung from a confusion of rigging and sails.

She saw the blurry lights of Plymouth receding. The sea swelled like a living thing about them, rocking the boat and dampening her face with spray. The captain saw her first and pointed. Bairn strode to meet her in three long steps. The rain pounded on the deck, creating a curtain between them. "Anna, stay below. You could get hurt up here."

She shielded her face from the rain with her hands. "I need to talk to the captain."

"Why?"

"He needs to turn the boat around and sail back to Plymouth."

A short laugh burst out of Bairn. "That's nae goin' to happen. The sails have caught the wind and bellied out." He took a step closer, annoyed. "And 'tis a ship. Not a boat. Do ye ne'er listen to me, woman?"

"But someone on board is having a baby."

Even with rain streaming down his face,

she saw his eyebrows shoot up in alarm. "Now?"

"No. Not right now. But she is only two months from her time, she tells me."

"Well, see then, there's naught to fash about. Surely we'll be in Port Philadelphia by then." A gust of wind nearly took her prayer covering right off and he gave her a wry grin. "With wind like this, mayhap we will arrive by morn."

"Then, you won't ask the captain to turn the boat around?" Anna said quietly, a cold realization dawning.

" 'Twill be fine. Anna, you need to get below decks."

A great swell raised the stern under their feet. It sent the bow plunging into a towering crest, and as the huge wave continued to roll beneath the *Charming Nancy,* it sent the ship listing to larboard. The stern settled with a roaring splash, plunging it into a blanket of spray that doused Anna and Bairn. She lost her bearings and stumbled. He reached out and held her steady, righting her. She felt him balance with the roll of the deck. One leg braced, the other knee bent, he leaned into the ship's heel, then straightened, keeping himself steady in order that she might lean against him.

Holding tight to his forearms, she had a

clear view of the storm. Below, the ocean rolled white with foam. "Wouldn't the b—" she stopped herself just in time — "ship be safer in the harbor?"

"Nay. Safer out to sea than in the channel."

"Bairn!" Captain Stedman shouted above the wind. "Set all plain sail. Pilot us out of the channel, and then set the topsails and jib sheets on a course southwest by west."

"Aye, Captain!" Bairn turned to Anna. "You must go below. Tell everyone below to mind their lights."

"To do *what*?"

"Douse their lantern flames. Dinnae light them again until the sea is quiet. Secure everythin' that is movable. 'Tis a mighty gale comin' upon us. We have a long stretch ahead." He put his hands on her shoulders to direct her. "Yer already soaked. You dinnae want to get a chill."

"But so are you."

"I'll have time for that later, after we ride out the gale. A seaman gets used to workin' in wet clothin'."

"Bairn, are you frightened?"

For a split second, his eyes softened. "Nay, lassie. 'Tis just a storm. Dinnae fash yerself. Trust me, I won't let anythin' happen to you." His hands as gentle as his voice now, he grasped her shoulders and guided her to the companionway, lifting the hatch to let her climb down. Off in the horizon flashes of white-hot light appeared, illuminating the ship, followed rapidly by a deafening boom. Anna startled and grabbed the top ledge of the companionway to steady herself. When the lightning struck again, that was when she noticed that Bairn was barefoot, pant legs rolled midway up his calves. His ankles were covered in thick red scars.

Bairn had once been shackled.

Chains rattled. Yards creaked and groaned. Wind shrieked through the rigging. Felix flashed open his eyes, waking to a clamor of activity above deck. Feet pounded around him, above him.

The ship had sprung to life, and he heard hurry in the movements of the crew and their shouts. A searing flash of light shone through the cannon portals, lighting the lower deck with a moment of glaring brightness to reveal his mother's slumbering form beside him. Felix was glad she was sleeping deeply because this storm would terrify her. He scudded over to peer out the cannon portal at the storm and gasped in awe. A greenish-gray sea lashed violently. Rising,

rising, rising, then curling into a foaming, towering crest that crashed down in an explosion. It was a frightening, terrifying sight, and Felix loved it.

Not long ago, he had seen Anna slip up the companionway and leave the hatch slightly ajar, so he hurried behind her, waited until a big wave hit the ship and everyone went topsy-turvy, then he crawled behind the capstan. As soon as the captain's back was turned, he made a mad dash to the bowsprit, his favorite spot, where he could stay for a while, unnoticed. He saw the guns of the Grand Battery on Lord Mount Edgecumbe's estate slide past and he leaned over the railing, watching England pass by, trying to absorb everything, to remember everything, so he could tell his father all about it when he saw him.

He stayed put as the ship made her way through the narrows and then progressed through the lower bay and out finally into the Atlantic, where she began to roll slightly as she made a sweeping turn to port. And then he was so soaked and chilled that even he couldn't stand it any longer, so he carefully wormed his way back to the lower deck. As the *Charming Nancy* sailed into the stormy darkness that enveloped her, venturing out into the churning open waters of the Atlantic Ocean, Felix was sure life couldn't get any more exciting.

A couple of hours out from Plymouth Sound, the *Charming Nancy* cleared Penlee Point and headed west toward the open waters of the Atlantic. Leaving and entering port were the busiest times for Bairn, for the entire crew: between those two moments of frenetic activity, as long as nothing untoward happened, life on board a well-run ship sailing at the right season was fairly uneventful and full of typical, mundane chores — trimming the sails, cleaning, disinfecting, cooking, mending sails and nets.

Bairn wondered if, down below, the passengers were frightened. The first moments of a ship's voyage, from when she leaves port until her course and sails are set, could be terrifying to those who weren't familiar with the sound of each activity. Sails flapped deafeningly until the wind began to fill them, ropes cracked, urgent commands were shouted incomprehensibly, seamen ran from one side of the ship to the other. When the sails were set and the ship was in good order, her motion settled and shouts on deck became fewer.

But this wasn't a time when things were

in good order and passengers had the luxury of getting accustomed to a ship at sea. There was a drenching pelt of rain, and a cold, stiff wind whipped against them. The ocean was a heaving mass of rollers, the water dark and oily. These were exactly the kinds of conditions that seamen dreaded most, not because of the pounding rain, but because of the peculiar sideways motion of the water when wind-driven waves interacted with a tidal current. Wind driven, Bairn suspected, by a severe storm they were heading into.

The passengers, who had just barely gotten over seasickness and found some pattern to life on a ship, would be back to square one, trying to gain their sea legs.

He wondered how Anna would fare in this storm, if she was anxious. He didn't know what had possessed him to promise he would keep her safe. Ever since he'd met her, he'd been saying and doing and feeling things against his better judgment. Certainly, he had the desire to keep her safe, to keep all the passengers safe. It was the means he lacked.

He wished he could bring Anna comfort. He wished he could give all the passengers a word of comfort. In the midst of this kind of a tempest, he had no comfort to give.

A crack of thunder roared through the lower deck, renting the air like a shot of cannon, waking many passengers with a cry. Another rumble sounded from above and the *Charming Nancy* lurched to larboard. A few women shrieked and Anna nearly did.

Lizzie, lying close to Anna's hammock, began to sob. "I'm going to die. Oh, I've been so wicked."

Anna hopped out of her hammock and crouched near Lizzie. "Hush, now. It's just a storm. It'll soon pass. Bairn told me so himself. He promised he would keep us safe." She spoke each word with care to keep the panic edge from her tone. But panic clenched at her middle with the notion of confinement in the lower decks, enduring the tumult of the raging storm, for who knew how long? The whining, the stale air, the sickness.

Rain dripped down on them, seeping through the cracks of the planks and holes in the hatch covering, pouring in with blasts of wind and spray through the cannon portals. Anna saw Felix sit up on his pallet to peer out the portal and went over to sit by him, tiptoeing carefully around Dorothea, who was sleeping soundly. God's mercy. Her melancholy had taken another turn for the worse after she heard details of Decker's death, and she went about her days teary-eyed, silent, exhausted.

"Are you scared?"

"No. Are you?"

Felix shook his head a little too vigorously, but she knew he'd never admit to feeling frightened if she didn't. "Do you think we're sinking?"

Such a thought hadn't occurred to her. Not yet. She hugged her knees to her chest and tried not to think about the thunder and lightning that was rocking the ship. " 'All shall be well, all shall be well, all manner of things shall be well.' "

"Who said that?"

"St. Julian of Norwich. An English mystic. When she was young, she was very ill. She said that she had sixteen visits from Jesus during her illness."

Felix turned toward her. "Maybe Jesus will come visit us and still the storm."

"But that's exactly the point. That's exactly what St. Julian of Norwich discovered. Jesus was right in the midst of her distress."

Felix pressed his knees together. "Solid-gold fact?"

"Solid-gold."

He turned back toward the cannon portal. "Maybe I should go help Bairn."

"Help how?"

"Shorten sails. Tie knots. Cook has taught me some."

"I heard that Cook woke one morning with his feet tied together." She reached into her trunk to take out a tin of crackers and held it out to him. "You're not going anywhere."

"Bairn told me that working a ship in heavy weather was dangerous. He said that even the most seasoned sailor could be snatched off the deck and dragged into the sea. He said the sea has buried many a friend and shipmate."

"All the more reason for you to stay below deck until the storm passes. You are not yet a seasoned sailor."

Thunder pealed above the trembling ship, so loud Anna's ears hurt. The *Charming Nancy* rose on a heavy swell, lunging left, tilting the ship to such an angle that passengers were pitched, bodies and bed linens, onto the deck. The tin flew from Felix's fingers and landed on Dorothea. Felix's mother rose onto her elbows in fright.

"It's nothing to fear, Dorothea," Anna said

in her most soothing voice. "Just a little rain."

"A little rain?" Dorothea asked. "It sounds like a deluge." She sat up. "Felix, come away from the window. You'll catch a cold."

It was nearly as wet above the ocean as it was below. Everything felt wet: clothes, shoes, beddings, books, hair, skin. They were cold, and the sea's roughness sent their belongings sliding back and forth across the floor so much that they gave up putting them back. All they could do was to huddle together in the dark and gloomy lower deck.

Felix spent some time tending the animals, then brought cups of water to Anna and his mother. "Did you know that Georg Schultz didn't return with the captain?"

"Really?" Anna was delighted. "How do you know that?"

"I heard Captain Stedman tell Bairn that Georg Schultz had learned of one more ship to sail, the *Townshend,* so he set off to Cowes to round up additional passengers for the ship. The captain said that Georg Schultz is always following a pot of gold."

Dorothea frowned at him. "Felix, what have I told you about eavesdropping?" She lifted her chin. "Wer lauert an die Wand, heert sei eegni Schand." *He who eavesdrops*

by the wall will hear that which shames him-
self.

Anna didn't mind Felix's eavesdropping so much. He had a talent for it. In fact, she couldn't help but smile at this turn of events. One thing, at least, was going in the right direction.

12

July 19th, 1737

The rain that had begun as a light wind and drizzle as they left Plymouth did not stop. It had rained as it had never rained before. Captain Stedman jested that they could turn the ship upside down and row without making much difference in their progress.

Bairn was relieved that the captain was able to make a jest. That meant that he wasn't too worried. Not yet.

On the afternoon of the second day, a hard rain continued to pound the decks and lashed in windswept fury against Bairn's face and chest. "Hard-a-lee," he shouted to Miles Carter, who was struggling to man the wheel. Bairn went to help him put down the wheel and turned the ship's head. Bairn followed the circuit of the *Charming Nancy*'s bowsprit as she came round, then snapped his gaze to the sails as she picked up the wind from her other quarter. Gusts wailed through the rigging with a shrill loud enough to curl an old salt's toes.

As the ship swung past the eye of the wind, his trained and discerning eye took measure. He ran down the deck to the top of the ladder. "She still carries too much sail," he yelled to the captain, who stood on the waist.

"Aye. Reef the main upper topsail."

Cupping his mouth, Bairn shouted to repeat the order over to the half deck, where three crew stood waiting. The wind carried back the faint echo of "Aye, sir!"

The three agile seamen started up into the rigging. It was precarious business to climb on those lofty, slick footropes, balancing against the roll and pitch of the sea, but Bairn had faith in the skill of them. The wind whipped ferociously around them, filling the sails and turning them into snapping sheets of unforgiving canvas, heavy and wet with spray. Twenty . . . forty . . . sixty feet and upward they continued to scale to reach the main mast. Reducing sail was tricky business in fair weather. In a gale like this, such a feat could seem near impossible. In the midst of this, a fierce wave exploded against the ship's topsides, straining every timber that held the ship together, and a loud crack vibrated through the entire deck. Instantly, Bairn and the captain locked eyes.

"I'll find out what it was," Bairn shouted.

He walked the entire deck, checking spars and masts.

A sailor emerged from the hatch that closed the companionway and met him with frightened eyes. "A beam cracked below deck."

Nay. He must be wrong. "What d'you mean, a beam? Which beam?"

"The center beam that holds the ship in one piece."

"Are you sure?"

"I seen it crack with me own eyes. You can go below and see it for yerself."

Bairn went to the lower deck, holding a kerchief over his nose and mouth to mask the stench. He lit a lantern and waited until his eyes adjusted to the dim light, then he strode quickly to the center beam.

The structural timber had a split running lengthwise through its center, cracking like a dried twig. The sailor's corner of his mind, developed over the last eleven years, realized the imminent danger they were in. If the timber split in two, the ship would blow apart into pieces.

Panic clawed at his stomach, his heart started to pound, his legs were shaking so that he had difficulty standing upright. He wambled, felt himself swaying.

But he must not show any reaction. He conjured Captain John Stedman's voice in his head, telling him to remain calm in the face of the direst situation. *Never let your crew know if you're flustered, scared, distraught.* He had seen his share of perilous situations in the years he had been on a ship and not once had Bairn seen the captain become flustered. "You may have hysterics afterward," Captain Stedman would admonish Bairn, "but not during the crisis."

"Vas dat de loud noise?"

Bairn looked down to see Felix peering up at the beam. "Aye. Dinnae fash yerself over it, laddie."

"Can you fix?"

Bairn ran a hand along the crack. "I ken not."

"My papa says the right . . . Waerkzeich . . ."

"Tools?"

"Ja. Tools. Tools can fix all tings."

Bairn gave him a pat on the head. "Your papa is a wise man." Unfortunately, there wasn't a tool on board able to fix a crack like that. "The captain is waitin' fer me. Get in bed and hunker down. The storm hasn't worn itself out yet."

Bairn bolted up the companionway to scud carefully along the deck, holding on to the railing, to reach the Great Cabin. The captain sat at his table, his hands gripping the edge of the table as if holding it together. He didn't look up when Bairn came in. "Tell me. Nay, dinnae tell me."

" 'Twas the beam that supports the main mast. A crack through the center." He paused to allow the captain a moment to absorb the gravity of the situation. "Sir, the structural integrity of the ship 'tis at stake."

The captain covered his face with his hands. "I made a serious error in leaving Plymouth when we did. I was eager to get the voyage under way and thought we could outrun the storm. I dinnae give enough consideration to the boxy hull of this ship. And here we are in the middle of a fierce storm, with a cracked timber. I dinnae ken what to do." He dropped his chin on his chest and covered his hands with his face. "Mayhap we should turn back," he muffled.

Turning back posed as much danger as pushing forward.

Giving this captain a suggestion was tricky business, so Bairn treaded carefully. There was an invisible boundary around the captain that he would not let others cross, and he could be sensitive about his authority. You could never quite be sure what might set him off or shut him down. "As I see it, sir, we have two problems. The beam we can do naught about fer now, but the storm we might be able to do somethin' about."

The captain dropped his hands and lifted his head. "Such as?"

"There was a time when your brother faced a storm like this, when he had run out of options."

"What did he do?"

"He had the ship lie ahull."

"Dinnae talk mince."

"I'm not talkin' rubbish."

The captain leaned back and folded his arms across his chest, gripping himself hard. "All sails down?"

"Aye."

"What happened?"

"Then her helm was secured leeward and her shoulder was kept to the sea."

"And what if she just wallows in the great troughs? What if her masts threaten to roll out?"

Bairn leaned the palms of his hands on the tabletop. "Sir, 'tis already happenin'."

"What happened to John's ship?"

"The ship stopped fightin' the elements. She was perfectly balanced and sat like a contented duck."

A ray of hope lit the captain's eyes. "That would take pressure off the beam. At least for now."

"Aye. One crisis at a time."

The captain dropped his head for a moment. Bairn wondered if he was thinking or praying. He lifted his chin and looked straight at Bairn. "Do it."

Bairn rushed outside. "Furl the sails. Tie everythin' down on deck."

The sailors stared at him with blank looks on their faces, as if he might be crazy, so he repeated himself, even more loudly. "Have her topgallants and courses sheeted down." His booming voice projected over the creaks and groans of the ship's timber and the wind as it whistled through the sails. Seamen leapt to their tasks, some working the ropes, others beginning the lofty climb up the ratlines.

As soon as the sails were furled and secured, everything on deck tied down, he ordered the helmsman to secure the ship leeward.

He squeezed his eyes shut. "Oh God, please help." It occurred to him that he was praying, though he wasn't a praying man.

Something remarkable happened as soon as the ship's bow swung into the wind. Her topsides, under empty masts, steadied the ship's motion. The ship found its balancing point, lying more or less quietly, bobbing like a cork on the water's surface despite the tumult of the squall. After being ruthlessly tossed and turned by the waves, after suffering an injury as serious as a cracked beam, the little ship was finally at peace.

In the lower deck, a sudden change occurred. Instead of the dramatic movement that lashed passengers from side to side, hurling them out of beds, the movements became as gentle as a cradle. Anna crept on hands and knees to the cannon portal, shocked by what she saw outside. Outside, the howling gale continued to rage and whip the sea with astonishing violence. Inside, the ship had somehow found her still point.

Anxiety had bubbled in Anna's belly all morning, but it started now to give way to a delicate sense of calm. Her thoughts were with Bairn out in the gale. She'd seen the look of concern on his face. Life was so precious, so tenuous. It could be altered in an instant. She had never believed this to be more true than she did right now.

Keep Bairn safe, Lord. Please keep him safe.

She looked around and saw people return

to their bunks and pallets. A gentle quiet settled over the lower deck. The ship felt easy under them, sleek and lithe. It seemed to be past time for words, until Christian rose to his feet in the middle aisle and read from Psalm 91 in his Bible, offering heartfelt thanks.

" 'He that dwelleth in the secret place of the most High shall abide under the shadow of the Almighty. I will say of the LORD, He is my refuge and my fortress: my God; in him will I trust. Surely he shall deliver thee from the snare of the fowler, and from the noisome pestilence. He shall cover thee with his feathers, and under his wings shalt thou trust: his truth shall be thy shield and buckler. Thou shalt not be afraid for the terror by night; nor for the arrow that flieth by day; Nor for the pestilence that walketh in darkness; nor for the destruction that wasteth at noonday . . . For he shall give his angels charge over thee, to keep thee in all thy ways . . . With long life will I satisfy him, and shew him my salvation.' "

A sudden revelation paid a visit to Anna. This was the point of the story of St. Julian of Norwich and her long illness.

Even in the midst of great gales, they could know peace.

■ ■ ■ ■

July 20th, 1737

After such a night, how could she sleep a wink? And yet Anna woke to a piercing beam of bright sunlight pouring through the cannon portal. Her eyes blew open. The storm was over.

By midmorning, the lower deck was cleaned, chamber pots emptied, soiled clothes washed and hung to dry. While the air was dank, it wasn't nearly as fetid as it had been the last few days. She was just about to call Felix and Catrina together for an English lesson when she saw Bairn come down the companionway ladder with the captain and first mate behind him. He looked exhausted, his long hair was tousled, and a day's growth of beard — maybe more — darkened his chin. Bairn cast her an enigmatic glance as he strode over to examine the cracked beam.

The captain, Mr. Pocock, and Bairn gathered around the beam, murmuring together, then Christian approached, motioning to Anna to join them to translate.

"I doot we can keep going, not with a cracked beam," the captain said. "I fear we will have to turn back to England."

Christian waited for Anna to translate, then he gave her an answer.

"Christian might have a solution."

The captain stared at Anna solemnly but said nothing, arching one thick brow.

"We brought a tool to help build houses in the New World. It's a device used to lift heavy objects."

Bairn cocked his head. "A screw jack?"

"I don't know," she said. "It's a roof raiser."

"Aye," Bairn said. "I ken what it is. Where is it?"

"Down in the hold."

Bairn frowned. "It could take days to find it."

Felix emerged from the shadows and tugged on Bairn's elbow. "I know vhere it sitz."

"And how do you know?" Bairn whispered. "Have you been prowlin' down in the hold as well as up in the holy of holies?"

Felix shrugged.

Christian leaned over to tell Anna something. She listened, then turned to Bairn. "Christian says he is confident it could hold the beam together."

"What do you think, Bairn?" Captain Stedman asked, pulling a handkerchief out of his pocket and covering his nose with it.

"We've got nothing to lose by givin' it a try. And if it works, we have everything to gain."

Bairn and Christian and Felix disappeared down the hatch into the hold to find the barrel that contained the screw jack. If Bairn thought the stench of the lower deck was bad, being so close to the sour bilge was enough to make a grown man weep. He covered his mouth with two handkerchiefs and wished for more. Christian and Felix carried none and he marveled at their endurance. Felix pointed out the barrel that held the screw jack, blessedly close to the hatch. Christian and Bairn attached the barrel to chains while Felix held the lantern above their heads. Christian's hands, Bairn noticed, were big, blunt-fingered, rough farmer's hands, yet he seemed to manage the tangle of chains hanging from the capstan as if he had wrestled many a barrel.

As soon as the barrel was secured, Bairn called up to hoist the chains. Seamen high above pulled and pulled, and soon the barrel was lifted to the lower deck. Bairn and Felix and Christian climbed the ladder and unhooked the barrel. As Bairn jammed his adze under the lid of the barrel, he hoped Felix was right and that this was the barrel that held the screw jack. He couldn't tolerate the thought of descending to the hold again. As the lid pried off, Christian lifted it, peered inside, and smiled broadly. "Ja, ja."

The screw jack itself wasn't a heavy piece of equipment, but it did a powerful job. Like a rudder of a ship, Bairn realized, as they rolled a barrel of water under the cracked beam. Small but mighty. The screw jack would be elevated on top of the barrel for sustained support to the beam, assuming it worked.

Bairn lined it up under the beam, his experienced eye telling him where it needed to be. The captain watched nervously as Bairn turned and turned and turned the handle with help from Christian and Josef. It turned easily at first, straining and squeaking toward the end. This, Bairn knew, was the moment of truth. The lower cracked portion of the beam must lift. He turned with all his might, Christian's large hands covering his to provide more strength. There was absolute silence in the lower deck as the passengers gathered to watch. The only sounds were those of Bairn's and Christian's panting breaths, sweat streaming down their faces, and the sound of wood shifting: creaking, creaking, creaking.

Until the open wound of the beam slid

together with a sweet *ahhh.*

Bairn released the handle of the screw jack and stepped back, his eye studying the beam, running a hand along the crack. It was barely noticeable. Satisfied, he gave the captain a nod, and then he scanned the crowd to find Anna. Her eyes were shining bright and soft as spring sunshine, and as soon as their eyes caught, he couldn't help but give her a slight smile. Then he turned his attention back to the makeshift repair.

As soon as Bairn hammered in a post for support, the captain decided, with a pleased look on his face, that the beam was seaworthy. The *Charming Nancy* was sound enough to continue on.

After Captain Stedman hurriedly returned to the main deck, Bairn packed up his tools and pondered the unshakable resolve of the Peculiar People. They knew next to nothing about the sea or the land for which they were bound, and despite all they had so far suffered — delays, seasickness, cold, and the scorn and ridicule of many sailors — they did everything in their power to help him repair the fractured beam.

"Why?" he asked Anna as she walked beside him toward the companionway ladder. "Just to own a piece of sod? Is that really why yer people would sacrifice so much to head to America?"

"The land is important, yes. But we are willing to endure almost anything if it means we can worship and serve God as we please."

It baffled him. Bairn was accustomed to money and ambition as the driving forces behind a man. Not a desire to worship.

Anna seemed to read his thoughts. "The love of God is like the ocean. You can see its beginnings but not its end. How can we not worship such a great God? How can anyone?"

She spoke with such confidence he was tempted to believe her. Almost. But he didn't know how to answer her. He never did. She had such profound thoughts and he cared naught for the things she spoke of. In fact, he felt extremely discomforted by her talk about God and worship. Instead, he gazed around the lower deck, and his eyes landed on a woman who was staring impassively out the cannon portal. She never moved, nor turned around to see what was going on, unlike the curious other passengers who crowded around the repair of the cracked beam.

Blue devils, he supposed. It was the seaman's term for one who floundered in

241

melancholy, gripped by a debilitating mental fatigue. Even among experienced crew, it was not unusual for a sailor to be caught by the blue devils, to lie in his hammock for most of the day, unable or unwilling to stir. "Is she ill?"

Anna looked in the direction his chin jutted. "No. Well, yes, in a way. She's grieving. That's Felix's mother. Her son died right before we left in April and she hasn't quite been herself." A look of worried uncertainty flashed across her face. "She'll be better after we reach Port Philadelphia and she is reunited with her husband."

"He's already there?"

She nodded. "The church sent him ahead to purchase land for everyone. He's the bishop for our church. Our leader."

"I thought Christian Müller was the leader."

"No. He's a minister. We're blessed to have both in the New World. A church can only survive a new settlement if they have leadership."

"Why?"

"For the sacraments. For communion or baptisms, or marriage."

Bairn's gaze shifted beyond Anna to the woman at the cannon portal. There was something familiar to him about the set of her shoulders, the way her head tilted to one side as she peered out the portal, but then he heard his name called and his attention turned to the captain, waiting for him at the top of the companionway.

As he reached the top step, the captain said, "Well, that might be a miracle in the making."

"Aye."

The captain suddenly keeled over and retched a dry heave. "Sorry, I —" He bent and retched again. "I thought the crew was only exaggerating about the stench." He wiped his mouth on his coat sleeve. "The pigs smell better."

Bairn felt the same way. The stench of the lower deck — urine, animal manure, body odor, vomit — always roiled his senses. He couldn't blame Anna or Felix for getting above deck whenever they could.

" 'Tis worse after a storm. The seasickness, that is." Dare he say something? "One of the Peculiars, that lassie who speaks English — she asked if the passengers could come to the upper deck. Take a turn around the deck each day. To get a bit of sunshine and fresh air and exercise."

"There's over one hundred people down there! 'Tis safer down below for them."

Two hundred and seventy-nine passengers, Bairn thought, twice as many as should be allowed. "Mayhap just a few at a time. Not during watch change, o' course. And only in fair weather."

The captain didn't say yes, but he didn't say no. Bairn decided not to press it. The captain tended to believe that his opinion was inevitably the right opinion, the only opinion, and he did not have patience for those who thought otherwise.

"They are a Peculiar people of a peculiar sect. Nay, a fiercely determined people." The captain held his thumb and index finger an inch apart. "I was *this* close to turning back, despite the loss we would face." They walked along the deck toward the fo'c'sle deck. "Assuming we make it to Port Philadelphia in one piece, the ship will need to be careened in a shipyard for repairs to that cracked beam."

"I doot the repair will be quick. This might be the opportunity to have the *Charming Nancy* updated." Bairn paused, folded his arms over his chest. Timing was everything with Captain Stedman. "Sir, I'm sure yer aware that the ship is overdue to have her bottom cleaned and the copper sheets near the water line replaced."

The captain rubbed his jaw, pondering Bairn's recommendation. "Mayhap you're right. 'Twill be too late in the season to chance another Atlantic crossing." He brightened. "My brother said he had outfitted his ship with three bunks in the lower deck, floor to ceiling. I believe there is room in the *Charming Nancy* for such an arrangement. That could also be done this winter."

Bairn stifled a groan. The *Charming Nancy* was seriously overcrowded as she was, so many passengers crammed in with no room for an apple to fall. And the captain wanted to fit in even more passengers?

Bairn had assumed the captain had been pressured into overcrowding the lower deck by the profit-hungry ship owners of the *Charming Nancy*, and Georg Schultz had been happy to oblige by finding willing Germans. But now he realized it was the captain himself who had instigated the overcrowding. What would next summer's passage be like for those poor pathetic souls?

"Mr. Pocock wishes to return to England as soon as we reach Port Philadelphia. If we winter the ship, I'll stay with her." The captain glanced at him. "I'm going to need a new first mate for next summer's passage of the Germans. Bairn, I'm counting on you."

This . . . *this* was what Bairn had been aiming for. First mate! After that, captain. It was right there, right in front of him. So close he could reach out and grasp it.

And yet a knot formed in his middle.

13

July 21st, 1737

This morning, Maria was in a fuss in that way she had, telling Christian exactly what was on her mind. Felix crept behind a leather trunk to have a listen. He took great care to remain unseen, especially by Maria. You wouldn't want to provoke her, to cross her or speak out of turn. Not that he was all that interested in anything Maria might have to say to Christian, but he was already bored and it was only nine in the morning. Then he heard Anna's name and his ears perked up.

It seemed that Maria didn't like the turn things seemed to be taking between Anna and Bairn.

"Cut to the cackle. What exactly is your point, Maria?" Christian said, because she was going on and on, no end in sight.

"Love."

"Love?" Christian echoed.

"Anna might be falling in love with him," Maria said. "That carpenter is a stranger, not one of us. An unholy and proud man. We don't know a thing about him. They're spending altogether too much time together and you started it."

"Me?"

"All this interpreting and translating keeps throwing them together. It troubles me, Christian. She's desperate to find a man by now — poor girl, after all, she's nearing twenty. But she must hold out for somebody else. Somebody right."

"Who?" Christian said in his longsuffering way. "There is no one else."

"Exactly. This is why she needs our help. You need to intervene, before it's too late."

Christian's bushy eyebrows shot up. "You think it's that serious? Maybe you're mistaken. Maybe he doesn't want to marry her at all."

"And that's another worry." Maria adjusted her shawls to cover her expansive middle. No one, Felix thought, could ever call Maria a dainty woman. "Anna's grandmother gave me the responsibility to watch over her. There's a problem brewing and we need to solve it."

"Oh for pity's sake, Maria. Perhaps it's not a problem at all. Perhaps you've created something out of nothing." He blinked through his spectacles and fingered his long beard. "Anna has always displayed a great deal of common sense. She knows how to conduct herself."

Maria snapped her fingers in the dusty air. "Men don't know about these things. Christian, something must be done before things go any further between that carpenter and our Anna. It must be stopped." She pointed to him. "And you are the minister. It is your duty to protect our Anna from a life of wicked debauchery."

Felix crept back behind the trunk before he could see Christian's reaction to that order from his bossy, know-it-all wife. Felix didn't think anything should be stopped between Anna and Bairn. He liked Bairn, quite a bit. But then Squinty-Eye's awful dog spotted him and started across the aisle toward him, toenails tapping on the wooden planks, letting the whole world know about his hiding spot. Felix reached into his pocket and tossed a piece of hardtack to the dog, distracting him just long enough to scoot away and head over to the stairs to go above deck, and all thoughts of Anna and Bairn slipped away.

Felix may not be able to speak English quickly and fluidly, but he could understand much of what was said. Especially what the sailors said. Some shook their heads north and south at him, some shook their heads east and west. There were others who simply pointed him to the hatch. The time he spent above deck greatly expanded his vocabulary, mostly with words that would horrify his mother and sorrow his father.

Even if one of the sailors sent him back down the companionway, which they did quite often, he much preferred that insult to watching Catrina and her little sisters play tag around the lower deck.

After the midday meal, Christian found Felix and asked to be led to the carpentry shop. Squinty-Eye's awful dog came along, uninvited. They stood at the door, waiting quietly until Bairn noticed them. Christian had something to say to Bairn and needed someone to translate, which made Felix feel very important. Bairn looked up, surprised at the sight of the two of them at his door, and invited them to come in. He offered seats on upturned nail kegs, but Christian declined.

Felix cleared his throat. He was here on official business as translator for Christian, and his chest stretched with pleasure, though he had no idea what was on the minister's mind. He hoped it had something to do with increasing the quantity of food the passengers were given. Hunger rumbled in his stomach and he crossed his arms against his middle to stifle the growling sounds. "Christian Müller has a ting to tell you."

Christian took off his hat and paused, with his hand resting on the crown of the hat, as if he had to collect his thoughts and carefully choose his words. When he lifted his head, he was very much the church minister, his eyes all solemn, his mouth stern. Felix knew that look well. As the minister, it was Christian's duty to be sure everyone followed the straight and narrow way and conformed to what it meant to be a church member. He began to speak in their dialect, expecting Felix to interpret. "I am here to tell you to keep your distance from Anna."

Bairn tilted his head, confused.

Felix looked from Christian to Bairn, thinking fast. "Christian says Anna likes her new shoes."

Bairn's eyebrows lifted in surprise.

Christian continued. "You are not of our faith. You will lead her down a path to the wicked world and all the evil that's in it." He motioned to Felix to translate.

"He vants you to be happy and live a long life."

Bairn looked at Felix as if he could not bring himself to believe him. "Herr Müller —"

"Christian. Call me Christian." His head jerked up and around as if he was pointing around the shop with his beard. "A relationship with those who are not of our faith can only bring dishonor." He glanced at Felix to translate.

"Call him Christian, he says. He vants you to . . ." He searched for the right words, and then a brilliant idea popped into his head. "He vants you to teach me all about ships, so I can be a sailor one day."

Christian stared at Bairn, his face settling into deep lines, and Bairn stared back, his head held high, erect. "Truly?" Bairn's glance traveled from Christian to Felix and back to Christian. "This is truly what he wants?"

"Truly," Felix said, nodding vigorously.

Christian nodded, pleased. "Do you understand what I have asked?" His arm swept in a half-arc, to indicate all that he was insinuating with his request. To stay away from Anna and not tempt her to a life apart from the straight and narrow way.

Felix was just warming up. He was enjoying himself. "He vants to know if you are in need of a helper. An apprentice." He swept his arm in a big arc, just like Christian had. "For yer shop."

Bairn nodded. "I do."

"He does," Felix told Christian in the dialect.

"Then I expect you to abide by my request." Christian clasped his hands together. "For the rest of the journey, you must do your best to avoid her, unless it is a matter of communication between the passengers and the ship's officers."

"He vants me to vork for you. Any time." Felix clasped his hands together. "I can be helper. For free." He tried, but failed, to keep his gaze from drifting toward Bairn, not quite sure how the carpenter would receive this bold offer.

Bairn was watching the two of them with a thoughtful look on his face. The only change, Felix noted, was that his eyes grew as cold and gray as the sea beneath the *Charming Nancy.*

Slowly, Bairn dipped his chin to give a nod of approval.

That was all Christian wanted, and he let out a breath of relief. "Excellent." He nodded to Bairn, put his hat back on his head, and left the small shop.

Felix gave Bairn a salute goodbye, just like he had seen the sailors give to the captain, and broke into a jog behind Christian to keep up with his long strides, grinning ear to ear. The awful dog trotted at his heels.

What just happened? Bairn sat back on the barrel top, flummoxed. Felix had ignored the unsuspecting minister's words and fed him lines of malarkey, his eyes wide and round and innocent. He'd have thought the boy to look like a living angel if he didn't know better. But he did. What that sly scamp didn't realize was that Bairn could make out Christian's intent.

He crossed his arms against his chest. How dare that Peculiar minister, with his spectacles perched primly on his nose, work-worn hands folded like he was praying, order him to stay away from Anna. As if his intentions were not honorable! After all the girls in all the seaports, the one girl for whom his intentions were nothing *but* honorable was the one he'd been warned away from. Intentions? Frankly, he had no intentions regarding Anna at all. She was nothing to him, a mere distraction during the tedious delays of waiting for the ship to be watered and wooded in Plymouth.

Perhaps he did admire the girl. But admiring someone didn't mean he had intentions toward her.

And what would Anna have to say if she knew what Christian had to say? And if she knew what Felix had been up to? He grinned, thinking of the tongue-lashing he would receive if she knew. But she must never know. The last thing Bairn wanted was to have Felix kept away from him — he was partial to the laddie. Besides, Christian's request was a ludicrous one to make on a tiny, confined ship. The lassie needed fresh air and sunshine. He would never stop her from coming above deck. Why should he?

Keep away from Anna, he scoffed. *As if I had any more than a passin' flirtation for a Peculiar girl.* Keep away from Anna? Not a problem.

He walked to the galley to see if Cook had any hot water to spare. As he did, a crushing awareness came over him, a burden of guilt. Christian Müller was right. Bairn *was* tainted by the world, by wickedness and evil. By what he'd seen and certainly what he'd done. He didn't deserve the attentions of someone like Anna. She was pure and wise and good.

Had his life carried on the way it had begun, had there not been a dramatic upheaval that altered his universe completely and permanently, someone like Anna would have been his. But his life did take a dramatic turn, a before and an after, and he wasn't the same person. He was forever changed.

He'd discovered one thing of importance during what he'd come to think of as his time of survival. He would make his own way, find his own route to happiness. He would never again let himself depend on people, not on a woman, not even the captains, nor on anyone else. He would survive, and he would do it on his own.

He found the galley empty and the kettle simmering on the furnace. He took a long-legged stride back down the deck toward his small carpentry shop, holding the kettle of hot water with a rag, pondering Christian's request. He wondered what made him think there was something brewing between him and Anna. Had she said something about him? Had Felix told him about the shoes?

Nay. It probably had more to do with that meddlesome wife of his. Hadn't Felix told him the minister's wife was on a mission to see that Anna meet and marry a worthy Peculiar? Bairn was about as far from being a worthy Peculiar as a man could be. It was a thought that should have made him grin, but instead, it gave him a sense of inferiority, of loneliness and self-doubt, as if he had lost something precious and didn't know how to reclaim it. He agreed with the minister about one thing: he needed to distance himself from that girl, starting now . . .

As he crossed the threshold, he stopped abruptly. Heat climbed up his neck. Anna stood in the middle of his shop and all words and thoughts dropped out of his mind.

Anna's gaze roamed slowly from the tools hanging tidily on the wall to the barrels that held up the workbench, to the tall carpenter that filled the door space, feet spraddled wide as if against a heavy wind. With his fancy coat removed and his sleeves rolled back to reveal his strong forearms, his white shirt tucked loosely into his trousers, he was as fetching a sight as any she'd ever seen. Her breath caught. He looked so *right* standing there.

She held out her palms. "I found these in Felix's pockets." Handfuls of tacks. "I was concerned he might have taken them without permission. He can be . . . dishonest in small ways."

"A pettifogger in the makin'?" A corner of Bairn's mouth lifted. "Nay, he was cleanin' the floor of me shop and asked if he could keep them."

"If he were to keep them, I fear Catrina Müller would find herself sitting on them at an inopportune moment."

Now a full grin spread across Bairn's face. "I've heard him bring up that name once or twice." He walked around her to his workbench. "Ne'er with much fondness."

He nearly surprised a smile out of her, the way he took note of people. She set the tacks in a pile on top of his workbench. She smoothed out her apron and said in a quiet voice, "I thought perhaps you might want to join us for church tomorrow. Christian is holding a special service." She saw him stiffen and regretted her words. She had felt so happy about how the ship weathered the storm, about how the cracked beam had been fixed, and the thought occurred to invite him to church to thank God for what He had done. She'd had plenty of time to think down below. It seemed right to invite him to church, but now, it seemed like she had made a terrible mistake. The silence stretched long and uncomfortable. Why had she come? She shouldn't have come.

Bairn turned away from her and set the hot kettle on two bricks, letting her words and her smile hang suspended in the air, until they both began to fade. "What makes you think I'd want to go to yer preachin'?"

"So that you can come to know us, to see how we are, what we're like."

He picked up the kettle and poured the water into a barrel, his face an impassive mask.

"Why do you put hot water in the barrel?"

"Dried-out barrels will leak when they're first filled with liquid. Addin' hot water is a quick way to get the wood to swell so the joints become watertight." He set the kettle back on the bricks and looked up at her. "I ken more than you give me credit for. I ken enough about yer people to know I would nae be welcomed."

She couldn't deny the truth of that. What purpose would it serve for him to know their ways when he could never be one of them? "I suppose I thought it would be an opportunity for you to gather with us to worship God. To thank Him for delivering us through the storm."

His gaze lifted from his workbench to her face, and she saw something in his eyes, a sort of wary pride. "I have nothin' at all to do with God."

"You may think so, but God has everything to do with you."

He blushed red as a beetroot, but he answered coolly enough. "Y'know nothin' at all about me."

"I know enough," she said gently. "I know you are not the unfeeling man you would like people to believe you are." She dipped her chin. "And I know you need to make peace with God."

His head rocked back a little, as if he'd just been slapped. "Are all Peculiar lasses like you? Bold tongued and bossy?"

"No, not most. But some." She lifted her head and looked out the tiny window. Sun wash flooded through the window, limning the floorboards with planes and angles. "My bold tongue has always been my weakness."

He said nothing. Squaring his shoulders, he turned back to his workbench and picked up a barrel stave. She wondered if he had a response to give her, but he kept his head down, silently shaving the stave with an adze. She should leave. She should. She knew her curiosity didn't excuse her staring or prying. She should have kept her curiosity to herself; she should not stare at his long black eyelashes and tanned skin. But before she had a chance to look away, he caught her staring at him.

"What?" He spoke calmly.

"What is it you want, Bairn? Out of life?"

He sat down on a barrel and laced his fingers behind his head. "To be captain of me own ship one day. Don't misunderstand. I'm loyal to Captain Stedman." He cast her a sly grin. "I'm a completely loyal man. Entirely devoted to me own interests."

"Why do you want to be captain?"

"To be rich."

"And then what?"

"What more is there?" His mouth took on that teasing look of his. "Surely even you can understand a man's desire to seek wealth. Isn't that what yer all doing by goin' to America? Y'said you want to own land, didn't you? I suspect it's the finest land yer pious church leaders are after. To get it before it's gone."

"Yes, I suppose you're right. But it's not our way to take pride in one's own worldly possessions, nor to covet those of others."

"But yer fine morals won't stop you from grabbin' the best land. To claim it and tame it."

A silence came between them, and he regarded her with inquiring eyes, his head slightly tilted, as if he was waiting for her to defend her people, but of course she wouldn't. He didn't understand. It hurt her to hear the bitterness in his voice, the hard assumption that their faith didn't set them

261

apart, that they were just like everyone else. She struggled to find words to fill the silence and break the uneasiness that lay between them.

She turned and started toward the door, when suddenly he bolted around the bench, blocking her exit. "Anna, wait." He was looking down at her, his face serious. Time seemed to slow into a breathless stillness, and Anna thought she could hear her own heart beat. She stood too close to him, close enough for her to smell the scent of sandalwood, close enough that she noticed a smallpox scar on his right temple.

He raised one hand, tracing the path of her chin with the back of his hand.

The way he touched her, the lazy afternoon light streaming in the window, the silence in the air — the setting suddenly felt too intimate. She backed up a step, withdrawing to a safe distance, and wiped her damp palms on her apron. She couldn't let this man with those compelling and mysterious gray eyes think she thought a thing about him. Because she didn't. Hardly at all. Maybe once or twice. "I'll let you get back to your work."

She was almost out the door when she heard him call her name.

"Anna, they dinnae want me. They'll

whisper to each other in that peasant dialect and you'll be the one they whisper about."

She spun around. In the dimming light of the day, his face was awash with concern, doubt, maybe even a bit of frustration. "You underestimate my people."

Then he said, "Mayhap I'll come. Not tomorrow, but before we reach Port Philadelphia, mayhap I'll come to yer preachin' one Sunday morn."

14

August 5th, 1737

A week passed. Then another. The air had grown cold. So cold that Felix's nose seemed to stop and not let him get air.

"Ahoy! Whale to the larboard!" All hands on deck rushed to the larboard rail for a look. Felix took the opportunity to climb up the tangle of ropes that Bairn called the ratline. Four feet, six feet, ten feet, fifteen feet. He stopped at that point and looked over the larboard side to view the whale. She was enormous, as big as the *Charming Nancy,* and he was sure she turned her curious eye toward him.

"Felix!"

He looked down to see Bairn peering up at him from down below. "You need t'come down before you hurt yerself."

Felix descended the sturdy rope ladder to within six feet of the deck and then dropped onto the wooden planks with a respectable thump. He was thoroughly pleased with himself and more convinced than ever to be a sailor as soon as he was old enough. He wondered if his father might let him apprentice to Bairn. After Squinty-Eye died, he'd heard the captain talk to Bairn about choosing a new carpenter's helper. Felix would rather apprentice for Bairn on the high seas than go to Penn's Woods and cut down trees to plow and plant fields and tend woollies. He'd had enough sheep tending to last him a lifetime.

He thought of the summers in Ixheim, laboring under pale blue skies in the hills with Johann and his father. His father would cut hay with a scythe, he and Johann would fork it onto wagons and hoist it into the loft of the barn. They would work from sunrise to sunset. His father believed that work was an end in itself, that it straightened a wayward soul, and that no amount of it was too much.

He doubted his father would agree to a life at sea. Dooted it, as the captain would say. Felix's father was a landlubber. That was another sailing term he'd learned. His English vocabulary had increased tenfold from being around the sailors, but he wasn't always sure what the words meant. Especially the words used when the sailors slipped on the wet deck or dropped a tool on their bare toes or when a fight got started between them, which happened rather often. Johann would have known what those words meant. If not, he would have borrowed books from the baron's house to find out.

Felix would like to call the baron a few choice sailors' words. He thought of how the baron had accused Johann of stealing books from him and that wasn't true. Johann always put the books back. His clever brother knew how to slip over the garden wall and pick the lock of the window in the baron's library to borrow and return books. He did it carefully and he did it frequently.

On that April day, he was returning a book — the last book he would ever borrow from the baron — when he was caught. The baron had a dog — an ugly, vicious dog — and he came after the boys. Felix, quicker and more agile, scaled the garden wall and slipped away, but Johann had trouble getting his breath when he was startled or frightened. He couldn't move fast enough and the big dog cornered him against the garden wall. Felix climbed a tree to see what was going on. To his horror, he saw the baron order his servant to beat Johann.

Once, twice, three times, four times. Johann cried out, but by the tenth time the whip hit his back, he went still.

Felix hated the baron. He hated the servant. Even though he knew he wasn't supposed to hate, that it was a sin. He would like to kill them, even though he didn't know how to go about killing anyone and his church didn't like killing. He wondered if Bairn had ever killed anyone — because Maria said he was worldly and unholy and probably wicked — but he decided that no, Bairn was too nice to kill anyone. And then his thoughts drifted to a sermon his father had given right before he left for the New World, how he had told everyone to forgive their enemies. The baron, his father had meant. The sailors had an easier time forgiving their enemies than Felix did. One time, when the ship was anchored in Plymouth, Felix had peeked into the seamen's quarters and watched two sailors drink from a brown bottle. They grew loud, then angry, then started pushing and shoving each other. One sailor bit off part of the ear of the other sailor, and then that sailor punched him so hard in the mouth that he lost a tooth. But the next time Felix saw them, the two sailors were friendly again.

"Where have you been?"

Felix jerked his head to find Anna staring at him, an annoyed look on her face, as he made his way down the companionway. "To the top." To the very, very top, the crow's nest, but he didn't think she would be happy to know that. He thought that if he could just look over the curve of the earth, there America would be. But it wasn't.

"Again?" She shook her head, then grinned. "They are going to sign you on to be cabin boy soon."

"Anna, did you know that birds who live on the side of a hill lay square eggs so they don't roll away?"

Anna had turned around and didn't hear him over the din of the noise in the lower deck. But horrible Catrina did. She appeared out of nowhere, like she always did. She could never wait to stick her nose into anything that might be happening. "Who told you that?"

He scowled at her. "Cook." Squinty-Eye's awful dog found him and panted beside him.

"That sounds like twaddle to me."

Felix ignored her. "Cook said that when it gets very cold and still, the smoke from his galley stove goes straight to the moon."

Catrina rolled her eyes. One of them,

anyway. "That's ridiculous."

"What do you know about it?"

"I know plenty," she said, hands on her hips. "I know your mother isn't right in her head."

Felix whipped around and stuck his tongue out at her, but unfortunately Catrina's mother, Maria, saw him. She raced down to them, clucking and fussing like a barnyard hen. He always did think Maria looked like a big chicken with a tiny head and sharp beak. He braced himself.

Anna hurried over and gave him a gentle push. "Get your slate and wait at the table. I'll handle Maria."

Felix found his slate and piece of chalk and sat down at the table to wait for Anna, grateful to narrowly escape another lecture from Maria.

On the slate he wrote: *cabin boy.*

Later that afternoon, Anna was hanging wet laundry up on a rope tied from the chickens' cages to a hook in the beam when a loud explosion rocked the ship. There was a moment of utter, eerie silence, then a hazy smoke drifted through the lower deck. Orders shouted from above and feet started running along the deck. Off-duty sailors emerged out of their quarters, stunned looks on their sleepy faces. "Are we under attack?" one of them said, dazed.

Bairn rushed down the companionway and stood planted at the bottom, sweeping the room with his gray eyes. "What in the name of God happened down here?" He waved away smoke with his hand. "Who shot off a cannon?"

Oh no. Oh no. *Where is Felix?*

"Which cannon?" Bairn thundered.

"Over here." A deckhand pointed to the far corner in the shadows, the cannon nearest the bow of the ship. Crouched behind the cannon was Felix, with his hands clapped over his ears.

Bairn stood with his feet parted, hands on his hips, bellowing. "What have you done, boy? Y'could blow the ship and everybody in it to smithereens!"

The boy quailed, then lifted his shoulders in an exaggerated shrug.

"Have you nothin' to say for yerself?"

Felix pointed to his ears. "Vat? My ears not vork."

Bairn raised his arms in exasperation. "What have you done?" he shouted.

"It jost . . . exploded . . . or someting."

Christian walked over to Bairn. He motioned to Anna to come join them. "Tell him that we will discipline Felix."

Bairn lifted a hand. " 'Tis nae as simple as a talkin' to. 'Tis a dangerous thing he's done. How did he find gunpowder? How did he have the time to figure out how to light it? 'Tis no one ever watchin' over this laddie?"

Felix's hearing was starting to return. Tears filled his eyes as he grasped what Bairn was saying.

Bairn's anger softened at the sight of Felix's tears. "Now, laddie, no harm has come. But you must think before you act." He scowled at Anna. "Is he not yer charge? You ought to do a better job of it." He stormed down the aisle and bolted up the companionway to placate the captain.

The air grew thick and heavy, as before a storm.

Maria stood with her shoulders pulled back and her bosom lifted high, as if she'd just sucked in a deep breath and didn't want to let it go. "And a Bauer at that."

Dorothea was looking up the empty companionway with a sweet, bewildered look on her face, as if some wheel finally clicked over in her brain. "I feel all fuzzy headed, as if all my senses are wrapped in wool. I'm starting to see my Jacob everywhere."

Felix's father would often warn his sons that

trouble didn't show up all at once, that it usually eased its way in with steps. He would point out that the worse the trouble was that the boys got into, the more steps it took to get them there. Then he would remind them to notice the little warnings on the way to trouble, little reminders that if they really wanted to, they could still turn themselves around.

The first warning Felix should have listened to was when he decided to load the cannon ball into the cannon and it was so heavy it dropped on his fingers and smashed them. The second warning was when the ball rolled straight toward Catrina, who was carrying a load of clean laundry in her arms. She tripped and went headfirst into a wooden tub filled with water for the animals. The laundry went with her. She emerged from the trough sputtering and wailing, which brought her mother sailing down the deck to rescue her. Felix spent half the afternoon cleaning out the pigpen.

After that it was hard to count how many warnings he got, because with the trouble he ended up in, he must've had dozens of them. Step by step he kept easing into trouble until he finally was knee deep in it. He had found a small container of gunpowder in the galley and assumed Cook was tossing it out because it had gone bad with mildew. It hadn't.

Then the last warning came when Felix was snooping around the captain's Great Cabin and found a box of wooden matches. Just as he held up a match to examine it, he heard the captain's voice heading toward the Great Cabin. In Felix's haste to hide, the match ended up in his pocket.

He couldn't stop thinking about how a cannon worked. That ball might be small, only about the size of a man's fist, but it was heavy and the gray gunpowder was fine, like ashes from his mother's kitchen fire. How could such an unlikely substance possibly push an iron ball out of that long muzzle? Even as Felix scraped the match along the muzzle to light it, and held it to the fuse to ignite, he doubted it would ever work. Surely, it was impossible.

But it did.

And then pandemonium broke loose.

The look of disappointment in Bairn's gray eyes was bad enough. Felix's legs seemed to turn to cornmeal mush. And then Maria Müller gave him a long lecture, pointing her bony finger at him, holding a stiff broom in the other hand. "You sow the seeds of destruction wherever you go." She shook her head. "You'll go too far one of

273

these days, Hans Felix Bauer, and you'll suffer then, for your proud and willful ways."

Felix didn't think it was such a bad thing to go too far, to go toe-to-toe with the rules, to see how far he could push things. Unfortunately, he might have said so out loud.

Maria lifted the broom to bop him on the head, but his reflexes were too quick. He jumped up quick and startled her good. The tip of her broom handle hit a tall sack of white flour behind her and knocked it over, pouring out on Squinty-Eye's awful dog, a dog that was everywhere and underfoot. The dog shook and shook, making a cloud of flour. Maria was having a conniption, and Catrina got into it and pretty soon all of them, including Felix, were white, white everywhere. Clouds of white! They sneezed and coughed and pretty soon Felix couldn't see his own hands.

Anna spun around, laughing at them, with them, just laughing. Even his mother was smiling. Then Christian started chuckling and, shock of all shocks, Catrina found the humor in the moment and giggled. Everyone laughed except for Maria, who had lost a sack of flour. She was fussing around and peeved at Felix, who was still shaking flour from his hair. Maria had out some wet washing on a line and he covered it with flour as he shook. Dorothea was chuckling away at the sight of floured laundry, which annoyed Maria to no end and she took it out on Felix, hissing through her teeth, "You and that senseless mother of yours take up more time and effort than the entire rest of the church."

That comment brought Felix up short.

Maria rewashed her clothes while they were all sweeping up flour and putting things to right. The next thing everyone heard was the sound of hollering. Maria's wet washing line was tied to the tail of Squinty-Eye's awful dog and he was dragging the line through the floor of the lower deck, picking up mud and coating laundry with unswept flour and dirt and who knew what else.

Felix made himself scarce.

August 8th, 1737

Up above, a bell rang and a scurry of footsteps could be heard on the deck. Down below, Anna was trying, without much success, to teach Catrina how to spell out numerals in English.

Catrina set down her piece of chalk, exasperated. "Why can't I just use figures?"

Anna rubbed her forehead. "I'm trying to teach you what you're going to have to know in the New World." No small task, because Catrina thought she knew everything.

Felix had finished his lesson quickly and left to go tend to the animals, and Catrina was miffed that she was alone at the table. "Have you noticed that Felix is trying to sound just like the ship carpenter you're sweet on?"

Provoking girl. "Have you noticed that Felix can carry on complete conversations in English with the sailors?" Anna shot back.

Catrina rested her chin on her fists. "Why don't boys ever want to be themselves? Why do they always want to be someone else?" She frowned. "He needs a firm hand, Anna, because he's headed for trouble. He's wilder than the wind."

"Catrina, perhaps you should stop worrying about Felix and finish writing out your numerals."

Catrina ignored her. "Felix would risk his silly neck to be above deck and near that carpenter."

True.

"Why, he's practically turning into a miniature version of him."

True, true. Catrina could be most bothersome, but she had a point. Anna should try to keep a closer watch on Felix. He had adopted an awful version of a Scottish accent, dropping off syllables. He shadowed Bairn, talking like the poor man, even matching his stride to his. Just this morning, Anna caught Felix drawing a picture of the ship on his slate, drawn with remarkable detail. There was more to this old ship than she had imagined. He knew far more about the ship's layout than she did, which probably meant he had explored it from top to bottom. Becoming a sailor was all that was on his mind. She knew what he was thinking. She always knew. No matter how many times she told him not to go to the upper deck without permission, she would see him make for those stairs and peer out the hatch, then ooze away like a barn cat.

"You would do well to try and speak more English," Anna said. "You're the only one in your family who is studying it. They're going to be dependent on you in the New World."

Catrina shook her head. "No. We'll have you to do the translating for us."

"I won't be around to translate for your family. You, everyone" — she swept her arm around the deck — "should be learning English. At the very least, they should be learning how to count. To buy and sell goods and not be cheated."

"Mama says you'll be able to figure it all out for us. She said you'll live with our family so that you can trade for us. At least until she finds you a proper husband, she said."

Anna froze. She'd accepted that her prospect to return to Rotterdam on the next ship sailing back to England was quite dim, but she hadn't given any thought to whom she'd be living with in Penn's Woods. She certainly didn't want to live with the Müllers and be subject to Maria's endless haranguing. She decided to speak to Christian at the earliest opportunity and suggest the adults join Felix and Catrina for English lessons.

"Anna, do you think Felix will ever love me the way I love him?"

Startled, Anna looked at Catrina. She was gazing at Felix, who was over at the animal pen, feeding the pigs and the goats. "Catrina, you're only ten years old. What do you know about love? When you're all grown up, you'll meet someone else."

Catrina looked at her solemnly. "Felix is the only one I'll ever love. There are some things in life you just know."

She was only ten! How could a child know such a thing? Yet that was just like Catrina. She was always so sure.

Then Anna caught sight of her basket,

over by the cannon portal, and she thought of Hans, Felix's older brother, the one who had brought her the rose.

15

August 11th, 1737

As Bairn settled himself on the floor of the lower deck on Sunday morning, many heads turned in his direction and then just as quickly turned away. One stern woman with a disapproving face gave him a look that could wither a hardened pirate and he wondered if he had made a mistake. He didn't know why he was in church that morning, why he bothered, although he knew why. It had to do with Anna. Last night, tossing and turning, he decided he would go, if only to keep her from asking again.

Out of the corner of his eye, he caught Anna's reflective gaze. Encouraged, he held her gaze. She lowered her lashes; a hint of pink tingeing her pale skin assured him she was not immune to him and the thought pleased him.

But then there descended a terrific silence.

It was ominous in its abruptness. He sneaked a look around him. Many had their eyes closed. But just as many had theirs open, fixed upon some point in the distance, though there was not much worthy of attention in that lower deck.

The man next to him fell asleep. He thought about elbowing him, but decided that if he made a cry upon waking, it would be too costly a gesture.

Those people actually sat around waiting to hear from God. Bairn practically snorted. As if the Almighty weren't busy enough attending to other matters.

He glanced across the room to observe Anna. She was looking at the minister. She bent over to smooth her skirt and that was when Bairn saw the woman sitting next to her and recognized her as the blue-deviled one. She was an older woman, eyes closed, face careworn and etched with worry lines, gray hair drooping down her forehead. It surprised him to realize she was much older than he would have expected, considering she was Felix's mother. Most passengers were young or middle-aged.

And then she opened her eyes and a forgotten image flashed into Bairn's mind. This woman looked nothing like the picture in his mind, and yet, something seized him.

He could feel his heart start to pound. Deep down in his gut, something surged — grief, anger, disappointment, resentment, he wasn't sure what, but it was old and familiar and painful.

Then a large woman shifted in front of the gray-haired woman and Bairn realized how foolish, of late, was the road his thoughts were on. His head felt full of strange thoughts and feelings that flickered and were gone like moths darting at a lamp.

He blamed Anna. She was an exasperating woman. They both knew he didn't belong here.

He bolted off the floor and rushed toward the companionway to get fresh air.

Anna found her heart beat faster whenever she caught glimpse of Bairn. It distressed her, it shamed her to admit it, but she couldn't help it. She knew that as soon as the journey came to an end, she would never see him again.

She wasn't entirely sure what had prompted her to invite him to church, once, twice, three times, and then for him to accept her invitation. She hadn't thought through that there would be consequences to face over what she had chosen to do. It was one thing to speak to the ship's officers on behalf of the passengers, but it was another thing entirely to invite him into their world.

"He shouldn't be here," someone whispered angrily in her ear.

Maria. How annoying. "It's not forbidden," Anna said.

"He'll not understand a word he's hearing," Maria said.

Lizzie, seated on the other side of Maria, leaned forward to add, "He'll be bored to tears." She looked quite bored herself.

"You're treading in dangerous waters," Maria whispered.

That, Anna felt, was a comment of staggering irony coming from a passenger on a ship. She could barely stifle a smile.

"Don't think I haven't noticed how often you go above deck when there's no need," Maria said. "Christian has noticed too."

A blush scalded Anna's cheeks. Christian wouldn't send the carpenter away from church. He wouldn't. But when she turned her eyes to Christian, concern shadowed his face as he watched Bairn find a spot to sit down among the men.

Then Anna wondered about herself, what her own thoughts and hopes were on this day. She had wanted Bairn to see this because it was so much a part of them, the backbone of their life. And yet she had known that even seeing it, he would never really understand. It could never matter to him anyway. She unconsciously smoothed her apron again.

When Bairn bolted up from the floor and rushed to the companionway, Maria wasn't done. She turned to give Anna a smug "I told you so" look.

Anna felt a nervous quiver in her belly when Bairn rushed away from church. She wondered what he had been thinking that would make him dash away like that, as if he couldn't tolerate another moment. But then, she could never tell what he was thinking. Not during all his teasing talk and cautious smiles that drew her to him — she never knew what he was really thinking or feeling.

Lizzie was right. He was probably bored.

Ten minutes in Bairn's bunk told him sleep would not visit him this night. He went outside, gulping huge drafts of the frigid air, watching the white-capped water turn into a soft blur of colors as tears filled his eyes.

He turned his face to the water, fiddling with the cleats on the railing so the others on watch would not see. He didn't know where the tears had come from, what they were all about. But something inside him had shifted. Something inside him had woken up from a long sleep, if only for a few moments.

The temperatures had fallen, and it felt even colder out on the deck. Bairn hardly noticed. He climbed the rigging, the noise of the ship fell away, and he entered into a world completely silent except for the rhythmic barking of the sailors in the stern.

Dark clouds fringed with silver moonlight scudded by overhead, carried briskly along by the winds. He stared at the water, pondering what Anna had tried to impart to him earlier this evening, running her words over in his mind.

She had slipped into his carpenter's shop to ask him why he had left church so abruptly.

"I have no need for it." He looked straight at her. "Nor of yer wrathful, mercurial God." Nor of nosy, pushy women.

"But that's not true, Bairn. Each one of us has a need to know God. Everybody needs people. It's the way God made us. We need to depend on each other to see us through."

He snapped at her then. "And I have no more patience for talk of true faith. You asked me to go to yer kirk and so I went."

Anna stared at him for what seemed like forever. "Oh Bairn, who hurt you so?"

"Lassie, yer not listenin' to me." He intended the words to come out with anger. Instead, his throat closed and the lantern light blurred.

"Yes, I am," she said softly. "I'm listening to what you're not telling me."

She was infuriating! Why couldn't she just leave him be? He paced up and down the small carpentry shop, then finally stopped. His shoulders dropped a fraction as if something settled in him. He turned quietly to face her. "You have lived *loved.* You and Felix and Christian and all those others down there. They have lived *loved.* That God of yours has His favorites. And I'm nae one of them."

"But you are loved by God, Bairn."

He shook his head vigorously. "Nay. Not me. I dinnae ken what I've done to earn the wrath of God the way I did, but I am not loved by Him."

She stared at him a moment in that intense way of hers. Then, to his shock, she moved toward him, to where he stood, moved her hand to his face, stroked his cheek so the rasp of his whiskers sounded like dry leaves. "Bairn, when you start to trust, when you go through that door, you will feel a peace within you that is far beyond anything you've ever imagined."

No one had touched him in comfort since he was a boy. His chest tightened. His throat thickened. It took everything in him to resist the urge to hold her close, bury his face in her hair, and weep. He could barely suppress the shudders that ran through him from her gentle, maternal touch. Instead he put his hands on her shoulders and pushed her away. "Go back. Back to yer people, Anna. Don't think twice about me." His tone held an edge.

Suddenly self-conscious, he struggled into his frock coat. Jerking his gaze away, he stepped around her, not waiting for her to respond, and strode off to the officers' quarters. Jaw taut, he jerked the door open and exhaled a weighty sigh, grateful Mr. Pocock was on watch. He slammed the door behind with a grunt.

He knelt down and pulled out his trunk, took out his father's red coat, and held it to his face, breathing in deeply. He thought he could still smell his father's scent of pipe tobacco. But maybe he was just imagining it.

Oh Papa, Bairn thought, the bitter sorrow pinching his gut as it always did when he thought of his father's grim fate. His last memory of his father was when he woke with a fever and chill, and his father had placed this coat over him to keep him warm.

For Bairn, who had spent the last eleven years doggedly making his own way in the world, who had forged his identity on stoic self-reliance, nothing was more frightening than allowing himself to depend on others. People let you down. People left you behind. Depending on people, trusting them — it's what got you hurt. But trust seemed to be at the heart of what Anna felt he was lacking.

Trust was something that was once second nature to him. His father would stop work to point out migrating geese as they flew in a crisp, perfect V, instinctively working together to maximize energy for the long journey ahead. He had marveled at his father's team of horses, pulling a heavy wagonload effortlessly, like one creature.

A shout from down below jolted him back to the present moment. Bairn descended from the ratlines and landed on the wooden deck with a soft thump. He crossed to the fo'c'sle deck and took the wheel to give Miles Carter a rest at the helm. If he wasn't going to sleep, he might as well let someone else do so. The night winds howled and the wrath of a bitter Atlantic beat against the *Charming Nancy.* And a great loneliness overwhelmed Bairn.

His relief helmsman arrived at midnight, and he retreated to his bunk. He slept long and deep until he began to dream of being hauled away, grasping the red coat that his father had placed over him when he had first taken ill. He was being sent from the ship to be auctioned off, to redeem his passage. Panic filled him and brought him jerking upright, his head foggy from sleep, fear and dread going bone-deep. That was the first time he knew he was entirely alone in the world.

August 13th, 1737

A day, then two, slipped by. Beneath the shadow of an overcast sky, the sea had turned a dark olive gray. A shout rang overhead. "Sail ho!" Heads turned on the *Charming Nancy* and all those sailors not on watch raced to the larboard side. They had sighted their first vessel since leaving Plymouth.

Bairn sprinted for the side, caught hold of the shrouds, and began to climb the ratlines. In seconds, he squeezed onto the crosstrees and snatched the spyglass from the lookout to peer through it. The ship's topgallant sails grew visible over the horizon, along with her flag. A grin spread across his face. " 'Tis the *St. Andrew,* Captain!"

Captain Stedman paused at the rail and cupped his mouth to give the order to furl the sails and drop anchor. There was great commotion as dozens of sailors crawled up the rigging to furl the sails and bring the *Charming Nancy* to a stop as the *St. Andrew* forged up alongside.

Bairn leaped to a backstay and slid to the deck, shouting an order before his feet hit the ground. "Johnny Reed! Go fetch the speaking trumpet for the captain."

Before Johnny returned with the trumpet, a familiar voice rolled over from the ship. "Ahoy! I request an audience. I am coming in a boat." Though low-pitched, John Stedman's voice was unmistakable with its highland burr. Captain Charles Stedman, who rarely betrayed much glimmer of emotion, couldn't contain a grin at the sight and sound of his older brother. Bairn handed him his speaking trumpet, which he caught up to shout, "Then make haste and come forth!"

The crew on the *St. Andrew* readied the longboat for the captain to scale down the rope ladder and drop into the ship. The oarsmen made quick work of rowing the longboat over to the *Charming Nancy,* despite a stiff crosswind and heavy chop, closing alongside the massive hull. Mr. Pocock secured the boat hook to the *Charming Nancy*'s chains. Bairn dropped the rope ladder over the side and one of the oarsmen caught it.

"Welcome aboard, Captain," Charles Stedman called down as his brother scaled up the rope ladder that hung along the ship's wooden side and hoisted himself onto the deck of the *Charming Nancy.*

"Captain Stedman." Captain John Stedman snapped from the waist into a bow, grayed hair flopping over his forehead. His brother did the same. Then John extended his hand, which Charles eagerly accepted, and they clapped each other on the back.

"How far out are you, John?"

"Twenty-one days from Cowes."

"We left twenty-seven days ago. We ran into a storm that slowed us down."

"You always were prone to run headfirst into trouble, brother." Captain John, eyes dancing with amusement, turned to Mr. Pocock, who made a slight bow before him.

"Mr. Pocock, you look well."

"Very well, sir." He lifted his foot. "Other than a bit of gout that troubles —"

Captain Charles coughed to cut off Mr. Pocock before he could expand on his ailment. "Bairn brought some of your luck with him, brother."

Captain John turned toward the carpenter. "Bairn. You look well. My brother is treating you reasonably well?"

"Aye, sir. He is a fair and generous captain. Like his brother."

"What is this luck you speak of?"

Bairn colored. "Somethin' I learned from you. To let the ship lie ahull during a severe storm."

Captain John looked pleased. "Aye. It goes against seafaring logic, and yet it works." He clasped his hands together. "Charles, there's a matter I must discuss with you."

"Let's go to the Great Cabin."

"No time to tarry. I'll tell you now and then I must return at once. I've received information that you have a passenger aboard ship who is wanted for thievery, back in Germany. There's a recruiter on my ship who is determined to come aboard and bring the individual to justice."

"How does he expect to do that on the open seas?"

"The recruiter plans to return to Rotterdam with the criminal immediately."

"A criminal? Among the Peculiars?" A

scoff burst out of Charles Stedman. "You know these people better than I do, John."

"Aye. And unlikely for one to be a thief."

"Who is the recruiter? Do I know him?"

"Georg Schultz."

"Schultz," Captain Charles said flatly. "I should have known. That man will go to no lengths for gold."

"He wishes permission to come aboard."

"Why? To sniff out the thief?"

Captain John nodded. "He thought he might be on the *St. Andrew,* but I have only Mennonites. Yours is the ship with those followers of Jacob Amman. The thief, he is convinced, is a follower of that church."

"And then what? We are bound for Port Philadelphia. As are you."

"He hopes there will be opportunity to speak a ship with a returning vessel. But frankly, I ken not and I care not. I'd like to hand this to you, Charles. My ship is over-crowded as it is . . ."

"As is mine."

"Still. He won't leave it alone. You know Schultz as well as I do. He's practically foaming at the mouth for the reward. I'll be glad to be rid of him." He glanced at Bairn. "And I did let you take my best carpenter from me."

Captain Charles blew air out of his cheeks.

"You will throw that in my face at every opportunity, won't you, brother?"

Captain John grinned. "I will."

"What exactly did the thief take?"

"A pocket watch. Pure gold."

"John, this has already been a taxing voyage. Two storms, a cracked structural beam. And now this."

Captain John's wooly eyebrows lifted in concern. "A cracked beam? Should you not be turning back to England?"

"We think we have it repaired. Temporarily at least."

Captain John rose and patted his brother on the back. "Well done. 'Twas no accident to have Bairn aboard your ship, no doot. The Almighty was looking out for you."

"Aye, that, and the passengers had the right tool. A screw jack, Bairn called it."

"I'm not surprised. Those Germans are a resourceful people." He picked up the speaking trumpet and shouted through the mouthpiece. "Send Georg Schultz over."

Over on the *St. Andrew,* Bairn saw Schultz find a spot for his foot on the first rung of the rope ladder before continuing with his descent.

"Will you stay for tea? Or something a wee bit stronger? A dram, mayhap?"

"Nay. I must leave immediately while the

westerly gales are with us."

Captain Charles looked disappointed. "Then I'll see you next in Philadelphia."

The brothers shook hands again, thumping each other on the back, a Scottish version of a hug.

Below, the longboat bobbed and rolled on the waves splashing against the *Charming Nancy*'s side. Three pairs of seamen sat at the oars, patiently remaining in the longboat as it rolled with the choppy waves, fidgeting in their seats, adjusting their grips on the oar handles, waiting for the captain to return.

Captain John Stedman descended to the longboat and stood at the bow, a captain at heart whether it was a mighty ship or a humble longboat. The oars were lowered and they shoved off, all six crewman putting their backs into rowing across a foamy, choppy sea.

They passed the other longboat containing Georg Schultz. When it reached the *Charming Nancy*, Schultz struggled to scale the rope ladder. He was huffing and puffing, his face a purplish red, as Bairn hoisted him over the weather-smoothed railing.

"Thank you, Bairn. Where is Captain Stedman?"

"I'm here, Schultz." The captain climbed

down the ladder of the fo'c'sle deck to meet the portly recruiter.

"Captain Stedman, did Captain Stedman —" Schultz frowned and shook his head — "did your brother inform you of my duty as a German citizen?"

Wind buffeted the captain's face, forcing his eyes to narrow. "He mentioned something about it. You're convinced there's a thief on board."

"I am. Without a doubt. Word was all over Cowes about the very generous reward."

Captain Stedman waved a hand dismissively. "A pocket watch is hardly a reason to upend a life. It can be replaced."

"This one holds great value. It is a family heirloom." He leaned forward to whisper to the captain. "It belongs to a baron. Terribly influential."

"To you and your purse, Schultz."

Schultz only laughed at the insult. He pulled his waistcoat over his large belly. "I would like to look over the passenger list."

"And what will happen to the thief?"

"He will be brought to justice."

"And?"

"The watch will be returned to the baron and the thief will be punished." Schultz shrugged. "What does it matter?"

"As long as you receive your reward."

Schultz gave him a smug smile. "After you and your brother, both, have overcrowded vessels with these sheep, you dare to accuse me of greed?"

A streak of red started up Captain Stedman's cheeks, then his entire face went as red as an autumn apple. He turned to his first mate. "Mr. Pocock, weather us a course southwest by south and fetch me those sails. Carry her as close to the wind as she'll bear, full and by."

Mr. Pocock relayed the order in his slow, exacting way and several of the crew went clambering up the ratlines.

The captain appraised the remaining sailors, standing at the railing, watching the *St. Andrew.* "Bairn, the crewmen are idle. See everyone returns to his duties. Let us be quick about it. The *St. Andrew* is nearly off the horizon." He narrowed his eyes to a slit. "And then you may show Mr. Schultz the passenger list."

As Bairn spun around to get to work, a flash of red hair caught the corner of his eye. Felix.

The boy disappeared down the companionway as though the devil himself were hot on his heels.

When Felix had heard that a ship had been

sighted, he dashed up the companionway to the main deck and crouched low in the bowsprit, his favorite hiding place, to listen to the captain talk to Bairn about speaking the ship. He had learned from Cook that to "speak a ship" meant both vessels would approach each other at a distance of about two hundred yards, drop their sails, and send officers back and forth in small boats.

He found it amusing to watch the two captains talk to each other. The brothers enjoyed each other, that was obvious. They made a show of bowing to each other, then clapped each other on the back. And their laughs! Nearly identical, though they didn't look at all alike. John Stedman, the older one, was taller and oozed self-confidence. Charles Stedman sounded as if he was trying to impress his brother. Felix felt a tug of sympathy. He knew what it was like to try to seek attention from your older brother. Johann always liked to sound as if he had enormous experience in life, though his knowledge only came through books. Books that didn't even belong to him.

On the heels of that thought came a wave of sadness, followed by guilt for thinking badly of Johann. Felix no longer had a brother to complain about, or play tricks on, or to wrestle with, or chase lambs down the hillside. Johann was gone.

Felix's interest in the captains' conversation quickly waned when he heard of Georg Schultz's return and saw for himself that the stout little man had returned to the *Charming Nancy.* He disliked Georg Schultz, though he knew his mother would scold him for thinking such a thought. But he knew his mother would feel the same way if she understood English and realized the kinds of remarks he made about Anna when he watched her with those eyes of his, eyes that looked wrong. Felix asked Cook what a few of Schultz's words meant and Cook practically boxed his ears. The sailors watched Anna too, but with a look of adoration on their faces. Schultz stared at Anna as if he hadn't eaten a meal in quite some time and was very hungry.

Felix liked the way Bairn looked at Anna. As if she was made of delicate china.

And then he heard Georg Schultz tell the captain that he was looking for a thief who stole the baron's watch, and his heart thumped hard.

16

August 16th, 1737

The days passed by, one after another. The only variety was the wind. At times it went with them. Other times it went against them and they lost hard-won miles.

Anna thought her patience might snap if one more person pressed her to ask the ship's officers "How much longer?" She had yet to ask Bairn that question; she dreaded the answer. Finally, Christian requested that she try to find out their distance to America. They had been relaxed about drinking water, using what they needed when they needed it. During rain squalls, they were able to refill barrels to have fresh water on board, but there had been little rain to collect since the first big storm, three weeks prior, and Christian wondered if they should be more judicious about its use.

Bairn told her that they were not even halfway across the ocean.

When Christian heard that report, he decided to ration the water, which caused ripples of grumbling, mostly by his wife Maria. "We have plenty of fresh water," Christian reassured everyone. "I just want to make sure we stay that way until we reach Port Philadelphia."

As irritating as Maria's petulance could be, Anna understood what drove her complaints. They were all growing weary, tired of salted meat and hardtack, missing home and frightened of what lay ahead. Anna alternated between abhorring this endless sea journey and blaming herself for failing to have the strength to tolerate it. She sorely missed home and its comforts — her grandparents, the farm, sleeping in a soft clean bed, drinking milk, baking bread, eating fresh cheese — and the longer she was gone, the more intense her yearnings became. Those few times when she was above deck after dark to gaze at the night sky, it seemed impossible that her grandparents saw the same stars she did. She felt too far away to share the same heavens.

Felix was catching on to English with remarkable ability, far ahead of Catrina. Today, when she went above deck to ask Bairn how far along they were in the ocean, she overheard Felix speaking to Bairn in a charming mix of German dialect and English, as the carpenter gently corrected him.

As Anna listened, she realized that Felix didn't translate. He listened, watched, repeated, and put the pieces of the puzzle together. No wonder he was catching on so quickly — language, for Felix, was about communication, not about perfect grammar.

Anna might have perfect grammar, a large vocabulary, and conjugated verb tenses, but she was constantly translating in her mind from one language to another and back again. Actually, three languages — now that Georg Schultz was back. He spoke only German and English, disdaining their dialect as a peasant's tongue. By the end of each day, her brain hurt.

Georg Schultz pored over the passenger list and still hadn't found his thief. He was frustrated and convinced the passengers were protecting someone, so tonight he called for a meeting with the men in the middle of the lower deck, right after supper. He stood on top of a trunk to get their attention. "It will do you no good to protect the thief who stole the baron's gold watch. He must be found out. I will find him. Where is he? Who is the man named Bauer?"

Before Anna finished translating, Christian and Josef exchanged a glance. Christian formed his words carefully. "There is no man named Bauer on this ship."

Josef stepped forward. "Perhaps the name is in error. Bauer, Byler, Beiler — there are many similar-sounding names among our people."

Georg frowned. "I'm sure I heard the name Bauer." He scratched his greasy hair. "He's here. I know he's among you." He stared at each man. "Now who is he?"

No one responded. Even the Mennonites were silent. They stared at Georg Schultz with blank looks on their faces, until he grew so exasperated that he jumped off the trunk and stomped away. "I will find him! Mark my words."

The story of the stolen watch plagued Anna all night. A memory tickled at the edges of her mind. Right after Johann's funeral, as they were hurrying to depart for the boat to Rotterdam, Felix had disappeared. When he reappeared, Anna asked where he had gone and he said there was something he had to do for Johann. She assumed he had gone to his gravesite for one more goodbye.

But something occurred to her tonight as she lay on her hammock. His proper birth name, the name stated on his records at Ix-heim, was Hans Felix Bauer. As was their custom, he had been named for the brother who had died before him. Not Johann, but Hans, the brother who had gone with Jacob to the New World. She looked below her hammock to the basket. The one who had given her that rose.

It also occurred to her that Captain Sted-man only wanted the names of male heads of families on the passenger list. Dorothea and Felix's names, Anna's, too, were folded into Christian's family. There was no Bauer on the passenger list.

The next morning, she asked Felix, point-blank, if he knew anything about the baron's watch — anything at all. He looked her straight in the eye and said no, but she also knew him to be a skillful liar.

And then Georg Schultz came strutting down the lower deck and the boy vanished, something he seemed to do whenever the Neulander was in proximity. Felix seemed to be everywhere and nowhere at once.

August 18th, 1737
The sea was glassy. When wind was scarce, there was more work for the men among the sails than when it was blowing strongly. Sailing through a windless stretch meant

trimming sails every few minutes to catch the latest cat's-paw of wind, each blowing in a different direction from the last.

The men at the sheets came off watch tired and demoralized by the log readings — a mile an hour, even less. Captain Stedman recorded fretfully one evening that they had gone ten miles back again from where they were yesterday.

Bairn ran a discerning eye over the ship, inspecting her three towering masts, her lines, and the rigging and unfurling of the square sails. In his mind, there was only one option to make way when the air was becalmed and none — to water the sails to make the canvas heavy, allowing them to hold more wind. Bairn was on his way to the Great Cabin to speak to the captain about watering the sails, thinking of how to word the suggestion carefully so as to make it seem like the captain thought of it himself, when he stopped abruptly. A foul odor wafted in and over the *Charming Nancy.*

Cook came out of his galley, sniffing the air. "Is it a dead whale?"

"Nay. Worse." Bairn had smelled this particular stench before. A knot of dread formed in his middle.

Soon, a lookout gave the cry, "Sail to windward!"

Sailors climbed onto the rails, pushing for a view.

The captain hurried out of his cabin and up to the fo'c'sle. "Lookout, what's the status of the ship?"

"Approaching larboard, sir," came the faint response.

The captain took out his spyglass. " 'Tis a slaver," he said to Mr. Pocock and Bairn as he peered through the spyglass. "Mr. Pocock, furl the sails and slow the ship in the event that the captain of the slaver requires assistance. But if not, I do not desire a speak-to. I'll be in my cabin." He handed the spyglass to Bairn and strode back to his cabin.

Mr. Pocock glanced uncomfortably at Bairn. "My gout's been acting up. If you don't mind . . ." He handed the speaking trumpet to Bairn and hobbled away to the officers' quarters. Bairn was left to act on behalf of the officers with the slave ship.

Seamen gathered to the larboard side to watch the approaching ship. Even the most hardened sailors were silent, mouths covered with their kerchiefs. The stench from the slave ship sucked the air from Bairn's lungs and he wished for a cloth to mask the odor, but dared not. He felt he must look the part of the officer. When the sails were furled and the ship slowed, he steadied the powerful spyglass on the edge of the foretop to take a closer look at the slave ship. He felt a tug at his elbow and turned to see Felix.

"Have I nae told you to ne'er come up on the fo'c'sle deck without permission?"

"I vant to see."

Bairn's gaze swept the deck to make sure the captain and first mate were nowhere in sight. "Have you ever seen a slave ship?"

"No."

Anna appeared at the bottom of the ladder, scrunching her nose. "Felix!"

"He's here, Anna, looking through the spyglass. Come on up. You can rest assured that the captain won't be comin' out of his cabin until we've long passed the slave ship."

"A slave ship?" Tentatively, Anna climbed the ladder and joined them. "Is that what the smell is?"

Bairn nodded. "Aye, and 'tis windward, so we're gettin' a full dose with what wind we have." Though cold, there was a stifling absence of air. "It's not so unusual to see them in the summer months. They come from the south, from the western coast of Africa."

Anna stood at the railing. "Where is it going?"

"Possibly t'the Caribbean islands. But this one is west and quite far north, so mayhap 'tis headin' to the southern colonies."

"Can I see slaves?" Felix asked.

Anna gave him a sharp look.

Bairn adjusted the spyglass for the boy to peer through. " 'Tis not a pleasant sight, laddie. Hell has taken up residence on earth. This one is ridin' low in the water. My guess is it must have five or six hundred Africans on board." Then he went silent.

Fascinated, Felix peered through the scope. "Vhat are they throwing in the vater?"

Bairn didn't bother to look. "Dead Africans," he said stiffly. "They throw over the day's dead."

"But . . . some are still moving."

Bairn kept his eyes averted. "And those who are near dead."

The closer the ship got, the stronger the smell, the more horrific the sight. Soon the ship was close enough that they could see the faces of the slaves — gaunt, hopeless. Most were naked. The slaver's crew poured buckets of salt water over them.

Felix lowered the spyglass and looked at Bairn with troubled eyes. "Vhy do dey not get up?"

"Because they are in chains."

He caught the pitiful wince in Anna's eyes

as they flickered straight down to the jagged raised scars on his ankles, bared from his boots after climbing the ratlines this morning to fasten a mooring to a spar. He hadn't thought to put them back on. He knew what was running through that quick mind of hers: Was he once someone's slave?

"I did not know that human beings could do such a thing to each other," Anna whispered, tears running down her face. "How do they bear it?"

He lifted his gaze back to her face. "Where is your just and loving God now, Anna?"

She spun on him, eyes flashing sparks at him. "God? You think this is God's handiwork? You blame God for this tragedy? This is not God's doing. This is the Devil's deed!"

The slave ship was approaching, drifting westward. The captain of the slave ship shouted out, "Ahoy! We are low on water. Have you any to spare?"

Bairn sent Johnny Reed to the Great Cabin to ask the captain for permission to release some barrels of casked water to the slaver. Back came a prompt and terse reply: "Nay."

Bairn's eyes closed, then he picked up the speaking trumpet. "We have no water to spare." Silently, he added, *May God forgive me.* He kept his head down.

Anna stood right next to him. "But what will they do without water?"

"Most likely, they will reduce their cargo."

"What does that mean?"

"They will start winnowin' the cargo."

"I don't understand what you mean."

He turned to face her, angry for what she was making him say. "They will chain a group of Africans together and shove them overboard, one by one." He pointed to the slave ship. "As they are doin' now."

She gripped her elbows, hugging herself as if she felt a sudden chill. "To die."

"Of course! 'Tis a more merciful death for the cargo than dehydration." He had heard recently of a slaver that started with six hundred Africans and reached port with only two hundred.

"They're not cargo." Anna's voice trembled as she spoke. "They're human beings."

Bairn stiffened. "Slavery 'tis the backbone of the British empire." And a lucrative trade for the captain and investors. He defended it, but in truth the practice sickened him, especially conditions on a ship like this one.

"If they need water, why can't you give them water?"

"Because we have a responsibility to our

own ship first. The passengers and the crew. That is the captain's orders and captain's orders are law."

She stared at him. "Felix, geh un holl mir Christian. Aa Levi Wenger. Yetz!"

Felix hopped off the fo'c'sle deck, ran along the upper deck, disappeared into the lower deck, and returned in a moment, dragging Christian and the Mennonite minister Levi Wenger along with him. Anna met them at the ladder and spoke rapidly to them. Christian's face went blank, then he climbed up on the fo'c'sle deck and took the spyglass from Bairn to peer at the slave ship. Slowly, he lowered the spyglass and passed it to Levi Wenger. Then the two men spoke together in quiet voices.

"Geb ihnen unser Wasser," Christian said.

Bairn looked at Anna, stunned.

"He wants you to give them our water."

"I cannae do that. The captain wouldn't allow it."

"Not the crew's water. Just the passengers'."

Bairn shook his head. "You don't know what yer asking. We're already running low on water. I cannae allow that."

Christian and Anna exchanged a look. "Would you ask the captain?" she said.

Curious Germans emerged from the mustiness and the dankness of the lower deck, blinked warily, and looked about for the source of the smell.

Bairn blew a puff of air out of his cheeks. "I will ask the captain. And he will say no." He crossed the deck to the Great Cabin in three strides, such was his confidence that the captain would dismiss this ridiculous request.

But the captain surprised Bairn. Surprised and disappointed him. As long as the passengers agreed to pay full passage for everyone now, the captain would allow them to share half their water supplies with the slave ship. The crew would be under strict orders not to share water with the passengers. "If that's how the Peculiars want to use their resources, so be it," Captain Stedman said to Bairn with a curt dismissal.

Anna explained the condition to Christian and Levi, and both men nodded, then spoke to those who were on the upper deck. Most of the passengers held handkerchiefs over their noses. Some were weeping. Bairn couldn't hear them from the fo'c'sle deck, but he saw beards and prayer caps nod in agreement.

Why? Why would they do this?

"Anna, the captain said he would put the crew under orders t'not share water. He meant what he said. Not even water for the animals."

"We won't ask any seaman for water. I promise."

He wanted to shake her, to make her see what danger they were putting themselves in. "Dinnae let this happen! Why would you put yer people in that kind of jeopardy? 'Tis tantamount to suicide."

"We believe that God will supply our needs."

"Remember that when you lie parched on your hammock, tongue swollen, eyes bulgin', desperate for a sip of fresh water."

"If that is what will become of us, then at least we will meet God with a clean conscience. We will have done all we could to help those poor people."

"Anna, you dinnae ken what yer doin' to yerselves! Why?"

She lifted her chin. " 'For I was hungry and you gave me no meal, I was thirsty, and you gave me no drink.' "

He felt a jolt run through him, as shocking as if she had struck him. "So that's it? Yer quotin' the Good Book to me like a preacher? Words on a page will bring dry comfort in a week's time if we don't get any rain."

She kept her eyes on the slave ship. "You

might be surprised by God's response."

Something so moving passed over her face, he found himself nearly holding his breath. She truly believed this, that God would answer her request as if He was at her beck and call. "More likely you will all die an agonizing death by thirst."

"We're not going to die of thirst," Anna said. "We're not." Though, she sounded less confident.

To that he only grunted. "So you say." They were oblivious to the dangers around them. He shook his head. Some people were too thick and too stubborn to heed advice.

He took a deep breath to calm himself before he picked up the speaking trumpet and shouted to the slave ship, "Aye. We have water to spare." He crossed to the center of the fo'c'sle deck to speak to the gathered crowd, gesturing to the companionway. "All passengers below, if you please."

Felix relinquished the spyglass to Bairn without any argument. He and Anna joined the other passengers at the waist as they drifted silently down the companionway.

Head down, Bairn ignored the stares of his crew as he gave orders to release half the casks of the passengers' water. They rolled the water over to the longboats while his anger simmered and stewed. After the water had been delivered to the slave ship, he directed the men to drop the sails, drawing the sheets taut so what meager wind there was could be caught in the canvas. The ship's bell rang, signaling a watch change.

For the rest of the day, the seamen talked softly amongst themselves, not joking for a change, not horsing around, just talking quietly about the slave ship, about the *Charming Nancy,* and about what lay before them. Bairn climbed the ratlines as high as he could, watching until the topgallant sails of the slave ship disappeared from view, downstream and downwind.

May Anna's God have mercy on them, he prayed, because the sun and the sea and the wind would not.

17

August 27th, 1737

One day had slipped by, then two, with not a cloud in the sky. Three days after the meeting of the slave ship, Christian had announced another cut in water rations for the passengers. They had already been rationed to four pints per day per person. Then it was two pints per day. Then one.

Four days later, the passengers finished the last of their casked water. Truly out. And not a cloud floated in the sky. After Christian finished morning devotions, the passengers drifted back to their sleeping areas. Most everyone lay on their hammocks or pallets or bunks, doing only what was necessary, tired and irritable. No one was fit to keep company with a grizzly bear.

Anna sought out Christian as he put his Bible back in his chest. "Did we make a mistake?"

"No," Christian said. His big and gentle

heart could have done nothing else but share water with the slaves. "God often uses the practical to lead to the spiritual. Scripture is full of such examples."

A few hours later, a shriek of happiness startled everyone. "I found another barrel of water!" Felix shouted from the center of the lower deck. He pointed to the barrel that held up the screw jack, grinning and nodding.

Indeed, it was a barrel and it seemed to be filled with liquid. The passengers gathered, laughing and clapping Felix on the back. Here they had been living amongst this barrel for weeks now and never gave it another thought. Right under their noses was the very thing they needed to survive. Anna grinned with happiness, trying not to feel smug. A fine example of the practical leading to the spiritual!

Christian worked his way through the group that surrounded the barrel. He seemed uncertain as he examined the screw jack. "Anna, go ask Bairn about this. We cannot jeopardize the safety of the ship."

Anna hurried upstairs and found Bairn in his carpenter's shop. After she explained what they wanted to do, he followed her below decks, ducking under the low beamed ceiling so he didn't hit his head. He went straight to the barrel, examining it. "Aye, 'tis water from Plymouth." He pointed out the water marking on the barrel.

Felix watched, fascinated, as Bairn checked the screw jack, the timber, and the barrel.

He knocked the top of it and heard a hollow sound.

"It's empty," Anna said, puzzled.

"Nay. Some of the liquid evaporates from a barrel. The headspace is called the *ullage*." He knocked the center of it and it sounded entirely different. "The bulging middle portion of the barrel is called the bilge. In the middle of the bilge is a hole in the barrel called the bung hole, which is corked with a bung." He walked around the other side of the barrel. "There. The bung."

"If we use the water, will it weaken the timber?"

"Perhaps if it were completely emptied, it could, but I think a few bucketfuls wouldn't hurt." He looked around. "Felix, go fetch me a bucket or pitcher. Even a cup."

Felix disappeared into the crowd and returned with a tin cup. Bairn used the claw of his hammer to pull out the bung. Water poured out of the hole. Sweet, blessed relief!

But not to Bairn. He jammed the bung back into the hole to stop the flow of water.

He sniffed the water, then tasted it and spit it out. " 'Tis brackish." He gave the cup to Anna with a trace of apology in his eyes. She sniffed it and passed it to Christian. It smelled foul.

"It would make you deathly ill to drink that." Bairn rose to his feet. "I'm sorry. I truly am." And he was. "Anna, come with me to the upper deck."

They walked side by side down the lower deck and up the companionway, and although Anna felt the stares of other passengers, she didn't care.

At the top of the stairwell, Bairn turned to her. "Anna, let me help. I'll give you water. Or beer. The captain didn't say anything about sharin' beer."

"No. Thank you, but no. You will need that water yourself. And we don't drink beer." She tried to swallow through the dryness in her throat. "It will rain soon. I'm sure of it." She *was* so sure of it. She *was* sure God was going to do this for them, but the situation was getting worse. And worse.

He wiped the sweat off the back of his neck and said, "Anna, yer the ones who have put God to this foolish test."

"It wasn't a test. We gave up our water because we are trusting in the mercy of the Lord to take care of us."

"And does He? Is your good Lord taking care of you?"

He wasn't mocking her, she could see in his eyes that he simply couldn't fathom why they did what they did. It was a question only an outsider would ask. Anyone from their church was born knowing the answer. "Bairn, our story is not meant to be read by itself. Think of the slaves. At least they have a chance to live now. They have a story of their own."

"Mayhap you put an expectation on the Almighty that He has no plans ta meet. What will you do when all hope is gone?"

"Broken expectations aren't meant to crush our hopes, but to free us to put our confidence in God alone. They aren't meant to make us give up, but look up."

He had a puzzled look in his eyes, etched with a type of hunger.

As she thought of what to say to make him understand, he reached out and cupped her cheek with his hand, gazing at her so tenderly, it hurt to look at him. In a voice that was deep and roughened with feelings, he said, "All you need to do is to ask, just say the word, and I will give you me water." His gaze broke from hers and he turned to leave her then.

She stayed at the top of the stairs, watching him stride down the deck toward his shop, his boots rapping across the deck planks. She found her growing appreciation for him blurred by confusion.

She had come to admire his tenderness and strength. His kindness too. But he didn't understand; he'd had such trouble understanding her and her faith. He told her that all she needed to do was to say the word and he would give her his water. But she could never, ever ask.

That evening in the lower deck, nobody spoke. Nobody said a word. There was nothing to say.

August 28th, 1737

Christian warned everyone not to ask the sailors for water, but he didn't say anything about *paying* the sailors for water. Felix had discovered that casked water fetched two shillings a pint; Cook's leftover water, gray from cooking, could be had for ninepence a quart. It worked for a few days. But then he ran out of money.

He dropped down on his knees to keep out of sight as he worked his way around the ship. In a corner, he saw a sailor slumped over a basket of oakum, snoring.

Queenie was peering down at him from the forecastle. The cat waved her tail back and forth. Felix glared at her. "Jump on me now, cat, and I'll lock you in the hold all day." The cat meowed as if she knew he was bluffing.

He noticed another seaman dip a tin cup into a cask of water and gulp it down, watched drips of precious water drain off his whiskers, trickle down his cheeks. Felix licked his dry lips. The seaman tossed the cup on the deck and Felix thought about scooting over to pick up the cup and lick the insides. He was *that* thirsty.

A hand reached out and doffed his hat off his head. "You sure do keep turning up where you don't belong, don't you, boy?"

It was the first mate with the jowly cheeks, Mr. Pocock.

Felix's arms went up to protect his head in case Mr. Pocock tried to box his ears the way Squinty-Eye did, but the first mate was already turning away. "Get on down below."

Felix snatched his hat from the ground and jammed it on his head, wondering how serious the first mate was about him going below. As if the ghastly cat knew what he was thinking, her hackles grew high and she started to snarl. She was making ready to pounce on him and claw his eyes out. Felix never trusted cats; they did that kind of thing. He scurried across the deck to head down the companionway. About halfway down the stairs was Catrina, sitting on a step. She patted the place next to her so that Felix would join her.

Catrina was being too nice, so Felix should have known that something bad was about to happen. Then he noticed a flask tucked by her side.

"Want some?"

Felix grabbed the flask and gulped down a mouthful of what he thought was warm water, but it was dark and bitter tasting. He coughed and coughed, then gagged.

A bell went off in his head. He recognized that particular flask. It belonged to the droopy-eyed first mate, Mr. Pocock. He handed the flask back to Catrina. She had stopped being friendly and looked straight at him, except for that turned in eye, and snapped, "Don't even think about telling. You drank from it too."

She had him. He couldn't tell on her, or else he'd be in as much trouble as she would. So he took another sip. Then another. Soon, he grew sleepy and went to bed without supper, worrying his mother.

In the middle of the night, Catrina complained about her aching stomach. She meowed and howled and turned in her hammock, clinging to her side.

Someone yelled out, "Quit it, Catrina. I can't sleep." But if Catrina couldn't sleep, then nobody could sleep, so too bad for her and too bad for everyone else. Maria just let Catrina carry on caterwauling while she rubbed her stomach.

Felix didn't sleep well either. He felt like someone had pulled all his teeth out with a pair of rusty pliers.

By morning, Catrina was in bad shape. She lay on her mother's sleeping shelf, pale and quiet. Anna cut up some tack for her, and added a little salted cabbage, which she knew Catrina was fond of. She left the plate by her shelf with a towel across it and went to get some chores done.

"Felix," Anna whispered, "would you read to Catrina or tell her a story? I want to take Maria upstairs for a moment to get some fresh air." She gazed over at the two of them, a worried look on her face. Maria was cradling Catrina in her arms, bone-white and frightened. She was stroking her daughter's hair, and murmuring to her, neither of which the sick child seemed to feel or hear. Christian was crouched beside the sleeping shelf, the Bible in his lap. "The suffering on her parents' faces is enough to break your heart."

It scared Felix to see Catrina just lying on

her bed, saying nothing. It was embarrassing but tears just exploded out of his face. "I hate her but I don't want her to die."

Anna wrapped her arms around him. "Then pray for her to get well. And be a good friend to her right now."

They walked over to Catrina and Anna put her hand on Maria's shoulder. "Come with me. We'll go upstairs for a bit of fresh air."

"I can't leave her."

"Just for a few minutes. Felix volunteered to stay with her."

Christian rose to his feet. "I'll go with you." He put a big hand on Felix's head. "Thank you, son." They walked side by side down the middle of the lower deck, around the barrel that held the screw jack, and climbed the stairs to the ship's upper deck. To Felix, Maria and Christian seemed suddenly so very old. Overnight, they had turned into old people.

Like his mother had.

Felix dropped his head, shamed. Now he understood the power of sorrowing and grief.

He kneeled down beside Catrina and listened for her shallow breathing. Be a good friend, Anna had said. "Catrina, I'm going to give you some solid-gold advice. For free, even though you got me whiskified yesterday."

Catrina mumbled something he couldn't understand.

"When you talk to people, you squinch your lazy eye kind of shut or you put your hand on your face to cover it. If you don't want people to look at your eye, you just do this."

One eye opened. Then another. She watched him suspiciously.

"Keep your head straight and look at me sideways."

She did it.

"See? You aren't cockeyed anymore. Your eye is straight as an arrow now."

Throughout the day, Catrina didn't get better but she didn't get worse. And Felix noticed she was watching people sideways.

August 30th, 1737
Two days without any water. Then three.

Anna's hands were raw and cracked open, her mouth dry like cotton, her lips peeling, her belly sour. The salted meat they ate only made it worse. She yearned for cool water to soothe her parched throat, a warm bath, clothes not stiff with salt.

Doubts plagued her. Had they made a terrible mistake? Had she misunderstood

God's leading? Yet she couldn't stop thinking of those tragic souls in the slave ship. She felt embarrassed over how sheltered and blinded she had been to the terrible plight of the lost and forgotten. It was right to share the water.

And yet to die slowly by dehydration was also a terrible plight. Two Mennonite toddlers had already died of sickness, aggravated by dehydration.

Over and over, she sent up her request:

Lord, hear our prayer. We need rain like the Israelites needed manna.

She wondered if perhaps she had not been praying properly. Surely if she was doing it right, God would heed her. But God did not.

"Anna, come quick."

She half-turned to see Felix waving to her from the bow of the ship where the animals were penned. He was in the pen with the goat and her kid, who was curled into a ball. Anna climbed into the pen and crouched beside the kid, talking to it, her voice soft and low. Poor baby was not more than a few weeks into this hard world. She picked its little head up and laid it in her lap, coddling the kid as if it were a child. The kid moaned: a pitiful, suffering noise. "Don't you go giving up now. They're going to need you in the New World. You'll have green grass and a still pond. All the grass you want to eat. All the water you need." She saw the kid's eyes sink, its body went quiet, and she knew it was dead.

As Anna sat next to the dead kid, right there in the animal pen, she pulled up her knees and cried.

Except she had no tears.

She wrapped the little kid in an old sheet and waited until dark to take it upstairs to send over the railing for burial. When she turned around from the railing, she found Bairn standing stock-still in front of her, a cold look in his eyes. "Where is yer God now, Anna?"

"God wouldn't bring us here if He didn't plan to sustain us. And to deliver us."

"You've put all yer trust in a God who dinnae care whether yer thirsty or not."

"You're trusting God by relating it to circumstances. Trust is much more than circumstances. Much, much more."

He took a step toward her. "The sky was red tonight. That means no rain on the horizon. Yer hopin' for somethin' that isn't going to happen."

"You don't . . ." She drew in a deep breath, her chest shuddering. "You don't understand about hope. About trust." What could she say to make him understand? "Even when there's not a spot of light in the east, you're still sure the sun will rise."

His eyes met hers and they were no longer cold. "Hope works like that for the sun, but other things aren't as sure as the sunrise."

She was helpless to argue given the dryness of her mouth. "Bairn, when I am most confused and unsure of the morrow, I remember something our bishop always quoted from the Bible: 'Be still and know that I am God.' "

At that, a grimace twisted his features, as if she had said something that hurt him. He took another step forward, grabbed her hand, and thrust a flask in it. "Take this water and drink it down." He swung around and walked off toward the forecastle.

Watching him, her heart felt as if it might burst. She looked down at his flask in her hands, touched beyond words by his unexpected tenderness. And to think she once thought that tall, fine man to be incapable of compassion and caring.

She looked up at the stars — so bright she felt she could reach out and touch them. She prayed, pleaded, begged for rain.

Then she went below deck, straight to Catrina, and made her take sips from Bairn's flask of water. Catrina swallowed as much as she could and then shook her head.

Anna gazed around the deck — at Peter and Lizzie with her swollen belly, at Josef and Barbara and their twin toddlers, at Maria and Christian and their stair-step daughters, at Dorothea and Felix, at the others. They were so much a part of her, as much a part of her as her hands, her heart, her soul. She squeezed her eyes shut. She couldn't bear to think of losing this little church, of losing any of them. Her throat felt so raw that her sigh hurt coming out. But it hurt even more to hold it in.

There were just a few teaspoons of water left in the bottom of the flask. Anna went to her rose, her withering, suffering rose, and thought of her grandmother's words. "If the rose survives, our people survive." She breathed, ran her tongue over her dry lips at the sight of those precious drops of water. And then she poured those few teaspoons into the dirt of her rose.

She dreaded the morrow.

Bairn lay awake in the heat of his room half the night. His only thought was of Anna. He hoped she had taken his flask and drank it for herself, but knowing her as he did, he was fairly confident she'd given it to someone in greater need. Such an infuriating female! He couldn't find a way to help her and he could see the toll a lack of water was taking on her. Dark smudges colored the skin beneath her eyes, cracked lips, her voice barely rose above a whisper.

She had been so confident that the Almighty would provide. Even desperately thirsty, her eyes were shining and her face was glowing. She had no doubts. And in a strange way, he had hoped she would be right. But dash it all! She'd made him hope. Made him believe.

And look at where things were now. For the entire ship.

After Bairn had discovered the brackish water in the barrel in the lower decks, he had checked the other water barrels and found they had also turned brackish. He wondered if Mr. Pocock had actually supervised the filling of the barrels at Drake's Leet, or if his gouty toe had sent him off to a pub for some liquid pain relief.

Captain Stedman had begun emergency consultations in the Great Cabin with Mr. Pocock and Bairn and ordered the seamen to be put on severe water rationing. In the back of Bairn's mind, he had thought he would be able to get water to the passengers before the situation turned desperate. Now it *was* desperate. He couldn't help them, even if he disobeyed the captain. There simply was no water to spare. Sixty passengers were on the sick list, some wee ones had already died.

A cold tremor rocked him to his very bones.

Why had this happened? Why would the Almighty punish someone like Anna, whose only crime was that her heart was broken at the sight of the slave ship?

"Be still and know that I am God," she had told him.

How many times had he heard those very words from his father?

I do know that You are God! That was the whole problem. The whole point! He was a God who wouldn't speak and wouldn't listen and wouldn't act.

And certainly wouldn't send rain when it was desperately needed.

18

September 4th, 1737

Anna woke in the night to a strange sound. A light pattering sound on the deck that grew steadier. Rain. It was raining! She crawled out of her hammock and peered out the cannon portal. Rain was coming down — glorious rain!

Others stirred, hearing the rain. They made their way up the companionway and pushed open the hatch to reach the waist of the ship. Felix was first on the deck and shouted for joy, lifting his face to the sky, as rainwater streamed down his face. The smell in the air was as good as a clean sheet just off the line, better than a cake in the oven, sweeter than pulled candy at Christmas. Sweet water. Oh Lord, sweet, good, cool water.

Passengers and sailors cheered and shouted like children, whooping and stomping. Anna stood in the center of them, smiling with happiness. Some passengers went back down to the lower deck to bring up cups and buckets and casks, anything that could catch rain. They held them up in the air, filling them with that good, clean water. She went over to the railing to watch the rain hit the surface of the sea.

Without any notion that he was nearby, she suddenly saw Bairn. He strode toward her and swept her up in his arms, and before she knew what was happening, he kissed her.

She was so happy about the water, so exhausted and happy, that she kissed him back. The commotion went on nearby, and though she didn't think it was more than a moment or two, it was a kiss. Her first. He let her down and released her, and her fingers flew to her lips, shocked at herself, shocked at him. Then he vanished into the crowd, and she was swept up into the celebration. They shook hands all around and slapped one another's shoulders until they were raw.

She filled a wooden bucket and took water down to Catrina for Maria to spoon-feed to her, and Felix took Dorothea two cups, one in each hand, spilling as he walked down the deck. Spilling drops of water! And praising God for every drop.

Christian held his cup in the air and everyone quieted down. "Thanks be to God, the giver of all good things." He upended the cup, letting it drizzle down his face and darken his shirt in streaks. "This is the most wonderful water I've tasted in all my life. Drink your fill!"

They drank and drank that water, like it had come straight from heaven. Indeed, she thought, watching all those people reveling, it did.

Anna filled two buckets to take down to the animals and poured the water into their dry troughs. Around her, Christian and Josef and a few other men were gathering empty casks from the lower deck to take upstairs to capture every drop of rainwater they could before the storm passed by. The noise went on around her, and for a minute, she was alone, watching the animals lap up the water with their parched, scratchy tongues.

Her thoughts floated up the companionway ladder, to Bairn's kiss. She felt embarrassed at the liberty Bairn had taken. At what she had given him.

It meant nothing. No more than if she'd been holding a puppy or a lamb in her arms; when the rain had finally come, she'd have kissed them too. She would need to talk to him, and tell him what the kiss meant to her. It was nothing more than happiness over the rainwater.

It wasn't right, what she'd done. To be friendly with an outsider, to kiss the way they'd kissed. She couldn't think of Bairn in terms of right and wrong anymore, of friend or stranger. She could only think of him with her heart, not her head. At some point during this long journey, he had become something more to her.

She should spend the morning doing washing that had gone waiting, so she rose to her feet. As she turned around, she nearly ran right into Georg Schultz. She gasped and put her hands to her face.

His beard rose on the sides, like he was grinning underneath it. "What's the matter? Do I make you . . . nervous?"

"You make me —"

"Anna!" Felix shouted down the lower deck to her. "Maria! Come quick!"

Maria walked out from behind the privacy screen where the chamber pots were kept. "Hans Felix Bauer, what have you gone and done now?"

"It's Catrina! She's up!" He pointed toward the sleeping shelf and there she was, sitting upright, dangling her feet over the side.

Maria and Anna rushed to Catrina's side, taking turns hugging and kissing her.

Another thing to thank God for — Felix's interruption. Georg Schultz was quickly forgotten as everyone crowded around Catrina, happy to see her well, with color in her cheeks.

Rain. Glorious rain. Anna would never look at a raindrop again without remembering that first pattering sound of relief as she lay in the lower deck of the *Charming Nancy*. What a beautiful sound, that of rain on the roof. Heaven sent.

September 7th, 1737
Every morning since the rain first started, Anna had awakened with the feeling of Christmas, just happy to have all that good water available. Better than gold, it was. Catrina recovered quickly and was back to pestering Felix again. The only lingering effect of her grave illness was how oddly she looked at people. Sideways.

All day, all night, for three straight days, it had rained. It wasn't a storm that would blow itself out within a day, it wasn't a hurricane, it was a gentle, steady rain. And with the rain came a prosperous wind. The *Charming Nancy* started to make quick progress. Felix overheard the captain say that if this fair wind kept up, they were but ten days out from America. Only ten more days!

And if that were true, then Lizzie's baby would be born in America, with a midwife. Not with Anna, who had no idea about birthing babies.

The only thing that nettled Anna was her momentary lapse of judgment in which she let Bairn kiss her. At least no one had seen them in the dark of night. Other than the Lord.

As for that certain seaman, she would just turn from her wicked ways and be sure never to place herself in a situation like that again.

She spent much too much time wondering what Bairn must think of her, of them. It changed things, made her look at her people differently as she tried to see them through his eyes. Did he still feel they were no different than anyone else? More importantly, did he believe that God had sent the rain, just in time?

Casks were filled, emptied, filled again. Passengers drank their fill and then some. The captain even allowed them to wash clothes using a barrel or two of rainwater, there was so much of it. And — wonder of wonders — to take baths! There was *that* much steady rain streaming down from the skies. Anna washed her hair in fresh water for the first time since they had left Rotterdam. As she twisted her hair into a bun and pinned it, her hair felt soft, not stiff and tangled.

Yes, it felt like Christmas. All was well.

Three days it had been since Bairn had seen Anna. He had been scrupulously avoiding her, which was no small task on a confined ship, especially one that was springing leaks like a colander.

As ship's carpenter, his job was to plug the leaks and that's what he and Johnny Reed had been doing since the rains began — jamming holes with oakum.

He wondered how Anna was faring. If the rain was coming through the planks or if his fixes had mended the leaks. Thoughts of her raced down like rain, pelting him. Was she thinking of him as he was thinking of her? As he was trying hard not to.

Still, what was she to him? Within a few weeks, she would be forgotten, like a tide washing out a message scrawled on sand. She was just an appealing, maddening woman. And the finest person he had ever known.

She wasn't just another girl, like those

he'd known in ports. Known, and yet not known at all. Whereas Anna he'd hardly touched at all, and yet he knew her well. He knew the way her mind worked, the way she craved being in the fresh air and hated to be confined below deck, the way her eyes shone whenever she spoke of her God.

He hadn't planned to kiss her. It was a stupid thing to do, exceedingly stupid. He caught sight of her that night, standing in the rain, with her head lifted to the sky, and the next thing he knew he had crossed the deck and scooped her into his arms. When his mouth came down onto hers, she flung her arms around his neck, kissing him back with a surprising intensity. And when he made himself pull away, she looked up at him through eyes welling with affection. Nay, with desire. It spurred a response in his chest that he had no right to feel.

Reason enough to avoid her. He knew the Peculiars would think he was bent on corrupting her, tempting her away from her sheltered world and into a life of wickedness and worldly temptations.

Still, with her constantly on his mind, it wasn't much surprise to see her standing at the top of the fo'c'sle deck ladder one evening while he took a turn at the helm. The world went cockeyed for him, and he was keen only on the red curves of her lips. More than anything in the world, Bairn wanted simply to circle her with his arms and rest his cheek on top of her hair, close his eyes for a moment, and feel her face pressed against his collarbone. But he didn't. He kept his hands gripped firmly on the wheel.

They both waited, and then at the same time, they said each other's names. Then they laughed, a little nervously.

She started over. "Do you think the rain is an answer to prayer?"

"A miracle sent down from the welkin, ye think?"

Her eyes lit with excitement. "Yes! Yes, that's it exactly. Rain from the vault of heaven."

A ragged laugh tore out of him, a laugh that didn't sound like himself at all. "More likely a typical storm encountered on the open sea."

"But you said yourself that the skies were red that evening. That there was no rain in the horizon."

"Just shows that a seasoned sailor can be wrong." In truth, he didn't know what to make of the timing of the rain. No one expected it, not even Mr. Pocock, whose gouty toe was usually an accurate rain predictor. He felt that old battle war within himself — the wariness he had developed over the last eleven years, the fragile hope that he couldn't stamp out. He wanted to believe the way she believed, and maybe that was all faith really was, he thought. Simply a need to believe.

She leaned forward, her voice softening. "It's possible to change, Bairn. With prayer and effort and the help of God."

"If yer up here tonight to preach me a sermon, you can turn right around and head back below."

Anna stiffened. "No. I came because I wanted you to know that the only reason I let you kiss me was because I was happy about the rain."

A wiser man — a smarter one, in any case — wouldn't have said anything at all, merely given a polite nod of acknowledgment. "What kiss? I don't remember any kiss." He tried to smile, but he knew it must've looked all wrong.

Hurt passed through her eyes and he regretted his callousness.

A gust of cold wind lifted the strings of her prayer cover and she shivered, crossing her arms over her middle. "I feel nothing but confusion when you are near." She said it as if she wished it weren't so. "I meant to say, there is no peace about you."

"There will be once I make my fortune."

"I don't think fortune will fill your emptiness." She looked away from his face and after a moment said, "Good night, Bairn."

What he wanted to say was that only when he was near her did he feel peace, that when he was away from her, he felt nothing but turmoil and trouble. He wanted to tell her that she made him feel like he could be a better version of himself, that she was the finest woman — nay, person — he'd ever met. But those words remained lodged in his throat. His vision blurred beneath a wash of unexpected tears and his chest was suddenly choked with feelings — feelings of love and anger and dismay and confusion, and a growing disgust with himself.

Why, if he wasn't the biggest fool to ever breathe sea air. What did he expect? Who did he think he was, hoping for some kind of ordinary life? No woman like Anna deserved him. They weren't the same kind of person at all. She should listen to that minister's wife and marry some eager young Peculiar, innocent and ignorant, who had already ventured to the New World. Someone who shared her views about home and hearth, someone who cared nothing for earthly possessions. Someone who hadn't done sinful and wicked things.

Someone who would probably never know what a treasure he had caught for himself.

Bairn welcomed the loneliness of the night, the darkness that engulfed him, as he listened to the keening of the wind and the rhythmic lapping of the sea against the hull. Peace and contentment, he'd long since decided and accepted, was something that happened to other people.

September 9th, 1737

A ruckus broke out in the lower deck. A rooster had gotten loose and half the lower deck erupted into flurries of hands, feathers, and screams. Felix leaped over two trunks to catch the rooster by the neck, and landed in the lap of a Mennonite woman.

"Well, this is a surprise," she said. "Two chickens for dinner tonight!"

A plump woman said, "Toss back the feathery one and we'll fry up the red-haired one. He looks a little plumper."

Felix, beet red, crept back to the bow of the ship with the bird tucked safely under his arm. The women continued cajoling as though they were sitting at home. Their cheerful mood was infectious, and Anna felt rather buoyant. There was plenty of water for all and the ship seemed to be sailing along as if it had discovered wings. Soon, they would be in the New World. Everything, she thought, was going to be all right.

She must not, must not, must not think any more thoughts of the ship's carpenter.

19

September 9th, 1737

That night, Anna had barely fallen asleep when she was woken by a woman's cry. The cries grew louder and louder. Then someone shook her shoulder.

"Anna, it's Peter. Lizzie needs you. It's her time."

Anna bolted from her hammock and hurried over to Lizzie's pallet. "Oh Anna . . . help me."

Anna watched a moment and then laid her hand on Lizzie's abdomen. "Perhaps they're just false spasms in your belly." *Oh God, please let it be false spasms.*

"No. This is different." Lizzie squeezed Anna's hands, hard. "You've got to help me." She let out a scream that echoed through the lower deck, waking everyone.

Maria lit a lantern and came to the pallet. "Perhaps it is a stomach worm, like my Catrina had. I'll get some ginger slices."

"No, Maria, she doesn't need ginger. She is going to give birth."

Maria looked at Anna with doubt and displeasure. "It's much too soon for that. Impossible!"

Anna watched Lizzie a few moments more. Contractions were coming every few minutes. "Very possible. And soon."

"Impossible," Maria said again, a little less confidently this time.

Annie helped Lizzie to her feet and they walked around the lower deck for the next hour. Her contractions were sharp and ir-regular, her breathing harsh. She ran with sweat and finally couldn't walk any longer, practically collapsing onto her pallet. She let out a bellow like an ailing cow. Peter was perched on the chest next to the pallet, look-ing as if he was experiencing labor pains along with his young wife.

"She'll need privacy," Anna said. "Can someone find a place for Lizzie?"

Christian rose to his feet. "I'll find a spot." He dragged the scarred wooden table that had served as the school for Anna's English lessons into the bow of the ship. Then he returned and motioned to Peter to help Lizzie up. One hand to her round tummy, she pushed herself to her feet and staggered toward the table. Maria crouched down and put a red ribbon around Lizzie's small wrist. "This will help draw off the pains." She turned to Anna. "I'll make up a potion."

Anna had to bite her lip to not snap at Maria about her odd Braucher beliefs. Some were harmless, silly superstitions, but some were dangerous. It amazed her that Christian tolerated his wife's practices.

Anna tried to remember what herbs her grandmother had in the garden. If only she'd paid more attention to her grandmother! Never had she felt so far from home. She remembered the herbs her grandmother used for the birthing process: birthwort for inducing contractions, lady's mantle to stop bleeding, wormwood to relieve pain, raspberry leaf to speed the last part of labor, hops for their calming effect. Of course, there were none of those herbs tucked in her trunk because her grandmother hadn't expected someone to give birth.

Maria hustled and bustled around her. She knew about chants and potions but surprisingly little about babies being born, and all her hustle and bustle did nothing to help. From all corners of the lower deck, women descended on Lizzie like a gaggle of geese, asking questions and offering suggestions, a sea of worried faces. Lizzie was struggling to sit up and was pushing so hard her red face looked near to bursting.

Anna looked to Christian. "Would you and Peter create a screen of some sort? To give her some privacy?"

Christian gathered sheets and hung them to provide some semblance of privacy. Lizzie's pale hair was spread out on the pillow like a silvery-gold cloud, and terror filled her wide brown eyes. She cried out, calling for her mother. Her pains seemed extraordinarily fierce, or else she was uncommonly poor at managing.

Anna sponged the girl's face with cool water. "You'll forget the pain once you hold your babe in your arms."

Peter came in and went out, returned and went out, unable to help but reluctant to leave.

After two hours, during which the spasms of labor grew closer and closer together, Lizzie wept and protested and declared again and again that she couldn't go through with the birth.

"It'll all be over with soon," Anna said in her most soothing voice. "Only a little while longer." But even as she said it, she shivered and prayed some more.

Finally, Anna looked at Peter. "Go upstairs to get hot water and clean cloths."

"But how — how do I do that?" His lower lip protruded as though he were about to cry.

"You go ask Cook."

"I don't know who Cook is."

"Someone will show you. Now go." The boy departed like she'd kicked him in the back of his breeches.

Moments later, Peter returned. "The man in the galley told me the galley fires have been doused for the night."

"Then ask Cook to light them again. Oh, never mind." Anna looked around for Felix and didn't see him, so she left Maria in charge of Lizzie, and Barbara in charge of Maria, and went up to the main deck to speak to Cook. She could use a little fresh air.

Upstairs, she felt disoriented. The sun was setting — the day had passed and it would soon be night again. And the baby hadn't come. Soon, she hoped. Soon.

She saw the lantern glow from the galley and went inside. But it wasn't Cook inside, it was Georg Schultz. He sat on a barrel, drinking from Cook's private stash of the captain's whiskey. He looked up at her, be-whiskered and bleary and red-eyed, and pushed to his feet, coming to stand quite close to her. She hovered on the coaming.

She must have hot water for the babe. She must.

Go, came a whisper of warning. As she thought it, Georg Schultz surprised her with his quickness, pulling her forward and shutting the door behind her.

"It's taken me awhile but I finally put it all together. The boy. The thief is the boy. Hans Felix Bauer. Son of Jacob Bauer."

She stepped back, moving out of reach of his touch. "Why do you say that?"

"I heard the minister's wife, Maria, call him by his full name. It was the day the rain came." He moved toward her. "Suddenly, it was so obvious. Of course, of course. The little redheaded brat."

She backed up a step, then another. "You said you wanted a watch. I'm searching for it."

"Have you found it?"

"Not yet."

"The watch is incidental, though it would be nice to be able to return it to the baron. Far better to return with the boy. More than double the reward."

A panic gripped her chest so tightly that she thought her heart might stop beating. "No. No!"

"The Baron of Ixheim has rancor with Jacob Bauer. He holds Jacob Bauer responsible for the death of his sons."

"The only thing Jacob Bauer did was to tell the truth. He saw the baron's sons kill that man."

"That's not the way the baron views the situation. He believes that justice is due him."

Understanding dawned on Anna. "So if he can't have Jacob Bauer, he wants his sons." She shivered. "He took Johann and he won't be satisfied until he has one more."

His smile was cold. "You are a clever girl."

"Felix is just a boy. A child." She stood like a statue, frozen to the spot. "I'll tell the captain. He would never let you take a boy away from his family."

His throat clenched around a harsh laugh. "So naïve, little Anna. The captain would never dare go against the baron's orders. Not with so many more Germans wanting passage to America."

"I will find the watch so you can get the reward. But leave Felix alone."

"I think we can make an arrangement that would suffice." His eyes were on fire with an unholy delight. "You know what I want from you."

Oh, she knew what he wanted. She saw him for what he was — a poisonous man in dire need of God's grace, and having none of it.

She spun around to leave when he grabbed her arm, his fingers biting deep, hauling her roughly up against him.

The sea was so calm that Bairn decided it was a good night to sharpen tools in his shop. Less chance of injury when the waters were quiet. He looked up to see Felix standing by the door, his eyes alive with panic.

"Anna! She's . . ."

Anna? Tension rose in him at the mere mention of her name. "What is it?"

"Georg Schultz. Galley." He pummeled his fists in the air. "He hurts her!"

Bairn cleared the deck in long strides, the alarm in Felix's tone raking his every nerve. He was barely aware of the boy on his boot heels.

The galley was so narrow that Georg Schultz had Anna cornered. He leaned nose-to-nose with her.

Her stomach soured at the reeking smell of his putrid breath. "Please. Let me go."

He laughed, exposing yellow teeth. "Come on, dear," he urged in an oily, smooth voice. "I just want a taste of you. You're a very pretty woman. Let me see you." He pulled

353

off her prayer covering, scattering its pins, and his hand was in her hair. "Let me touch you." His grip on her waist relaxed, but then his hand moved up her side. At his touch she felt soiled, nearly nauseous.

She tried to fight down the terror that was rising within her. Her chest had locked tight and her breathing was shallow. She tried to stay calm, to keep her wits about her, as his hand started to grope her and she pushed him away. "Stop!"

"Feisty little wench, aren't you?"

"Get your hands off me."

He drew back, watching her, brows raised, his voice nearly growling. "Am I so repugnant to you?"

She stood her ground, unflinching. "Yes."

Georg Schultz jerked back, stunned by her audacity. "Why you . . ." He reeled back his hand and struck her cheek. He raised his hand to hit her again and she screamed, so he pinned her against the wall with his other hand. He leaned toward her to press his mouth against hers, when suddenly the door almost flew off its hinges and in came Bairn. He pulled Georg Schultz off Anna and tossed him against the wall. Schultz sank to the floor like a bag of potatoes.

Bairn's big hands clenched and un-clenched rhythmically, his powerful chest shook. "If you dare lay a hand on her again, I'll cast you overboard. Don't think I won't."

Georg Schultz's breathing was strident, his beard bristling, as he pulled himself to his feet. He scrubbed at his mouth with his coat sleeve.

"The captain will be outraged when he hears of this. You'll be done totin' passengers across the ocean."

He thrust his finger at Bairn. "The captain won't hear a word. Don't forget what I know about you, Bairn."

"That has nothin' to do with hurtin' Anna."

Georg Schultz lifted his head and faced Bairn squarely. "Why do you care? Unless you want her for yourself?"

Bairn raised his arm to hit the man, but Anna grabbed his arm. "Don't! Violence violates the word of God. It will only turn you into him. Just make him go."

Georg Schultz gave Bairn a hostile glare and pushed Felix aside as he staggered out the door. "I'm coming after you, boy."

Felix jumped and paled, his eyes went wide with fear.

"Felix." Anna held a hand out to him. He startled when she said his name, then came to her. She put an arm around him. Then she remembered Lizzie. "Water. I came up here for hot water for Lizzie. Her time is here."

"Felix, go find Cook and tell him he's needed in the galley," Bairn said. "Tell him the orders come from me. Dinnae take nay for an answer."

Chin not quite steady, Felix fled.

Bairn closed the door behind him and pulled a stool out for Anna to sit down. He picked up her hair covering and her pins, then his eyes held hers for a moment. She couldn't stop shaking.

"Anna, sit . . ."

Instead of sitting, she wilted against Bairn, sliding her arms around him, her face nestled against the curve of his neck.

His arms closed around her, crinkling her prayer cap. "You're safe now."

He helped her to sit on a barrel top, examined her face, dipped a cloth in cool water, and pressed it against her bruised cheek. He never spoke, but there was nothing but kindness in his eyes as he tenderly put that cloth against her cheek where it was bleeding. "Does it hurt?"

"No." She drew back a bit. "He frightened me, but little else."

He leaned nearer, his calloused fingers grazing her cheek. Apprehension and anger were etched around his eyes. "I'll see t'it he doesn't touch you again," he whispered. "I promise you will always be safe with me."

She nodded. She knew that what he said was true. Somehow she had always known it. She had always felt safe with him. For a few seconds she was struck with the power of his presence, the unspoken feelings between them. She twisted her hair into a knot, pinned it in place along with the prayer covering. His eyes watched every move she made, almost reverently.

"Bairn, Georg Schultz says Felix is the one who stole the watch."

"But . . . Felix would never do such a thing." Less confidently, he added, "Or would he?"

"It's very possible. Felix blamed the Baron of Ixheim for his brother's death."

Bairn jerked his head up. "Ixheim?"

"Yes. That's the name of our village." She flicked her dangling capstrings behind her. "Georg Schultz plans to take Felix back with him, with or without the watch." He had the strangest look on his face, as if he had seen a ghost. "Bairn, did you hear me?"

"Hmm?"

"Georg Schultz says he is going to take Felix back to face the baron, with or without the watch."

"Aye, I heard you." He was peering at her

so intently that she felt pinned in place. "Anna, tell me about that rose."

"My rose? The one in my basket?"

"Aye. The one you gave water to durin' the drought instead of drinkin' it yerself."

Felix must have seen her and told him. "The rose was given to me by a boy I once knew. I'd fallen in the hills and broken my leg. He knew I loved roses, so he dug up the rose and left it for me."

"Left it?"

"He went to the New World with his father."

At that, Bairn shuddered, then quickly turned from her. He went to Cook's small window and gazed out at the sea. "Why . . ." He stopped, cleared his throat, started again. "Why does the rose matter so much t'you?"

Watching him, listening to his curiosity about a garden flower, made her wonder about the life he'd lived, the comforts he hadn't had. She wondered what was going through his mind as he stared out the small window. Whatever it was, she'd probably never know. "We were just children . . . but there was something special I felt for him."

Without turning around, he said, "And he for you?"

"I don't know. I was younger than he was.

He hardly noticed me." The ship rose on a swell, hung there, settled into a trough, then rose again.

He turned back to face her with a look in his eyes that was so tender, so loving, her feelings for him came close to surfacing and she struggled to tamp them down. "Anna," he said, his voice low and husky, "I doot the laddie would have left you the rose had he not noticed you."

A sailor's shout floated in the air and suddenly she remembered why she had come to the galley in the first place. "Lizzie! The baby is on its way and she's having a dreadful time of it." She looked up at him hopefully. "You're the ship's surgeon. Surely you must know something about delivering a baby."

He shook his head. "I've seen plenty of pox and scurvy, but I ken naught about how t'prevent it. The older women ken more than I about birthin' babies."

She scanned the open cupboards of the galley. "Has Cook any hartshorn or chamomile?"

"Nay. China tea with opium drops."

"She may need that after the child is delivered." She heard the stroke of the ship's bells. Had it only been a short time since she'd come up on deck? It felt like hours.

He helped her to stand. "I'll have the hot water brought down to you."

"Bairn, I don't know what to do. I've never delivered a baby."

"You said you raised sheep. I'm sure you've seen plenty of lambs come into this world. Could it be all that different?"

She looked up. "Maybe. But I don't know. Bairn, I'm so frightened. About Lizzie. About Felix."

His Adam's apple slid up, then down. For a moment he didn't say anything. He turned, then looked away and quietly said, "Let me do the worryin' about the laddie."

A kindness, but Felix wasn't his problem. Still, she could only handle one crisis at a time and Lizzie was her chief concern right now. "I don't remember a baby taking so long to get born. What if something goes wrong?"

He took a deep breath, fixing his attention on the top of her head. Her prayer cap. "Where is that strong faith of yers?"

She sighed. "Faith." At that moment her convictions fell away. "I don't know."

For a moment, he closed his arms around her, held her close, his lips at her ear, his breath fanning her cheek. "Well, I have faith in you."

He led her to the companionway and left

her there.

But his warmth remained, spilling through her, easing her fear. Momentarily, her hands balled into fists before she managed to relax them. She could do this. She must.

September 10th, 1737

It was after midnight. In his carpenter's shop, Bairn launched his frock coat and hat onto one of the brass hooks he'd screwed to the wall, then stalked to the workbench and slammed his palms onto the bench. Barrel staves rattled, stacked on floor-to-ceiling shelves he'd built on a better day.

And all that time he nursed a growing rage for Georg Schultz. The anger that flooded through Bairn turned the world red as hot, hot fire. Just the memory of Anna, pale-faced and trembling, so wounded and yet so brave, made him want to strike Schultz. He abhorred violence, always had. Yet violence was impossible to avoid — among men or among nature. The fury of a stormy sea, the brutality of the wind, the cruelty of some individuals. Even the act of giving birth, he realized, was a violent business in itself.

He thought of Anna and the suffering girl in the lower decks, and wondered how they were faring. He felt a strange surge of something unfamiliar — a sense of caring for someone, of protection. Something deep, long buried. He remained in his shop until the soft purple time before dawn, musing, until he realized that his hardened heart was betraying him. It had begun to shift — coming together like the individual wooden staves of a barrel, bits and pieces being moved around by an invisible hand to start to fall into place, to form a completely functional piece. A future he thought was forever lost to him was now right in front of him. Close but out of reach.

He loved Anna, yet he could never have her. Never *should* have her.

The knowledge that Bairn had faith in Anna had an extraordinary effect. All the tension and anxiety left her, and she felt calm and confident. Anna set about doctoring Lizzie with calm efficiency. She did every single thing she had seen her grandmother do and even invented some of her own, but dawn came and still the baby did not come.

Anna was so tired she could scarcely think. She tried to remember anything more she could do, but her brain wouldn't work. Barbara Gerber worried the baby was breech, Esther Wenger suggested Lizzie should sit on a birthing stool — of which they had none — and Maria recommended she climb stairs.

Lizzie snapped at them and told them to leave her be. She only wanted Anna. Minutes passed, hours, and Anna stayed by her side, cooling Lizzie's pale face with a wet cloth.

Then, as suddenly as it had started, it was all over. Lizzie gave a terrible cry, and a massive push, and a baby emerged, wrinkled and slimy, with a great gush of liquid behind it. Lizzie fell back exhausted.

Anna had very little experience caring for a baby, but Bairn was right — she had been present at the birth of many lambs. Her instincts told her what to do next: she checked the baby to remove the cord from around its neck and wiped any membrane from across its face, then turned it slightly downward so mucus drained from it.

She tore a coarse thread from the hem of her dress, tied the baby's cord, cut it with a small knife brought down from the galley. Having no cumin to seal the cord, she spat on her hand and rubbed the cut end. She wrapped the baby in clean linen and marveled at the sight: A tiny, perfect infant, a boy, with the blond hair of his father and the pale face of his mother. He looked like a tiny doll. His arms and legs were small, yet a miniscule nail completed each finger. He was red and wrinkled and heart-achingly beautiful.

At the sound of the baby's mewl-like cry, Maria pulled up the sheet flap and hurried behind Peter to see the ship's newest passenger.

"Here, Peter." Anna handed the baby to his father "No stomach worm," she gave Maria a glance with a lifted eyebrow, "but a boy."

Then Anna turned her attention to Lizzie and felt a spike of concern. Lizzie's breathing was rapid and her temperature high. She put a hand in the hollow of Lizzie's chest and felt her heartbeat, faint and irregular, but it was there.

"Lizzie needs to be cleaned up and kept warm," Anna said, trying to keep her voice steady. "She should have something hot to drink. Maria, hot water and honey would do nicely."

Lizzie's eyes flickered, and opened a little. "Baby. My baby. Where is my baby?"

Peter held the baby in one hand so that the child lay within Lizzie's gaze. You could see the struggle and the effort it cost her to lift her head, and with a sharp intake of breath she put out a shaking hand to touch the infant. She smiled a beatific smile, murmured, "My baby. My darling baby," her hand resting on Peter's hand and the baby.

That was when Anna noticed there was blood everywhere. She wiped it up, but it kept coming. In the flickering lantern light, it looked dark as pitch on the white rags. The bleeding wouldn't stop and Anna was starting to panic. She asked Maria for more fresh linens and wondered what kind of herbal remedy she could concoct from ingredients to help slow the bleeding.

Lizzie closed her eyes as if to rest. Then she fell quiet. Too quiet.

"Lizzie?" Peter asked. He shook her gently, trying to waken her.

Anna leaned down to listen for Lizzie's breathing. She didn't hear anything. She reached for her pulse and felt nothing. Slowly, she straightened and gave a slight shake of her head. "She's gone."

20

September 10th, 1737

As Anna and Maria prepared Lizzie's body for burial, she felt a tug at her elbow and turned to see Felix. His eyes widened in shock at the sight of Lizzie on the table. "Bairn said to tell you that Captain Stedman wants to see you as soon as you are able to come."

"Go ahead, Anna," Maria said. "I'll finish up."

Anna washed, changed her clothes, combed her hair, and put on a fresh prayer covering before heading up to the main deck. Bairn strode over to meet her at the top of the companionway. She was so tired she practically collapsed in his arms when he offered her a hand over the coaming. It seemed the only time she could take a full breath was when Bairn was nearby.

"Felix told me. I'm sorry."

"So am I," she said, her throat tight with

a wistful sadness. "If only I could have done more —"

He put a finger to her lips. "You did the best you could, under the circumstances."

She sighed. "Christian said the same thing. He said Lizzie knows a better life now, the eternal life, warm and safe in the glory of heaven."

Bairn looked at her with that slightly amused look of his, wanting to believe her but doubtful. She was too tired to pursue a discussion about the afterlife.

"Why does the captain want to see me?"

He bit his lower lip. "News travels fast on a ship." He led her down the deck to the Great Cabin.

The captain looked up from his table as Bairn led her in. "I was told of trouble in the lower deck."

"A child has been born."

The captain stared at her. "And lived?"

"Yes, though his mother passed soon after the delivery. I don't think the child will survive the day. He is small and his breathing is labored."

The captain pulled out his Bible. "I'll conduct a funeral service at sunset." He glanced at her. "Unless your minister prefers."

"I think Christian would want to lead the

service."

"Fine, fine." The captain looked more than a little relieved. " 'Tis customary at sea to have the child wrapped with his mother."

"But . . . that might be too soon." She looked from the captain to Bairn. "Surely you wouldn't wrap the child before he's passed." Anna sought Bairn's help. "Could you not wait?"

Bairn kept his eyes lowered. " 'Tis most merciful."

"Please," she whispered. "Please, wait."

Captain Stedman and Bairn exchanged a meaningful look, then the captain shook his head. "Only until sunset. 'Tis bad luck to keep a dead body aboard a ship."

To Anna's shock and dismay, Christian did not object to the custom of burying a babe with his mother. "It's the compassionate thing to do," he said when she explained what the captain had said. "Let us pray that the babe passes soon."

But as the afternoon wore on, the babe had not died. Death was near, Anna felt, as his breathing had grown more shallow and his skin had gone nearly translucent. The men had already taken Lizzie's body up on the upper deck.

As the sun was starting to drop low on

the horizon, Christian came back downstairs. "It's time, Anna."

She swaddled the babe in a clean cloth and handed him to Peter. The grief-stricken father held him close to his cheek, tears streaming. They went up the companionway and joined the group of mourners. Christian took the baby from his father and gently tucked him into his dead mother's arms. The baby looked even smaller now; only his downy hair was visible. As the other men started to wrap the body, a shriek stopped them.

"Don't you dare! Give me that child!" Dorothea stomped over from the top of the companionway and grabbed the baby out of his mother's arms. "It's a tiny living soul!" Felix trotted behind her, with Decker's dog on his heels. "Do we need another tragedy on this day?"

Anna put a hand on her shoulder. "Dorothea, the baby is soon to die. I'm sure of it."

The effect on Dorothea was dramatic and immediate. She looked wildly round at everyone, thrust the baby down between her breasts, and folded her arms over him. "No," she said. Then repeated louder, "No. He will not die."

Anna brushed the beginnings of tears

from her eyes. "Why do you say that?"

"Because I said so."

Christian held out a hand to her. "Dorothea, even skill and love and care cannot overcome God's will."

"Don't you *Dorothea* me, Christian. Let this child have a chance at life. Let him have a chance!"

Christian didn't seem to know what to make of Dorothea. Nor did Anna. Dorothea hadn't looked so spirited in . . . months. "But he is so small. How will he eat? There is no woman on the ship who can feed him." As many young families as there were on this ship, there were no nursing mothers.

Dorothea looked frantically around her, then her eyes rested on the companionway. "The goat. The one that lost its kid."

"The milk has dried up."

"Not entirely. Especially since we have water now." She jutted out her chin. "I will feed this babe. You mark my words. This child will live to see Port Philadelphia."

Anna whispered to Christian. "Would it be so wrong to let her try?"

Christian looked at young Peter.

"Please," Peter begged. "Please. For my Lizzie."

Short of tearing Dorothea's arms apart with brute force and grabbing the baby, which Christian would never have done, there was nothing he could do. He seemed astonished, then said quietly, "God's will be done." He nodded to Dorothea.

The men wrapped up Lizzie's body and resumed the burial. After the body slipped into the frothy waters, Anna turned around and saw Bairn standing at a distance, a stunned look on his face.

She walked toward him, sensing his disquiet. "The little baby may not survive, but at least he has a chance."

The baby was not on his mind. "Who was that woman?"

"Who? Which woman?" She turned to the clump of passengers as they made their way back down the companionway. She saw Maria and Barbara. "Those two?"

"No. The one who insisted on saving the babe. What is her name?"

"That's Felix's mother."

"Her name! What is her name?"

"Dorothea. Dorothea Bauer. Why?"

He looked at her strangely, all tight in the face as if it pained him to try to talk. She didn't know what had upended him. "What's wrong, Bairn?"

A terrible shadow fell across his face. He swallowed once, then twice. "Why is she going to Port Philadelphia?"

"To join her husband. Felix's father. Jacob Bauer. Our bishop."

A painful light flared behind his eyes. He looked . . . stricken. For a long time, he stared at the companionway, his face like a thunderstorm brewing. "Jacob Bauer is not dead?"

"Goodness, no." She took a step toward him. "Why?"

She began to see that all the color had left his face and his eyes had gone stark and hard. She tugged at his coat sleeve. "Bairn, what is it?"

He seized her hands and backed away from her, a fierce tension in his gray eyes. "Leave me be, Anna." He spun on his heels and left the upper deck, left her, without another word.

Felix's eyes were swollen and aching. He wiped the tears off his face with the backs of his hands as he returned the kettle to the galley for Cook to find in the morning.

He couldn't get the image of Lizzie wrapped up in that cloth out of his mind. And then the worst sight of all — the sharks that snapped and tugged at her shroud, pulling it into the deep water.

He wondered how Johann would have handled that sight, if it would have bothered him as much as it bothered Felix. He expected to have nightmares over Lizzie's funeral for a long, long time, like he did about Johann's. He often woke up with a start, sure he could still hear the clods of dirt that filled his brother's grave, shovel by shovel.

When he saw the baby being put in Lizzie's arms, he panicked. He flew down to the lower deck to find his mother and told her to get upstairs, fast, to save that little baby boy from being tossed overboard.

She was sitting at the little opening by the cannon, that awful blank look in her eyes.

"Now, Mem! Now! Get up and get upstairs. They're tossing the baby overboard to the sharks. That baby needs you!"

And to his astonishment, she did get up. She moved faster than he had seen her move in months. She took those stairs two at a time, and then she grabbed that baby just as Christian started to cover it with the sheet. She yelled at Christian. Yelled! His mother yelled at the minister.

What if that little baby had not been rescued by his mother?

Felix choked at the image, and his breath came in ragged gasps. His mouth was dry, his belly sour. He set down the kettle on a barrel and heaved into Cook's sink. It was the first time he'd been sick on the *Charming Nancy.*

21

September 11th, 1737

Anna's thoughts continued to whir as she climbed into the hammock. For long minutes she laid there, locked in prayer, her petitions a muddle of joy and disbelief. And terrible fear.

She gave thanks for the new life in the lower decks, nestled in Dorothea's arms tonight. She was grateful for the spark in Dorothea's eyes and begged God to let the child live, for both their sakes. She was glad, too, that she hadn't crossed paths with Georg Schultz all day.

But she felt a dread as she thought of the look of horror on Bairn's face. What was troubling him? What did he know about the Bauer family that gave him such a fright?

Her eyes lifted to the beams above her head. She recognized the sound of Bairn's footfalls pacing the deck above. She knew his gait, the sound of his boot heels on the wooden planks. Finally, she slipped out of the hammock, grabbed a woolen shawl off the top of her chest, and tiptoed through the lower deck to the companionway.

She found Bairn leaning on the railing, slumped forward with his head on his crossed arms.

"Sometimes it helps to talk about what's troubling you."

He startled at the sound of her voice and half turned toward her. "Not this. Not now. I've got to sort it all out meself." His dark eyes looked like two bruises in the paleness of his face, and she wondered what could be the cause of such turmoil within him. He tore his gaze away and stared past her to the vast, black ocean. He had vanished into that endless sea.

She moved her hand a fraction of an inch closer to his, wanting to comfort him as she comforted a child, but awkwardness crept over her and nearly closed her throat. The wind lifted the fringe of her shawl and slapped it across her face, biting at her exposed skin. "I just thought I'd see if you were all right."

He glanced at her. "Yer shivering." Suddenly he flung his arm around her shawl-wrapped shoulders, drawing her close to his side. "I cannae get warm. I was beside the galley fire for a full turn of the hourglass. Aye, a full half of an hour, and I couldn't get warm. 'Tis a chill deep in me bones."

The temptation to lay her head against his shoulder ran deep, to give him what comfort she could. But she resisted that urge and rubbed her hands together to warm them. "Bairn, isn't there some way I can help?"

"Tell me everythin' you know about Jacob Bauer and his family. Leave nothin' out."

"But why?"

He slanted an aggrieved look at her. "Please, Anna. Just tell me."

"Jacob Bauer is the bishop for our church."

"When did he go t'America?"

"A year ago, last May."

"What else do you know?"

"He is a fine man, I know that. A bit impulsive and headstrong, perhaps, but a man of convictions. He leads our church well."

"What about his family? What do you know of them?"

"There's Felix, of course, and Dorothea."

"Anyone else?"

"There was Johann, Felix's brother."

"Where is he?"

"He died, right before we left for Rotterdam."

Something cold seemed to shiver across Bairn's face. She had the notion that he'd just seen something, or thought something, that hurt him terribly. She wanted to touch him, just touch him. Just lay her hand against his cheek. Instead she gripped her elbows tighter and held her breath.

"How — ?" His voice cracked and he had to start over. "How did he die?" he rasped, a strange roughness to his voice. "Why did he die?"

"He was . . . trespassing, I guess you could say, onto the Baron of Ixheim's property." A sadness welled up inside her, choking off the words. She shut her eyes and pressed her fingers to her lips. She covered her face with her hands, but for just a moment. Then she let them fall to the railing where they made a single, gripping fist. She'd never spoken aloud of the beating, nor had anyone else. The Lord had taken Johann home, they all acknowledged. No one ever spoke of how.

But Bairn was waiting for her to continue. She swallowed and drew in a deep breath. "The baron was so angry with him, he had him beaten. Not just a little, either, but enough to teach him a lesson and to send a message back to Jacob Bauer."

"Why? What ill will did he have toward Jacob Bauer?"

"A year ago, maybe a little longer now, Jacob witnessed the baron's two sons as they brutally murdered a man. They ended up convicted of the crime and were hung."

"But a Peculiar would nae have testified against them."

She was always surprised by what he knew of their people, and what he didn't know. "No, he wouldn't testify. But he did tell the truth to the authorities. The baron's sons were quite wicked. They went too far." She paused. "Yet the baron blamed Jacob for his son's deaths. That's why Jacob left for the New World when he did — to escape the wrath of the baron. I don't think it occurred to him that the baron would seek revenge on his sons. And he certainly didn't know that Johann had been borrowing books from the baron's library. To be perfectly fair, I don't know if the baron intended to kill Johann with those beatings, or to frighten him and send a message to his father. The trouble was, Johann wasn't . . ."

"Strong."

"No. He wasn't strong. He had already lived longer than anyone expected. He had a weak heart." She tilted her head back, and it seemed she was falling into a big black bowl of a sky dotted with stars. "Yet he had a very big heart."

"So . . . there were two boys?"

Anna lowered her gaze to a star on the dark sea's horizon. "There was an older boy. He's gone."

"What happened to him?"

"His name was Hans. Years ago, when Jacob had first gone to America to seek land, he had taken Hans with him, but they both became very ill on the ship. Hans died. When Jacob recovered and learned that his son had died, he was heartbroken. He returned to Ixheim on the next ship." She told him more, about how Dorothea had slipped into melancholy, and it wasn't until Felix was born that she began to recover.

Anna grew quiet, although she didn't raise her head. Her gaze fell to her lap. She put a pleat in her apron with her fingers, then smoothed it out with her palm. "Nearly everyone died on the ship, Jacob said. Even the captain. The carpenter sailed the ship into harbor."

Bairn was shuddering and she suddenly realized it was not from the weather. With a sudden horror that almost made her heart stop, it occurred to her that he must have been on that ship. He had told her he was once a cabin boy.

"You knew them? Jacob and Hans?"

His harsh breathing made his words come

out as a gasp. "Aye."

"It must have been horrific, watching so many people die."

"Aye."

She picked up his free hand and wrapped her own hands around it as if she cradled a wounded bird. He tried to pull free, but she tightened her grip. "Is that why you don't sleep well? Why you're always pacing in the night?"

He pulled his hand away from her. "My dreams won't leave me be."

She put an arm around his waist. She had to touch him, to comfort him. "God can heal memories, Bairn. You can do that with God's help."

"God left me long ago!" he flung back. "And I kinnae blame Him fer that. I've done things . . . I'm not a man God should pay any mind to." His shudders continued beneath her arm.

"I don't believe that, Bairn. I believe that nothing is outside of God's ultimate purpose."

He raised his head, and ran his hands over his face in a weary gesture that broke her heart. With a shaky sigh he stepped back from the railing to face her, and she along with him. "You'd best go below. The ship's bell will ring soon. It would nae do for you to be seen up here with the likes of me."

She started to turn toward the companionway, but his voice stopped her.

"Felix said that you pray for me." Wonder warmed his voice. "That must take some effort."

She gave him a gentle smile. "I ask God to bless you and keep you."

"Save me, you mean." Then he looked at her again, with that same odd sadness welling in his eyes.

She watched him walk down the deck, head hung low, until he disappeared from view, and dismay filled her.

Despite her best intentions, despite all her precautions to the contrary, one thing had become clear to her. Somewhere along this sea journey, perhaps when he adjusted the heel of her shoe or thrust his flask in her hands to make her drink or burst into the galley to protect her from Georg Schultz, or just now, when he'd revealed some vulnerable part of himself to her . . . she'd fallen in love with Bairn.

September 12th, 1737
As soon as Anna dismissed Catrina and Felix from English lessons for lunch, Maria sat down across from her and rubbed her big red hands together. "Anna, you have

inherited your grandfather's ability to teach."

Anna shifted uncomfortably on her seat — an upturned nail keg that Bairn had given her to use as a stool. It wasn't like Maria to flatter. Anna much preferred her plain speaking, even her criticism.

"I believe I have found an ideal solution to Peter's dilemma." Maria rested her eyes on Anna. "Peter needs a wife, to care for him and the babe. You need a husband."

Anna's hands curled into a tight ball in her lap. "Peter is but a child still." Unfinished and rough-hewn, a man still waiting to happen.

Maria's brows seemed in danger of disappearing into her prayer cap. "He's quite fond of you." She lowered her voice and added, "Dorothea, tell her."

Dorothea was passing by them as she walked the baby around the lower deck to rock him to sleep. "I think our Anna knows her own mind."

"Peter wants to wed again, for his child's sake." And it should be to you, Maria's tone seemed to say.

"But I don't love Peter."

"Love?" she replied, a pinched expression about her mouth. "You've lost that luxury after dallying with the carpenter."

What good would it do to defend herself? Anna said nothing, only got stiffly to her feet. She pushed past Maria, but the woman grabbed her arm to pin her in place.

Maria leaned close to her ear. "The purity of a soul can be corroded by exposure to the world, the same way a shovel grows rusty if it's left out in the rain."

Anna stopped and turned to face her straight on. "I will not marry Peter, even for the sake of the baby."

She left Maria stuttering disapproval in her wake.

The last time Felix had gotten caught in a lie, his mother had cried over his sin. He had hated that most of all. He would almost rather she'd have given him a whipping, but she wasn't the type to pick up a switch. Which was why he had decided to avoid Georg Schultz like the pox and hope he'd give up trying to find the thief with the gold watch.

Felix wondered if the baron would have dared to hurt Johann if his father were still around. It was his father the baron was riled up with. He remembered his father and his mother talking together one night, in quiet voices he probably wasn't supposed to be hearing, and his father said that he needed to get his family away from Ixheim before it was too late.

And then it was too late.

He tried to swallow down the wad of tears that were building in his throat. He hoped Johann could pull back the curtain of heaven now and then and see that they were all right. That Mem was finally better, laughing and smiling and cooing over that little baby, and soon they would be with Papa in the New World.

He wondered what his father would think about having a new son. Last evening, Peter had asked his mother if she would take the baby for him, to raise him like her own. He had Christian's blessing, he told her. "I can't take care of him, not like you could."

"I'll need to ask Jacob," his mother replied, but Felix already knew the answer. The baby, if he lived, and it seemed like he would by the way he was squalling, would be his new brother.

Bairn angled his face in his mirror to shave his chin and nicked himself. He flung the straight-edged razor into a porcelain bowl with such disgust that soapy water splashed over the rim of the bowl and onto the floor.

He needed something to occupy his head and hands every moment, because when his hands were idle they started to shake, and he was too full of feelings to think. Each time he saw Georg Schultz, his belly clenched with a sick dread. He felt as he did before a storm, when there was an absence of wind but the horizon looked terrifyingly gray.

He dropped to the floor of the officer's cabin, his head in his hands. He couldn't take in all that he had discovered in the last twenty-four hours. He could hardly take in a deep breath. "Is this Yer deign on my life, this agonizing subtraction? Please, God, there must be some way."

He didn't know why he prayed. He expected no answer. Indeed, he had not received any answers to his petitions during that awful time, years ago.

He couldn't help it. Something deep inside him was asking for help. His chest ached with a longing — no, a need — to make things right. *Me sin's much greater than the laddie's. Please, God, dinnae let him suffer. There must be some other way.*

With those words, he felt an unexpected peace come over him; it seemed to enter the cabin like an unseen guest.

Bairn jumped to his feet, started pacing, working out the details in his mind. He felt his whole world shift and give way.

The next morning, he walked toward the galley to see what Cook was doing about supper. Mr. Pocock sought him out to tell him the captain wanted to see him in the Great Cabin and a knot of alarm tightened in his gut.

Here it was. He put on his frock coat and went to face the storm.

The captain had Bairn sit in the chair at the table while he paced up and down in the narrow cabin. "Georg Schultz said he found the thief who stole that baron's gold watch."

"Did he tell you that the thief is an eight-year-old laddie?"

"Aye. He did. And it sickens me, but there's naught I can do. A thief is a thief." The captain averted his eyes. "He says he will return to Rotterdam on the next ship and plans to take the lad with him."

"And yer in agreement with him?" Bairn was incredulous. "A mere laddie?"

The captain ran a hand across his whiskered jaw and groped for a sensible solution. "His mother may accompany him back." He waved a hand in a grand manner. "I'll see to it that she won't be charged full passage."

Bairn rose to his feet, towering over the captain. "Nay."

The captain looked up at him, surprised. He wasn't accustomed to anyone disagreeing with him, especially not Bairn. "This isn't our affair. We are merely the transporters for these people. We have plenty of work ahead of us to get the *Charming Nancy* shipshape for next summer's passage."

"Nay," Bairn said more emphatically.

"Bairn, I don't like Schultz any more than you do, but the law is the law. And mayhap this scare will keep the lad from a life of thievery."

Bairn raked a hand over his hair. "Sir, I was a laddie meself when yer brother took me under his wings. And then you did, yerself. You both gave me a chance."

"That's different. You were an orphan, all alone in the world. And you showed promise. Real promise." The captain strode to the window. "This boy has parents, a family, and yet he stole something of great value."

"Without meaning t'sound disrespectful, this isn't about the laddie, Captain. This is about money. Schultz wants the reward. You want plenty of passengers t'fill the lower deck."

Their eyes locked.

A knock on the door interrupted the standoff. Mr. Pocock stuck his head in the door and asked for the captain to come to the fo'c'sle deck for a moment.

The captain nodded. "We're finished here."

"No, sir, we're not."

The captain gave Bairn a tight smile. "Then wait here. I'll return and we can finish this discussion."

He opened the door and shouted for Johnny Reed to fetch Georg Schultz and bring him to the Great Cabin.

By the time the captain returned, Georg Schultz had already arrived and had settled himself in the chair.

Bairn stood in the center of the room, feet straddled. "Captain, sir, I have something to tell you. You and Schultz both."

"Perhaps Mr. Schultz wouldn't mind vacating my chair for this important announcement."

Georg Schultz slowly rose.

"I won't be stayin' in Port Philadelphia this winter. I'll be returnin' to Rotterdam with Schultz. I'll go in the laddie's place."

"Very nice offer, Bairn," Georg Schultz said, "but the baron wants only a Bauer."

"And so he will have him." He fixed his gaze on Georg Schultz. "My name is not Bairn. My name is Hans Bauer. I am Jacob Bauer's eldest son."

22

September 13th, 1737

Something had come over Dorothea. She was making changes and she was not a great one for change.

Anna had a theory that it was the baby that cured Dorothea. Her old indomitable spirit came back to her with the care of this infant boy. Her powerful maternal instincts had kicked in and told her that she was the protector, the provider. She didn't have time anymore to be sad or depressed. She couldn't afford to be woolly minded. The baby's life depended on her.

Dorothea was sleeping, the baby lying on her chest. One hand was protectively over him, the other lay limp by her side. She was smiling. The baby was never alone, day and night. He had the warmth, the touch, the softness, the smell, the moisture of a mother. He heard her heartbeat and her voice. Above all, he had her love.

The baby stirred and Dorothea's eyes flickered open. She reached for a saucer at the side of her and began to squeeze milk she had extracted from the goat, pressing out a few drops, which fell into the saucer. Then she took a tiny silver salt spoon, something Felix had found — Anna had a sneaking suspicion he had found it among the captain's things but she didn't really want to know the answer. Dorothea held the little baby in her left hand and touched his lips with the spoon she held in her right hand.

Anna watched, fascinated. The baby's lips were no bigger than a couple of flower petals. A tiny tongue came out and licked the fluid. She repeated this about six or eight times, then tucked him back between her breasts. She did this each time the baby woke, even through the nights. Then they both would catch a little sleep, and she would feed him again.

"She said he won't die, and he won't, you know," Felix told Anna. "She knows how to look after baby boys."

And what about bigger boys? Anna thought, but didn't say aloud. She had asked Felix again and again if he knew where that gold watch was and, each time, he denied that he knew anything about it.

She was almost starting to think he really didn't have anything to do with the watch, but then she remembered the morning of Johann's funeral, when he had disappeared for a time.

She looked through all of Felix's belongings to try to find the gold watch. She went through her own chest, through Dorothea's belongings, even Catrina's. She tried to think the way Felix thought. If the watch were left in Ixheim, she figured he would confess as much. But he wasn't budging from his denial, which made her certain that it was on this ship. But where? Where could it be?

Time was running out. They would be in Port Philadelphia soon. She had to find that gold watch.

September 14th, 1737

The rain seemed to come out of nowhere. At dawn, there was nothing more than a light chop on the waters, a typical gray, late fall day with light winds out of the southeast. An hour later, sustained winds were blowing out of the southwest. By noon, gusts were screaming over the sea.

From the fo'c'sle deck, Bairn caught sight of the waves swirling toward them, a mountain of water plunging across the sea to crash upon the deck. "All hands on deck," he shouted. "Topmen aloft."

Then the downpour changed to a gentle spray of water, and the lightning and thunder moved away. But it was too still, oddly quiet. Bairn searched the sky. The clouds had a funny green tinge that bled out into the air. The sailors stopped what they were doing and looked curiously to Bairn for direction.

Bairn didn't notice that Georg Schultz had assumed the storm was over and ventured from the lower deck to step onto the upper deck.

Suddenly the wind hissed like a snake in the sky and began swirling madly overhead, shrieking through the rope rigging. The bow of the ship lurched upward. Bairn heard a terrifying scream and spun around to see Schultz stagger to the ship's railing and tumble into the sea.

That should have been the end of him. Bairn rushed to the rail and saw Schultz gripping the topsail halyard that dangled over the side, holding onto the rope with a wild desperation.

"Hang on, Schultz!" Bairn yelled. He turned to the deckhands. "Over here. Come help!" Several sailors took up the halyard and hauled Schultz back in, finally snagging him with a boat hook and dragging him over the railing and onto the deck.

Georg Schultz lay on the deck, so still that Bairn thought surely *this* was the end of him. Then he coughed and sputtered and heaved, very much alive.

September 15th, 1737
Georg Schultz might have survived a toss overboard, but illness soon caught up with him. It started with a racking cough that curled his shoulders. And then chills set in. Passengers avoided him, fearful of any contagion. They all knew that ships could be easily quarantined for disease and wanted none of it.

"Anna, wake up."

"What?" Disoriented, she opened her eyes and lifted her head. "Christian?" Still fuzzy from sleep, her head bobbed slightly before she jerked erect and ran her hands over her face. "Christian, what is it?"

"Follow me."

Immediately, Anna rose from the hammock and came to her feet. She followed Christian down the aisle to the stern, where he stopped in front of Georg Schultz's sleeping shelf.

"Listen to his breathing. Doesn't it sound strange?"

It was an odd sound, like the bellows from a fireplace. Anna bent over and placed her palm on his hot forehead. "He's got a fever."

"Have you anything to help him in your remedy box?"

Fever. Fever. Anna bit her lip, thinking. What did her grandmother do to bring down a fever? Why hadn't she paid more attention? Because, she realized, she had never thought she'd need to know such essential knowledge. "Perhaps I could fix a vinegar compress for his forehead."

Anna and Christian stayed by the Neulander's sleeping shelf through the rest of the night, but by dawn, his fever and racking cough worsened.

Christian looked at her. "I think he has pneumonia."

She met his gaze. "I think so too."

As the day wore on, Anna checked on Georg Schultz. Late in the afternoon, she leaned forward and placed a palm on his forehead; it seemed even hotter. Christian wrapped him tightly in a wool blanket. Anna fixed a hot poultice for his neck and chest, but the constant wheeze of his breathing grew more labored.

After his last turn on watch that evening, Bairn came down to check on the patient. He hunched forward with his lips pressed to his thumb knuckles, staring intensely at the man's chest. His chest seemed to strain for each bit of air.

"He's growing worse," Anna said quietly.

"Aye, well, 'tis his own doing. 'Twas a foolish thing t'go above deck in a storm." He crossed his arms against his chest. "Anna, why do you bother nursin' a man like him back t'life? If he lives, he'll ne'er thank you for it." His voice fell to a murmur. "All ye need t'do . . . is . . . nothin'. No one would blame you."

Do nothing. The reckless thought had crossed her mind, had tempted her — she was no saint. Georg Schultz was repugnant to her. She couldn't stand being in the same vicinity of him, recoiled at touching him. Nor could the other passengers. He had alienated himself after those interviews to find the thief of the baron's watch and they were fearful of his illness spreading through the lower decks.

Anna thought Bairn would leave as quickly as he came, but he bent down and propped some pillows behind Georg's back.

Felix rushed to the bedside, eager for a chance to be near Bairn. "Vhy are y'doin' that?"

"So he won't choke."

Bairn settled down on the ground beside

Georg Schultz's bunk, bracing his elbows on his knees, bent forward, studying the man. As if he sensed Anna watching him, he glanced up. But her eyes skittered down; she was unable to look at him. The candle was nearly out, and Anna fetched a fresh one, lit it, and placed it in the holder, casting shadows that bounced off the corners.

"You dinnae answer me question. Why do you do it?"

Anna lifted exhausted eyes to him. There was no sting in Bairn's words, only gentleness in his eyes, softness in his curiosity. "Don't you know by now?"

The moment lasted but several seconds. "Aye . . . I guess I do."

Her eyes lingered on his — those compelling, memorable gray eyes of his — but she was conscious of Felix studying them both and she only smiled. That was Felix. Never around unless you didn't want him. He was quicksilver, there and gone again before you knew.

"I'll stay with Schultz for a while, Anna. Why don't you and the laddie get some sleep?"

Hours later, Anna woke. She found Bairn asleep on the ground next to Georg Schultz's bunk in the stern. His coughing had grown loose, and he mumbled incoherently, then fell still again.

Anna went to the side of the bunk, tested his forehead, found it cooler. She sighed and slumped her shoulders in relief. "He's going to live."

"You sound relieved," Bairn said, woken by the coughing.

"I am," Anna said.

Bairn sat up and leaned his elbow on his raised knee. "You make it sound easy."

"It's not. It's not easy at all to do the right thing." But she feared God more than she loathed Georg Schultz. "How could we face God one day, if we did nothing to help this man?"

Bairn gazed at her in quiet amazement and she wished he wouldn't credit her with such noble gestures. Keeping vigil over Georg Schultz was not easy.

"Where are the others who share yer beliefs?" He looked around the lower deck. "Fast asleep."

She felt her face grow warm. "Others have helped." Not many, but a few.

" 'Tis curious that when others are in need, yer the natural one t'turn to for help."

Just as she was about to object, to insist that her response came from a desire to please God, he put a finger to her lips. "Hush, lassie. Yer the one blessed with the gift of healin'. Souls as well as bodies."

Gift of healing? Me? she thought. *Me?*

September 17th, 1737

The day was cool but sunny. A seagull appeared in the sky, first one, then another, and Bairn rushed to the fo'c'sle deck. He picked up the spyglass to peer out to the horizon but saw no land in sight. The color of the water had changed from deep blue to pale green. Another seagull appeared and the seamen's shouts and cheers created such a stir that a number of passengers rushed up to the waist.

Bairn saw Felix and Dorothea, babe in her arms, stand by the railing, watching the seagulls dive for some hardtack that Johnny Reed threw on the deck. Watching and laughing.

An invisible cord yanked at his heart. He picked up the spyglass and studied his mother through it, finding her much changed. The lines about her eyes seemed more pronounced. And her fire red hair — could it be? — was now silver. The transformation shook him. She was but . . . how old was she, anyway? . . . he couldn't remember, but guessed she was but forty.

Over the last week, he'd observed the Peculiars every chance he could, with awe, with disappointment, mostly with fascination and wonder. They were not perfect, but they were his. *His* people. She, she was *his* mother. The laddie, he was *his* brother.

He felt a movement beside him and turned to find Anna standing at the top of the ladder. He felt a surge of emotion for her and blinked back tears.

She shielded her eyes from the sun to peer up at him. "Do you think this is how Noah must have felt when a dove returned with an olive branch?"

A smile tugged at his lips. "We will be seeing land soon. Very soon." His smile faded when he added, "Anna, tonight, meet me at the ship's helm at third watch." The time had come for a talk.

She nodded, looking puzzled.

The moon, round and creamy, had risen, shedding a soft light over the waters. From the feel of the air, this night brought the first hint of winter's coming. Bairn leaned against the rail and scrubbed his hands over his face. Beyond him a dozen feet away, he sensed the helmsman looking on with concern.

When he noticed Anna standing at the top of the ladder, with her hands linked behind her back, he turned to the helmsman and relieved him. "Carter, I'll take the wheel for the next hour." He closed the distance between Anna and himself and he held a hand out to her. "Come, lassie."

She stood at the helm, with Bairn behind her.

"I wanted a few moments alone with you."

She didn't press him, but he knew she was curious about why he asked her to meet him tonight. Curious and impatient.

His chest moved against her back as he eased out a held breath. "I'm n' good at this, Anna. It's like lettin' the wheel go free in a storm." His arms, which had been wrapped loosely around her, tightened a little.

"Maybe I can help. I have a question I've been wanting to ask you."

Bairn drew a shaky breath and ran a hand through his hair. "Ask away."

"Why do you have those deep scars on your ankles?" She dipped her head down, as if she could see through his boots.

Lord, where to begin? It occurred to him that he had just prayed again, that somehow he had developed a respect for the power of prayer. What change had come over him, headstrong and foolish, who only weeks earlier had found the whole idea of prayer to be a joke?

Start at the beginning, came the answer.

"Anna, do you recognize this frock?" He reached down and picked up his father's red coat to hand to her.

She held it in the air. "It's a mutza. A red mutza." She turned it over. "One or two men in my church have these red mutzas. Most of the mutzas are homespun brown. But those who came from Oberländer in the Bern of Canton, in Switzerland, they had these fine red coats."

"Do y'happen to remember if Jacob Bauer wore a red mutza?"

She tilted her head. "Why, yes. Yes he did. But it was long ago." She opened the interior of the coat and saw the initials *JB* embroidered into the lining. "Is this . . . Jacob's coat?"

Bairn nodded. "Aye."

"Bairn, were you the cabin boy for Captain Stedman on that crossing?"

Bairn lowered his head. He didn't trust his voice. He shook his head. "Nay."

After a lengthy pause, Anna said, "But you were on the ship with Jacob?"

"I was on the ship with Jacob Bauer, because . . ." He cleared his throat. It felt as if he had ground glass in there. "I am his son. Thought to have died from smallpox. I am Hans Bauer."

It took a moment for Anna to catch up to what Bairn was confessing. Then she spun around to look at him. Her face blanched, her hands flew to her mouth, her eyes widened in disbelief while she stiffened as if struck by lightning. "B . . . Bairn?" At last her hands fluttered downward and she stammered again in a choked voice, "Hans?" She closed her eyes. Though she made no sound, tears began to slide down her cheeks. She opened her eyes and sought his. "Can it be true? Is it really you? You are . . . Hans Bauer?"

He nodded.

"But . . . what happened? Why weren't you with your father?"

"We both took sick and became separated. The ship was in utter chaos, with ailin' bodies scattered everywhere. When I recovered, I was told my father was dead and I was taken off the ship. I'm guessin' that he recovered after me and was told his son had died. I'm sure he would've searched the ship until he was satisfied I was gone."

Bairn gave Anna an abbreviated version of a story that was etched on his mind. He still remembered the rain that was pounding the ship, the wind that moaned in the tops of the masts, the mournful sounds of other sick passengers. He remembered lying on his pallet after he had been told that his father had died. Set suddenly and unexpectedly adrift in the world, uncertain of what to do next, he was filthy, dazed, and hungry. Fear and loneliness weighed on him, pressing down on his chest, pushing him into despair. He did not want to get up, did not really care if he ever got up. Finally, though, he did get up and was led off the ship. Despite his despair, his body was healing.

And in a way, so was his determination to survive. His father had taught him that the very problems a man must overcome in life also supported him and made him stronger in overcoming them. Somehow, he would survive.

Her hand lighted on his arm, tugging him back with a questioning gaze. "Is that when your ankles were shackled?"

"Aye. I was handed off to a redemptioner to be auctioned off," he said, his voice gone flat and cold now. "Georg Schultz bought my debt and sold me off to a shipping agent named Otto Splettshoesser, who treated me like he treated his hogs. Worse. I ran away first chance I got, but he caught me with dogs that he bred for fighting. He dragged me back to his place and put shackles on my legs and chained me to a post in the barn.

"He kept me chained to that post in the barn when he wasn't workin' me like a coolie." His throat locked up for a moment. The darkness and the silence of the night lapped around them. He'd never told anyone this much before and he wasn't sure he could finish the tale. His voice felt raw, hoarse, as if someone had his hands on his throat. Anna held herself completely still, holding her breath, waiting for the rest of the story. As if she might've guessed the ending.

Sensibly, he hurried on, trying to get this story out while he had his wits about him. "It took me months to work a link loose. And on the day that I finally did, Splettshoesser came into the barn and discovered that I was free. He picked up a hayfork and threw it at me, but it missed. We tussled and I pushed him. His head hit the beam of the barn and he dropped like a stone. I dinnae mean to kill him. I dinnae ken me own strength. To my surprise, Georg Schultz was standing at the open barn door. He'd seen the whole thing. He told me t'get in his wagon and wait for him, so I grabbed the red coat and left the barn, sure I was heading straight t' the gallows. Awhile later, Schultz came out of the barn and said he'd buried Splettshoesser, and not to worry meself over it. Said he knew it was an accident but dinnae think others would see it that way. Said he would take care of everythin', that he would keep me secret. He took me t'the docks and promptly lost me in a Pharo Bank game. Thankfully, he lost to Captain John Stedman. The captain was the one who named me Bairn. It was the closest he could get t'pronouncin' me name." He let out a deep sigh. "And I think you know the rest of the story."

But he was leaving out the heart of his story, leaving her to fill in the blanks. How the burden of guilt over the terrible thing he had done to Splettshoesser lay heavily over him, how Georg Schultz frequently reminded him of the information he held over him, how he had made his way but his world had grown dark, narrow, and lonely. How a shadow had been cast over his soul. And how he had remembered another thing his father had taught him: Don't ever depend or trust Outsiders.

To Bairn, everyone had become an Outsider.

He could survive on his own, he figured, if he just kept his wits about him, if he kept his eyes open for opportunities, and if he didn't allow his life to be dictated by other people.

Anna was quiet for a long moment. The only sound was the sharp prow of the ship cutting through the seething sea. When she spoke, her voice was almost a whisper. "Was he good to you, this Captain John Stedman?"

"Aye. John Stedman has been very good to me. Fair and generous. He realized that I was capable of learnin' and saw to it I was educated."

"If the captain was so fair and generous to you, I don't understand why he didn't try to reunite you with your family."

"Most ships weren't sailin' to Rotterdam like they have been the last few years. They were goin' back and forth between England and the colonies, totin' goods t'sell and trade. Now and then I came across a German Peculiar —" he stopped himself — "Sorry. 'Tis a bad habit."

"Go on."

"I would ask if they knew of the Jacob Bauer family, but the German Peculiars were all Mennonites. No one knew of the Ixheim church. As time went by, I stopped askin'. It was too . . . difficult . . . t'hold on to hope. Each time me hope was dashed, it felt like a blow that might level me. Finally, I realized there might be a gift in acceptin' the end of my old life. It would sever me ties to my old life and free me fer this new one."

"You were a boy. Just a boy, hardly much older than Felix. All alone. You must have been so frightened. You couldn't even speak English."

"Aye. Well, I learned it quickly." He had to. "Anna, I dinnae want to tell my . . . mother." He spoke it as if it was a new word to him and in a way, it was. "I'm goin' to return to Rotterdam with Georg Schultz. I will go in Felix's place."

She spun around, eyes wide, trying to absorb what he was telling her. "But you'll go to prison. Or worse. This baron . . . he hates Jacob Bauer. He could find a way to see you hang for a trifle."

"Nay. He'll put me in prison but I don't think he will have me done away with. We have no history together — not like me father and the boys did. It will go easier for me than for Felix. The laddie must stay in the colonies with our father and mother. And I will nae allow Felix t'endure what I had to live through." He put his hands on her elbows. "I'll be fine, Anna. You taught me that. I dinnae think God was watching o'er me, but I see now that I was wrong. He never left me."

"Let Jacob decide what must be done.

He'll know what to do."

Bairn seized her by the arms, desperate to make her see, to understand. "Nay. My father is not t'be told of me. Not until I return. They've lost me once already. They don't need to grieve me twice. Not while they're still grievin' Johann's passin'."

"But, Bairn . . . you are his son. You belong to Jacob and Dorothea and Felix. They belong to you —"

His hand went to her cheek, stopping her words as effectively as if he had silenced her lips. "It's decided. I dinnae want to hear another word about it. I told you so you'd take special care of me mother. My family will watch over you and you'll watch over them."

"Oh no." She shook her head, and though she tried to pull away, he refused to let her go. "No, no, no. I'm going back with you. Dorothea will be fine once she is with Jacob."

"She's not fine, Anna. I can see that for myself. She's ne'er been strong, I remember that, and she's been weakened by the rigors of the ocean journey. She's not sturdy like you are."

"But I want to return to Germany. I've always wanted to return. I never wanted to go on this voyage. I was trying to get off the ship back in Plymouth but you forgot to let me talk to the captain."

"Ah well, that was auspicious. Nay. You must stay in the New World and help Dorothea. She thinks of you as a daughter."

"But I can't let you go, Bairn." Tears starred her lashes and spilled over.

"Shhh, dinnae fash yerself over me, lassie." He brushed the tears off her cheeks with his fingertips, then tilted up her chin. "I must do this. There's no dissuadin' me. I've done many things in me life that I'm not proud of, and mayhap this will atone for my sins. Some of them, anyway. It's just for a time, then I'll find you." He murmured into her hair. "Wherever you are, I'll find you." His arms twined around her, pulling her against the entire length of his body, his voice turning husky. This was hard for him, to say the words he wanted to say to her, needed to say to her.

He inhaled, and something inside him gave way, snapped, dissolved. "And now I have another confession t'make. I lost my heart to you the moment you gave me an order t'go get the captain and have him turn the boat around. Then I lost everythin' else to you when you gave water to the slaver. You have stolen me very heart away. I see yer face, I hear yer voice, I watch ye walk, even in my sleep."

She stood before him with soft eyes and softer lips. Eyes meant for gazing into. Lips intended for kissing. He bent his head to cover her lips with his. She tasted of ambrosia, of a future he didn't think he had. She clung to his shoulders and kissed him back.

And his heart softened from a sharp pain to a dull ache in his chest. If he kept on kissing her, the discomfort might vanish forever. He kissed her again and again, then held her in his arms, close to his chest. For a long time neither spoke. And then the ship bell rang and he knew their time together had come to an end.

23

September 18th, 1737

At daybreak, after eighty-three days at sea, land was spotted. On the fo'c'sle deck, the corner of Captain Charles Stedman's mouth twitched reluctantly into something vaguely resembling a smile. Standing next to him, Mr. Pocock clapped his hands together one time. It was the most enthusiasm he could muster, given his gout. Johnny Reed, in anticipation of good times ashore in Philadelphia, threw back his head and howled like a banshee.

Sheets of rain swept across the decks of the *Charming Nancy* as the ship finally sailed up the narrow Delaware River on a flood tide. Anna and Felix, standing by the larboard rail with other seamen, took no notice of the rain that was soaking them.

It looked so . . . new, so youthful, Anna thought, staring at her first sight of the New World. The harbor was filled with ships and fishing boats, nowhere near as crowded as Plymouth or Rotterdam. And the shoreline looked so unfinished, with random piers jutting into the harbor. Snug brick buildings, shoulder to shoulder, hugged the ground, but a few steeples reached to the sky, competing with iridescent orange-and-yellow-leafed trees. So many trees! No wonder it was called Penn's Woods.

Before the ship could enter the port, a health officer was sent out by the harbormaster. He gave a rudimentary physical to each passenger and miraculously everyone passed, even toddlers with runny noses. Then the health officer heard a noise that made his head lift in alarm: Georg Schultz's hacking, choking cough echoed across the lower deck. "Infectious disease!" the health officer pronounced, and ordered the ship to be removed one mile from the city, quarantined.

Felix was beside himself. "But I can see it! I can see Port Philadelphia! I see the ships in the harbor! I see the people on the docks! Papa must be waiting for us." That night, he sobbed himself to sleep.

"Felix is learning the gift of patience," Anna said. But they all felt travel-weary and disgusted with Georg Schultz.

It wasn't all bad for Felix. The captain had

ordered provisions of fresh greens and water to be sent to the ship, so the quality and quantity of food improved enormously. And because the ship was anchored on the Delaware River, life on the ship became make-and-mend days for the seamen. Accustomed to Felix, they let him roam freely above deck, Decker's dog following on his heels wherever he went.

Anna held an opposite view on the quarantine. She treasured it. She reveled in the unaccustomed luxury of being dry on this ship, clean after months of being splattered by ceaseless waves and wearing oily, salt-caked clothes. She cherished every stolen moment with Bairn. Each evening, she would meet him at the bowsprit, and his fingers would wrap around hers, warming her hand, thrilling her heart, and they would talk late into the night, lingering until the pale moon was high overhead. During those shared hours, she told him everything she could remember about Johann, about Felix, about Jacob and Dorothea. She caught him up on eleven years of life in Ixheim and helped him to remember things he'd buried in memories. Sometimes, she had discovered, the heart remembered things better than the head.

And she listened to him. He told her

about his life on the ship, learning English, studying mathematics so that he could unlock the mysteries of navigation.

Sometimes, they wouldn't speak at all. Their arms would circle each other for an embrace, a drawing of strength, of support. She discovered things about him — that in a way, he was more Amish than she. His childhood was his foundation, and even though he might have tried to forget the old ways, they were still a part of him — the very essence of him. It was no wonder he was willing to sacrifice himself for Felix. He was much changed from the boy she once knew, but much the same.

Joy and dread were Anna's constant companions. As the day drew near for the quarantine to be lifted, her time with Bairn would be over. He reassured her that he would come to Penn's Woods and reunite with his family, but she knew that was a promise he couldn't make.

On October 7th, the ship was cleared by the health inspector. Bairn lifted his eyes to Anna's when Captain Stedman made the pronouncement, and there was pain in the gray depths.

If all went well, tomorrow morning on the high tide, they would reach Port Philadelphia. Tomorrow eve, if all went well, Bairn would sail out on the high tide.

October 8th, 1737
The time had come once more to pack up for a journey. Maria was all aflutter in the way she got, ordering everyone about, accomplishing very little but stirring up a great deal. Anna unhooked the hammock from the hook in the beams, a simple thing, but it triggered a sob from deep within her. She hurried to the bow of the ship to put the hammock in the barrel where she had first found it, and then sunk to the deck behind the barrel and doubled up, pressing her head to her knees, hugging them. A downpour of tears exploded, tears for the moment she would say goodbye to Bairn, knowing she might never see him again. Tears for the years Bairn had lost with his family. Tears for what Jacob and Dorothea, and Felix, too, would be missing by not knowing that their son, Felix's brother, was alive. By the time her cry had been spent, her eyes were swollen and aching. She wiped the tears off her face with the backs of her hands and slowly rose to her feet.

"Something troubling you, dear?" Dorothea leaned in to whisper as they finished packing up their chests. "You seem far away."

416

Anna kept her head down. "There's a lot on my mind."

The dear woman gave her shoulder a squeeze of motherly affection. Anna breathed through her mouth to keep from crying again, but a fierce pain was pressing against her chest so hard it seemed her ribs would crack.

She took the rose out of the basket and unwrapped its base, then let it sit in a plate of water to soak up as much as it could. Its leaves were brown at the edges and there was little new growth, but it had survived. A small smile tugged at her lips. *It had survived, and so will I.*

They would need to make several trips to get their belongings out on the dock after the ship anchored. The more organized they could be, the better. She wrapped up her rose in burlap and set it in the basket. As Anna cleaned up around the lower deck, she found a stack of overlooked pewter spoons from the galley. Felix was nowhere in sight, so she took them up to Cook. She took her rose basket too, just in case it would get swept up with the other belongings that the men were taking from the lower deck and down to the docks. She had come this far with it — she wasn't about to lose it now.

In the galley was Bairn, saying goodbye to Cook. He straightened when he saw her and her heart started to pound.

"Cook, would ye mind if I had a moment alone with Anna?"

Cook simply clamped him on the shoulder in response. "Godspeed to you both," he said, before closing the door behind him.

"Mr. Pocock is waitin' fer me. He found a ship that is sailin' at high tide tonight. Georg Schultz will be on it as well." He took a step toward her. "Well . . ." The word hung in the cold air like the sound of the ship's bell.

"Yes, well . . . ," she answered, drawing out the words molasses-slow. She spread her palms nervously, then clutched them together. It was too much at once, and she heard Bairn thinking the same.

This would be the last of it, then. She would say goodbye, and he would sail back to Rotterdam to face the baron. And who knew what would happen next? She might never see his face again, a face that had grown beloved to her. The thought was so painful it was like a sliver of glass in the eye. Tears threatened, but she tamped the burning at the back of her throat and whispered, "Bairn, please, let me go with

418

you back to Germany. I don't want to leave you."

No longer able to stem the rush of tears, they flowed unchecked down her cheeks. Bairn wiped them away with his thumbs and pulled her into his arms, murmuring into her hair, "Just knowin' that you want to is all I'll need t'get me through and bring me back." The words came soft and unhurried. Then he kissed her, a silent reminder that no matter what the future, he loved her.

As his arms tightened around her, her hand released the rose basket and it dropped to the ground with a clink.

He pulled back, holding her by the arms. "What was that? Did y'hear that sound?" He bent down to grab the basket. "Of course. Of course, of course! This is the way Felix's sneaky little mind would work. Put it someplace obvious, because no one looks for the obvious." He pulled the wrapped rose out of the basket and laid it on the table, then carefully unwrapped it.

"The baron's gold watch? It's not there. I've taken the rose out often to check on it, to give it sun and keep it damp. I would have noticed."

Bairn was examining the basket. "You would nae notice . . . if there's a false bottom in the basket." He reached a hand in and pulled out a wooden oval. There, at the base of the basket, was a wrapped handkerchief. Bairn unfolded it carefully. Inside was the baron's gold watch, complete with a delicate gold chain. "He's a cannie laddie, that one." He started toward the door.

"No . . . let me. I'll go get him."

Anna hurried downstairs to find Felix. She brought him back up, grateful that Dorothea was occupied with feeding the baby. She bit her tongue for all the scoldings she wanted to give that boy.

Bairn had laid the watch out on a barrel top in Cook's galley.

Felix's eyes went wide, then he tried backing up toward the door, but Anna reached out to stop him by placing a firm hand on his shoulder.

"Am I in trouble?"

"Yes. You lied to me, over and over." Anna swallowed down a frustrated sigh. "Why did you steal the watch?"

"I dinnae vant the baron t'have the vatch," he said in his awful accent. He wasn't even pretending anymore; the accent had become part of him.

"But why the watch? Of all things, why would you steal a watch?"

Felix's eyes filled with tears. "The baron used it t'time the beatings his servant gave t'Johann. At the stroke of twelve, every minute, fer fifteen minutes, Johann vas lashed. He never cried. He just vent silent."

"His heart," Anna said woodenly. "It wasn't strong."

"So I took the vatch so he vouldn't hurt anyone else." He looked at Anna, tears running down his cheeks.

"I'm not angry with you, Felix. You meant well."

"I *alvays* mean vell. I am misunderstood."

"That's a question for another time. You go finish packing up. We should be reaching the harbor soon."

Felix looked up at Bairn, worry covering his small round face. "Do I have t'give it back t'Georg Schultz?"

"Ich gibt acht auf Georg Schultz," Bairn said. *I'll take care of Georg Schultz.*

Relieved, Felix jumped like a grasshopper into the air and out the door.

Anna tilted her head. "You spoke our language to him. Weeks ago, I realized that you could understand it, but this was the first time I've heard you speak it."

" 'Tis rusty. I'd forgotten much of it. I've forgotten most everythin', until you came along."

She had to touch him. She lifted her hand, at the same time that he reached for it. He kissed her palm, and then her wrist, where her pulse beat. He laid the back of her hand against his cheek. His smile was so tender and fragile, it hurt to look at it. "What I've learned of love, of life, I've learned from you." He breathed out a sigh. "And now I need t'give the watch to Schultz."

"Do you think there's any chance he will be satisfied with the watch alone?"

"No chance at all," said a voice at the door. They turned to find Georg Schultz at the doorjamb, standing spread-legged with his thumbs in his breast pockets, smiling to show off teeth that were yellow as corn. He reached out to snatch the watch from Bairn's open palm and dangled it in front of his face. "But I'm delighted the little thief finally confessed his crime."

"Schultz, I know yer not a man discouraged by conscience, but are you truly so hardhearted? So greedy fer gold that you'd break me family apart?"

"It's not personal, Bairn. It's just money. Quite a bit of money. That reward will set me up for . . . ," he snapped his fingers, ". . . for life. I won't have to work another day. No more tiresome ocean voyages."

"And Anna?"

"What about her?"

"You've ne'er thanked her for savin' yer

life, even after you manhandled her like a drunken schoolboy."

Georg Schultz bowed before her. "Danke sehr."

"That's not enough. Would you take so much from a woman who's shown you only kindness?"

"Why should the fate of a ship's carpenter make any difference to her?"

"Because we love each other. We plan t'marry."

Anna's teeth caught her lower lip and she stared at Bairn in disbelief for several seconds. She felt a lump gathering in her throat. She swallowed, but the emotion could not be gulped away. They had talked long in the night, but it was never about their future, only their past. It seemed too dangerous to assume they would be together again.

Bairn slowly turned to her with a sober expression, a streak of red running up his high cheekbones. "If she'll have me, that is."

Startled, she replied with the first words that came to her mind. "She'll have you."

"Bah!" Georg Schultz said, dismissing them with a wave. "Your heart belongs to the sea, Bairn. You could never settle down and become a farmer with those Peculiars."

Bairn looked at Anna and smiled. "The sea can't love you back."

The Neulander considered their plight for a long moment, then held a finger in the air. "I'll make a bargain for you two lovebirds. She can sail back to Rotterdam with you for . . . free! . . . and I'll watch over her in Ixheim while you are . . . incapacitated." He gave a lusty grin to Anna and smiled broadly when she shuddered.

"A devil's bargain," Bairn growled.

Just then Schultz was clutched by a spell of coughing that doubled him over and he sat down on an upturned nail keg. When the coughing passed, he was winded.

Bairn stared him down. "Schultz, do you mean to tell me that Anna gave you back yer life, after you treated her so badly, and you cannae give her back hers? Are you truly so heartless? So selfish as that? So greedy?"

A poignant silence fell.

"Ja. I am that selfish and that greedy."

"I don't believe anyone is without conscience, Georg Schultz," Anna said. "You're a man driven by your appetites, but I don't think you would have rescued Bairn from Otto Splettshoesser if you were entirely without mercy. I believe that, given the opportunity, you will choose good over evil."

424

"My dear, you can't teach a devil to be an angel."

"Schultz!"

Their heads snapped at the sight of Captain Stedman at the door, looking peeved. Felix was right behind him. Georg Schultz jumped to his feet.

"Schultz, I have a German passenger, a Christian Müller, who is waiting in my Great Cabin, greatly distressed. He said you had sold off most of their goods in Rotterdam to purchase new goods in lots of dozens."

Bairn looked at Anna with a question in his eyes. *It's true,* Anna mouthed.

Schultz licked his lips, stalling for time. "I only did it to help you, Captain. The new goods would be packaged tightly and require less space in the hold. More room for you to bring goods from England."

"At the time did you inform him that those new goods would be confiscated and sold by the Philadelphia port authorities? Because there is a customs officer in the hold right now, requisitioning all the Rotterdam purchases. Importing new manufactured goods, other than from England itself, is forbidden by English law."

You could have heard a pin drop. Georg Schultz's mouth moved and moved before a sound came out. "I'm sure I told him all that. Christian Müller does not speak German. Or English."

"Anna translated fer ye," Felix offered up in his dreadful accent.

Georg Schultz's face colored, but he smiled amicably. "Who can remember every detail? It was months ago." He batted his hand in the air at Felix like shooing a pesky fly.

Captain Stedman narrowed his eyes. "Apparently the captain of the ship is to be heavily fined for breaking the law."

Purple-faced, strangling for words, Georg Schultz backed up a step. "Just a simple misunderstanding."

The captain lifted his chin. "Schultz, come with me to the Great Cabin and explain yourself to the passenger. Bring your purse."

Schultz's smile was gone, and a crease appeared between his thin eyebrows. "My purse?"

"If you ever want to work on the ships again, you will make a full reimbursement to Christian Müller."

"A full reimbursement?" His voice rose to a squeak.

"And you can explain yourself to Otto Splettshoesser."

"Otto Splettshoesser?" Bairn asked, his

face suddenly blanching.

"Aye," the captain said. "The customs officer."

"Otto Splettshoesser is not dead?" Bairn thundered. He turned toward Georg Schultz, his fists bunching as he took one menacing step forward. "All these years, you had me thinkin' he was kilt?" Bairn advanced on the retreating Georg, whose mouth was pursed tightly while his eyes blinked rapidly in fright.

The little galley seemed to crackle in the silence before a storm, when the very air seemed to disappear, until the little man practically wilted.

Georg Schultz gave Bairn and Anna a weary, defeated, bleary-eyed look. "I suppose the watch will suffice for the baron."

October 8th, 1737

It was an ever-widening world for Anna König. The day was flawlessly clear, and seagulls scolded from an azure sky as the German passengers filed off the ship. On a day like today, with the sun bright overhead and the weather cool and crisp, the water still and calm, it was hard to imagine how perilous the crossing of the Atlantic had been.

Anna's thoughts spun backward to her old

life, on the far side of the sea to the little sheep farm in Germany. She remembered the day of Johann's death, of saying good-bye to her grandparents for what she suspected — and they knew — would be the last time she'd see them. Her head rattled with the events of the *Charming Nancy,* to the wild beauty of the endless sea, to the seaman Decker, to the storm that cracked the beam, to the slave ship and those thirsty and tragic souls, to poor Lizzie, to nearly losing Felix and Bairn to Georg Schultz. Her thoughts turned to meeting Bairn, to finding him in the most unlikely of places.

The Lord giveth and the Lord taketh, and she would never understand the mysteries of why.

Anna almost didn't feel the touch of a hand on her shoulder, so light it was, so tentative. Afraid even to breathe, she turned her head and looked into Bairn's face.

"You look cold. There's some winter in this wind." He took her free hand and chafed it between his, his gaze soft on her face, a sweetheart's caress with his eyes. "I was lookin' for you. What were you doin' up here on the bowsprit all alone?"

"Praying." She gazed into his eyes and smiled. "For you. For me. For all of us."

"Good. Prayers seem t'make a difference,

though I cannae pretend t'understand why." Bairn passed a hand over his whiskers. For a wisp of a second he looked like the boy she remembered. Focused. Intense. Now, strikingly handsome. Never in her wildest imaginings would she believe that he was here, standing in front of her, loving her. And yet, another part of her, deep in her soul, had felt an inexplicable bond with him from the moment she met him.

Felix waved furiously to them from the crowded upper deck of the ship, now a marketplace. He cupped a hand to his mouth and shouted, straining to be heard. Buyers had come on board to haggle and bargain with redemptioners, mostly Mennonites, over how many years of labor they owed in exchange for their passage debt. Only after accounts had been paid could the passengers go ashore.

"Look! Look!" Felix laughed gaily. "There is Papa!" He pointed to the crowded, chaotic dock, filling with cargo, casks, longshoremen, and pods of ponderous Germans who had come to meet their friends and relatives. He ran to grab Dorothea's hand and hurry her down the gangplank. Decker's dog barked and trotted on Felix's heels.

"There! There is your father, Bairn." She pointed to a tall man who towered above the others.

"My father," Bairn said, his voice breaking a little over the words. She saw his knuckles go white as his hands gripped the rail.

Jacob Bauer bolted to the base of the gangplank to meet his wife and son, arms opened wide to scoop Felix up.

Beside her, Anna heard Bairn inhale a deep breath, and it was plain that he was as eager as Felix. "Does your father look the same to you?"

"His hair and beard are mixed more with gray than brown now." Bairn swallowed, breathed. "But he holds himself tall and straight, just the way I remember."

"Tall and straight like you."

Anna watched the surprised look on Jacob's face as Dorothea showed him the infant in her arms. Then she realized she was telling him about Johann, because she saw Jacob still, and wrap his arms around Dorothea for a long, long time.

Felix ran halfway up the gangplank, skirting around passengers, and waved to tell them to come down.

"Let's wait," Bairn said, putting a hand on Anna's shoulder. "Let's give them this moment to grieve Johann."

"Are you ready?" she asked. "Ready to be

reunited?"

His eyes met hers and they were no longer cold, no longer hard. *Eyes, eyes,* she thought. *There is no forgetting eyes.* These were the clear gray eyes of the boy she once knew.

"Aye. Nay." He shook his head. "How do you tell a mother and father that their son is nae dead but alive? That a boy has a brother, after all?"

"By letting them see that you are changed, but the same."

Anna looked back over her shoulder with a strange feeling of parting, a tenderness for this old wooden tub. The ship had taken care of them and brought them safely across the ocean. She would actually miss the *Charming Nancy.* It was an odd feeling to care about the ship, one she didn't expect, similar to the sad feeling she got when she closed the cover on a book. She had finished with that part of her life and would begin a new book.

A chilly cross-course breeze circled around her, lifting her capstrings, pushing away the now familiar stale smells that hung about the ship. She thought of how often sea wind had refreshed and renewed her. She would never miss the stench of the lower deck, but she would miss the cleansing bite of tangy sea air. And she looked forward to the familiar and pleasurable scents that awaited her in Penn's Woods: earthy scents of soil and trees and horses.

Bairn turned to give her a hand to climb down the forecastle ladder and said, "Why such a solemn look? Dinnae you feel happy t'leave?"

"I am," she said. "I'm happy to leave. And a little sad. But more happy than sad."

Her gaze traveled lovingly over him and stopped when she saw his father's red mutza in his other hand. It was a quietly miraculous moment, Anna felt, one she'd never forget as long as she lived. She had thought, twice, they would be forever parted and now they had it all again, their lives, their love.

Bairn draped his father's red coat over his arm and bent down to pick up the rose basket. "Did you ever know where I found this rose?"

"I thought it was wild. I assumed you dug it up on a hillside."

"Nay. It came from the old baron's garden. He was quite a fancier of roses. I dinnae think he would miss one. Mayhap me brothers and me are not so very different. Always helpin' ourselves to the baron's treasures." He grinned, eyes sparkling in a way that reminded her of Felix and Johann, both. With the other hand, he gripped Anna's hand tightly and they walked the deck of the *Charming Nancy* for the last time, down the gangplank to join their family.

DISCUSSION QUESTIONS

1. In the beginning of the story, Anna struggled to leave the past behind. We meet her as she is digging up her most precious rose to take along to the New World. To her, the survival of the rose was a symbol of the survival of her people. Now that you've discovered why this particular rose was so important to her, what do you think this rose truly represented to her?

2. Context is key. Have you ever not recognized someone if you've seen him out of context? It might seem unlikely that Bairn didn't recognize his own mother, but eleven years had passed, and in his mind she was still a young woman, pleasingly plump, with russet-colored hair. On the ship, she was thin and gray from sickness and sorrowing. But how

could a mother not know her son? Dorothea thought her son had died, a boy at the age of eleven. She would never have expected an English-looking sea carpenter, complete with a long hair queue and bushy whiskers, to turn up as her missing son. Why is context so important to memory?

3. Usually, Amish fiction has a rural setting, a reminder to the reader that she is escaping to another world. This story had no such reminders. It took place almost entirely on a ship. Even seasons weren't relevant — though weather certainly was. Still, it was a challenge to create tensions in which the Amish showed a better way to respond to life's trials without the usual props. It stripped away what draws us to and distracts us about the Amish (such as a simple farm life) to show their depth and commitment to faith in their responses to crises. Challenging, and inspiring. If you were taken out of your ordinary setting, what would identify or set you apart as a Christian?

4. Anna wanted Bairn to see that faith

could keep a person, as well as a church, in the world but not of the world. When Anna and Christian offered to provide water to the slave ship, what were your initial thoughts? Did they waver when day after day went by and no rain appeared? What did the water symbolize to Anna? To Bairn?

5. God is often slow, but never late. Why is that? What was happening, spiritually, to Bairn during this drought on the ship?

6. Let's consider the water from a different angle. What could be a metaphor for the water in your life? And what could be a metaphor for the slave ship? Could you, or should you, offer your water to the slave ship?

7. Anna believed that God wouldn't bring them this far if He didn't plan on delivering them. She never wavered from that conviction, even as she started to suffer the effects of severe dehydration. Did she mean that God would deliver them by providing water? Or did she mean something beyond physical provisions?

8. There were some gruesome details in this story. The shark with Decker's body in it, for example. The horrific smells of the lower deck mingling with the bilge. The tradition of throwing a dead mother and her living child into the sea together. (A vivid account of ship mortality in 1750 is given by Gottlieb Mittelberg in his published *Journey to Pennsylvania.* In it he wrote that if a woman died in childbirth, the dead mother and the living infant were both thrown into the sea together. [Also documented in *Unser Leit,* page 271.]) You might be surprised to learn that those gruesome details were true! Have you had an event in your life in which fact was worse than fiction? (I have! A couple of them. But I'll save those for a book club discussion.)

9. One of the themes in this book is a basic question: Can I trust God? Bairn struggled with it. If we're honest, most of us do. Anna said, "We think of trusting God by relating it to our circumstances. Trust is much more than circumstances.

Much, much more." What do you think she meant by that?

10. Bairn believed in God, but a mercurial, unpredictable one. Understandably! He was only eleven years old when he was essentially abandoned, orphaned, and left to his own survival. Do you think God did abandon him for a season? Why or why not?

11. Another theme in this book was broken expectations. Bairn had endured many failed expectations of God. His despair and disappointment caused him to give up hope that God had any regard for him. In another scene, Anna said, "Our story is not meant to be read by itself." What do you think she meant by that — and how would it be applicable to Bairn?

12. During the drought, Anna was confident that God would provide water to them, though there were no rain clouds in sight. The situation on the ship grew dire, worse and worse. Anna might have been desperately thirsty, but she did not lose hope in God. "Broken expectations shouldn't make us give up," she

said, "but look up." Describe a time in your life when God did not meet your expectations, at least not in the way you had planned. Looking back on that time now, what are your thoughts about your expectations and God's response?

13. Bairn said that Anna and Felix and the other passengers "lived loved." And he did not. What do you think he meant by that? What difference does it make to you to "live loved"?

14. Eleven years later, Bairn had a miracle of his own — an amazing coincidence that his mother and brother were on the *Charming Nancy*. What does that reveal about God's timing?

15. What was the most interesting historical detail you learned as you read this story?

16. Have you ever had an experience in your life when circumstances converged and you knew it was an "Only God" moment? I have! Not many, but I can think of a handful of times when I knew that only God could have brought unlikely details together in such a remarkable way. Those "Only God" moments are

meant to build our faith, but our faith rests not in those moments, but in the supreme sovereignty of God.

AUTHOR'S NOTE

How much of this story is true? Little is known about the actual journey of the *Charming Nancy*. As Amish historian David Luthy wrote in a letter to me, "Many questions can not be answered with certainty."

So I started with a handful of facts, an amateur's interest in the history of this ship, and the intention to reconstruct it. To do this I worked with documents and books and newspapers, visited museums and historical ships.

Here are the few known facts of the group of Amish who crossed the Atlantic in 1737:

- They sailed on the *Charming Nancy*, a merchant vessel that was captained by Charles Stedman. The ship left from Rotterdam, made a stop at Plymouth, England (most ships stopped at Cowes for provisions), and arrived in Philadelphia on October 8 — after a three-week health quarantine in which the ship had to remain one mile away from the port.

- There was a passenger list with a mix of Amish and Mennonite names.
- Few eighteenth-century diaries have been preserved, but a fragment of a diary by one passenger was found and it described over twenty-four deaths, mostly children. (See below to read the fragment.)

Beyond those basic facts, I came across many conflicting ones. One source stated there were eleven Amish families on the *Charming Nancy* in 1737, another stated twenty-eight. One source stated that the ship arrived in Philadelphia on October 8, 1737, another indicated some passengers disembarked on September 18, 1737.

As I was constructing Anna's story, I chose to use those basic facts about the *Charming Nancy* to try to create a story that would give readers a sense of why immigrants left all that they knew to travel across the ocean to the New World, and what they endured along the way. I used common first names from the passenger list (Anna, Barbara, Christian, Maria, Hans, Jacob, Josef, Catrina, Felix) and intentionally avoided actual surnames. I debated whether to use names from passenger lists and, in the end, decided not to. Why? I didn't want to try to tell the story of anyone's cherished ancestor. I only wanted to tell a story of what this 1737 crossing might have been like, to show the grit and determination — and heart — of these people. And God's loving protection.

I made some assumptions to make the story read smoothly. For example, I couldn't find any authoritative documents to prove the Amish started to think of or refer to themselves as "Amish" in 1737. There were other terms used to describe Anabaptists (Täuffers, Mennites) and the followers of Jacob Amman (Avoiders). The split in the Anabaptist church came officially to light in the 1690s, only fortysome years prior, when Jacob Amman created division by introducing, among other things, more stringent church discipline (shunning). As *Anna's Crossing* grew, it became complicated for readers to not have a handle for the followers of Jacob Amman, so I chose to call them "Amish."

Another assumption: I don't know if the passengers of the *Charming Nancy* came from one German village or several. Again, to keep it simple and to create a sense of community, I chose one location.

In *Anna's Crossing,* there was one death among the Amish on the *Charming Nancy* — Lizzie Mast — but in truth, there were dozens of deaths on that ship in 1737, mostly children. The condition of passenger life in the lower decks of a ship was truly pitiful. It was a miracle they survived at all. A child of seven years stood only a 50 percent chance of surviving the ocean journey, while those under a year of age rarely survived.[1]

The following year, 1738, became known as "The Year of the Destroying Angels." It brought the largest year of German immigration, and the highest ship mortality. This is an illuminating paragraph from the book *Unser Leit: The Story of the Amish* by Leroy Beachy:

The overzealous solicitation by shipping agents had brought far more anxious emigrants to Rotterdam in that year than there were ships immediately available to transport them. Poor sanitation and immoderate weather conditions caused an outbreak of dysentery and fevers in the tent city at Kralingen, in an outskirt of Rotterdam, that was established for those awaiting the arrival of passenger ships.

Within a short time nearly eighty small children had died.[2]

The emigrants' anxiety about getting on their way and the opportunity this offered to greedy captains to increase their profits led to serious overcrowding of the passenger ships that sailed in 1738 with the result that an estimated 1600 to 2000 passengers, many already sick before they left, died en route. Among the most seriously over-crowded ships was the *Charming Nancy,* which embarked with 312 1/2 freights, at least thirty-three more than Captain Stedman had packed into his ship the previous year. About half of the ship's passengers had apparently died en route. Captain Stedman's ship may have still been contaminated with disease from the previous year's crossing when he had lost one out of nine.[3]

The following passage is from Klaus Wust's online paper "The Emigration Year of 1738 — Year of the Destroying Angels" and reveals more about the perils of the ocean crossing:

Next appeared the long overdue St. Andrew, commanded by the favorite ship captain of the Germans, John Steadman. [The spelling of Captain Stedman's name

447

was found to be both Steadman and Stedman.] Several letters of passengers on some of his previous five runs between Rotterdam and Philadelphia were full of praise for him. This time, on a voyage that lasted twelve weeks, almost 120 passengers had died before reaching port on October 29th. The same day, Lloyd Zachary and Thomas Bond, two physicians recruited by the authorities to tighten the inspection of the incoming Palatine ships, presented this report to the colonial council:

"We have carefully examined the State of Health of the Mariners and Passengers on board the ship St. Andrew, Captain Steadman, from Rotterdam, and found a great labouring under a malignant, eruptive fever, and are of the opinion. They cannot, for some time, be landed in town without the danger of infecting the inhabitants."[4]

There was disbelief in the German community that such a fate could have befallen a ship led by Stedman. The *Send-Schreiben* expressed the reaction as follows:

The two Stedmans, who had so far been renowned for the transfer of Germans and wanted to keep this reputation, also had to suffer the plight this time, one of them lost near 120 before landfall, although he had a party of the Hope's roughest and sturdiest folks, who had to succumb to sickness and fear of death. And the other one lost probably five-sixths, of 300 hardly 60 were left. His mates and some of his sailors he lost and he himself lay near death.[5]

It was the last emigrant transport that Captain John Stedman ever commanded. After his return to Europe, he settled down in Rotterdam in the shipping business.

Another assumption: I don't know if, in 1737, an entire ship could be quarantined or if only sick passengers would be quarantined — I found conflicting information about quarantines. With the fear of plagues and contagion, it made sense to think they would isolate the entire ship. Within a decade or so, there was enough of a steady stream of immigrants that Province Island became an official gateway, a predecessor to Ellis Island. On a note of trivia, the Philadelphia Airport now occupies that site.

A fragment of a diary was found that was written by Hans Jacob Kauffman, a passenger on the actual 1737 *Charming Nancy* sea journey. Altogether, Kauffman recorded the death of two adults and twenty-four children, four of which were his own. Perhaps a more skillful writer than I could have created a story that wove in such frightful deaths, but for me (and for my editor), sticking to the facts of such an horrific ordeal would have been far too depressing. See for yourself if I made the right decision to avoid writing a novel hinging on this scarce bit of information:

The 28th of June while in Rotterdam getting ready to start my Zernbli died and was buried in Rotterdam. The 29th we got under sail and enjoyed only 1 1/2 days of favorable wind. The 7th day of July, early in the morning, died Hans Zimmerman's son-in-law.

We landed in England the 8th of July remaining 9 days in port during which 5 children died. Went under sail the 18th day of July. The 21st of July my own Lisbetli died. Several days before Michael's Georgli had died. On the 29th of July three children died. On the first of August my Hansli died and Tuesday previous 5 children died. On the 3rd of August contrary winds beset the vessel from the first to the 8th of the month three more children died.

On the 8th of August Shambien's (?) Lizzie died and on the 9th died Hans Zimmerman's Jacobi. On the 19th Christian Burgli's child died. Passed a ship on the 21st. A favorable wind sprang up. On the 28th Hans Gasi's (?) wife died. Passed a ship 13 of September.

Landed in Philadelphia on the 18th and my wife and I left a ship on the 19th. A child was born to us on the 20th — died — wife recovered. A voyage of 83 days.[6]

There is truth to the facts about Bairn, a child on a quarantined ship, who was auctioned off to the highest bidder in the New World as payment for his passage from Europe. The traffic in redemptioners was profitable and even ship captains were prone to entice persons, including children, onto their vessels and to sell their services once they reached America. Emigrants were simple and trusting, and prone to be taken advantage of. There was also truth to the story about a ship being ravaged by smallpox, killing so many passengers and crew that the carpenter was left to bring in the vessel. However, the ship was called the *Davy* and sailed in that ill-fated year of 1738 (as reported in the *Pennsylvania Gazette*, October 26, 1738).

The incidents of persecution involving the Anabaptists on the *Charming Nancy* are taken from historical accounts, though events were fictionalized to fit into the story. It's hard to understand the discrimination that these people faced for their beliefs. They were, for the most part, families — men, women, and children — who were willing to endure almost anything if it meant they could worship and live as they pleased. In spite of everything, the amazing, rapid growth of the movement under very difficult conditions is fascinating. Today, the Amish are the fastest-growing population in North America.

Somehow, in spite of oppression and persecution and hardship, the Amish church has flourished as a rose among thorns.

Notes

1. Leroy Beachy, *Unser Leit: The Story of the Amish* (Millersburg, OH: Goodly Heritage Books), 270.
2. Ibid., 272.
3. Ibid.
4. Klaus Wust, "The Emigration Year of 1738 — Year of the Destroying Angels," http://homepages.rootsweb.ancestry.com/~marier/Germanna.htm.

5. *Send-Schreiben,* http://kinexxions
.blogspot.com/2012/06/jacob-berlin
-voyage-across-ocean.html

6. The diary was found among papers of
the late Dr. D. Heber Plank, who had
translated it into English. See S. Duane
Kauffman, "Early Amish Translations
Support Amish History," *Budget,* Febru-
ary 22, 1978, p. 11; and "Miscellaneous
Amish Mennonite Documents," *Pennsylvania Mennonite Heritage* 2 (July 1979):
12–16.

ACKNOWLEDGMENTS

It's a funny thing about books. You start out with an idea, a basic sketch drawn from a few facts, get a green light from your publisher, and then it's time to open a new Word document. For a while, it's just you and your computer.

But a book is never the work of just one person. As the story grows and expands, it includes imaginary people and places, but it also includes real people. Those who lend advice on research issues, those who help to proof and edit, those who take great care to design covers, those who market and sell the books, and of course those who eventually read the book. Each one deserves a felt thank-you from the bottom of my heart.

First of all, thank you to my dedicated first readers, Lindsey Ciraulo and Tad Fisher. Nobody could have better bird's-eye readers. Or encouragers.

In terms of print and paper, words cannot

express my gratitude for the team at Revell for your many efforts on my behalf. To Andrea Doering and Barb Barnes, my editing bookends, thank you for being such talented, wonderful people with whom to work. To the group in marketing, publicity, and art, thank you for using your talent in support of this and so many other books. Much of what you do to get books into readers' hands goes behind the scenes, but I notice! Thank you for your love of Christian fiction. To my agent, Joyce Hart, thank you for taking these literary journeys with me over the years.

To David Luthy, a thank-you for answering my questions as I began this story. To Ervin Stutzman, for sending me Gottlieb Mittelberger's *Journey to Pennsylvania.*

I thank the Lord for giving me the love of writing, which I enjoy immensely. I'm deeply grateful to be able to do something every day that I love so much. God's way of connecting people is, indeed, the most magnificent part of any story.

Last of all, but never least of all, I am grateful to so many reader friends far and near. Thank you for all the sweet emails, for recommending my stories to your friends. You can't imagine how much it means, when the story goes out into the world, and people make room for it in their reading life. May each of you find your "Only God" story!

RESOURCES

The following books and sites provided helpful historical information about life in the eighteenth century, seafaring or otherwise.

Amish Society, 4th ed., by John A. Hostetler (Baltimore: The Johns Hopkins University Press, 1963).

The Floating Brothel: The Extraordinary True Story of an Eighteenth-Century Ship and Its Cargo of Female Convicts by Sian Rees (New York: Hyperion, 2002).

Johann by Everett J. Thomas (Goshen, IN: Woodgate Pond Publishing, 2012).

Mayflower II (and her wonderful staff), State pier, Plymouth, MA 02361; www.plimoth .org.

Mayflower: A Story of Courage, Community and War by Nathaniel Philbrick (New York: Penguin Books, 2006).

Unser Leit: The Story of the Amish, vol. 1, by

Leroy Beachy (Millersburg, Ohio: Goodly Heritage Press, 2011).

Some helpful websites about the eighteenth-century sea crossings for Amish and Mennonite immigrants:

"Beyond Germanna" by Klaus Wust; http:// homepages.rootsweb.ancestry.com/ ~marier/Germanna.htm.

Kinexxions blog by Becky Wiseman; http:// kinexxions.blogspot.com/2012/06/jacob -berlin-voyage-across-ocean.html.

The Palatine Project by Progenealogists; http://www.progenealogists.com/palproj ect/.

"Soul Seller: The Man Who Moved People" by Louise Walsh; http://www.cam.ac.uk/ research/features/soul-seller-the-man-who -moved-people.

ABOUT THE AUTHOR

Suzanne Woods Fisher is the author of the bestselling Lancaster County Secrets and Stoney Ridge Seasons series. *The Search* received a 2012 Carol Award, *The Waiting* was a finalist for the 2011 Christy Award, and *The Choice* was a finalist for the 2011 Carol Award. Suzanne's grandfather was raised in the Old Order German Baptist Brethren Church in Franklin County, Pennsylvania. Her interest in living a simple, faith-filled life began with her Dunkard cousins. Suzanne is also the author of the bestselling *Amish Peace: Simple Wisdom for a Complicated World* and *Amish Proverbs: Words of Wisdom from the Simple Life,* both finalists for the ECPA Book of the Year award, and *Amish Values for Your Family: What We Can Learn from the Simple Life.* She has an app, Amish Wisdom, to deliver a proverb a day to your iPhone, iPad,

or Android. Visit her at www.suzannewoods
fisher.com to find out more.

Suzanne lives with her family in the San
Francisco Bay Area.